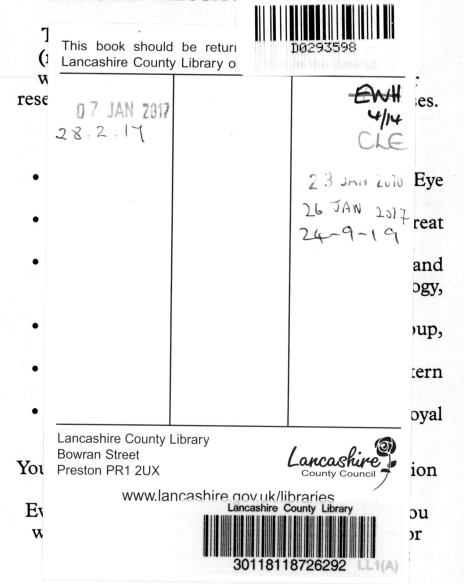
THE ULVERSCROFT FOUNDATION
The Green, Bradgate Road, Anstey
Leicester LE7 7FU, England
Tel: (0116) 236 4325

website: www.foundation.ulverscroft.com

Augusto Cury is a psychiatrist, psycho-therapist, scientist and best-selling author. The writer of more than twenty titles, he is published in more than fifty countries, and is currently one of the most widely read authors in Brazil, where he has sold over twelve million books. *The Dreamseller: The Calling* is the recipient of China's 2009 Weishanu Award for Best Foreign Novel. Through his work as a theorist in education and philosophy, he created 'the theory of multifocal intelligence'. which presents a new appraoach to the logic of thinking, the process of interpretation and the creation of thinkers.

For more information, visit:
www.thedreamseller.com

THE DREAMSELLER: THE CALLING

Wherever he goes, the dreamseller enchants, stirs up trouble and inspires his listeners to search for the most important thing: the heart of the human soul. Every person he meets is someone who has abandoned their dreams and is struggling through life: a professor who has stopped pursuing his ambitions, an alcoholic who has no family, the elderly who have lost their zest for life. Through his questioning and wisdom, the dreamseller helps them to look into their silent hearts and get to the root of their unhappiness . . .

AUGUSTO CURY

THE DREAMSELLER:
THE CALLING

Complete and Unabridged

ULVERSCROFT
Leicester

First published in Great Britain in 2011 by
Simon & Schuster UK Ltd.
London

First Large Print Edition
published 2014
by arrangement with
Simon & Schuster UK Ltd.
A CBS Company
London

11872629

A catalogue record for this book is available
from the British Library.

ISBN 978–1–4448–1820–8

Published by
F. A. Thorpe (Publishing)
Anstey, Leicestershire

Set by Words & Graphics Ltd.
Anstey, Leicestershire
Printed and bound in Great Britain by
T. J. International Ltd., Padstow, Cornwall

This book is printed on acid-free paper

I dedicate this novel to the readers in every country where my books have been published. Especially to those who in one way or another sell dreams through their intelligence, critical approach, sensibility, generosity and kindness. Dreamsellers are often outsiders in the social nest. They are abnormal. For what is normal is to wallow in the mud of individuality, egocentrism and personalism. Their legacy will be unforgettable.

Contents

Preface

This is my fourth work of fiction and my twenty-second book. My novels do not have as their goal plots that merely entertain, amuse or arouse emotion. They all involve theses, whether psychological, psychiatric, sociological or philosophical. Their intent is to foment debate, to journey into the world of ideas and go beyond the borders of prejudice.

I have been writing continuously for over twenty-five years and publishing for slightly over eight years. Perhaps it is because of the voyages into the territory of the unfathomable world of the human mind. Sincerely, I do not merit this success. I am not an author who can produce texts easily. Striving to be an artisan of words, I continually write and rewrite every paragraph, day and night, as if I were a compulsive sculptor. You will find in this novel thoughts that were sculpted after having been rewritten ten or twenty times in my mind.

Some books come from the core of the intellect; others come from the viscera of emotion. *The Dreamseller* came from the depths of both. While writing it, I was bombarded with countless questions, I smiled a lot, and at the same time reconsidered our follies, or at least my own. This novel journeys through the realms of drama and satire, through the tragedy of those who have experienced loss and the ingenuousness of those who treat existence like a circus.

The main character is endowed with unprecedented daring. Nothing or no one succeeds in controlling his acts and his words, except his own conscience. He shouts to the four winds that modern society has become a vast global madhouse in which it is normal to be anxious and stressed, and abnormal to be healthy, at peace, serene. With his Socratic method he challenges the thoughts of all who meet him. He bombards his listeners with countless questions.

My dream is that this book will be read not only by adults but by young people as well, many of whom are becoming passive servants to the social system. Unenraptured by dreams and adventures, they have become, despite some exceptions, consumers of products and services, not of ideas. Nevertheless, con-sciously or unconsciously, they all want a life peppered with effervescent emotions, even as babies when they risk leaving the crib. But where in society can such emotions be found in abundance? Some pay large amounts of money to achieve them and yet live in anguish. Others desperately seek fame and renown but die in boredom. The characters in this novel reject the crushing social routine, yet experience high doses of adrenaline daily. Still, the 'business' of selling dreams comes with a high price. That is why risks and windstorms are their companions.

The Encounter

On that most inspiring of days, a Friday, at five p.m., people usually in a hurry stopped and congregated at a downtown intersection of the great city. They stared upward, frozen at a corner of the Avenue of the Americas. A fire truck's ear-splitting siren announced danger. An ambulance attempted to break through the jammed traffic to reach the building.

Firemen arrived quickly and cordoned off the area, keeping any onlookers from approaching the imposing San Pablo Building, which belonged to the Megasoft Group, one of the largest companies in the world. Curious pedestrians lined the streets and soon the area was buzzing with questions: *What's going on? Why all the commotion?* Others simply pointed upward. On the twentieth floor, on the ledge of the stunning mirrored-glass building, stood a man ready to jump.

One more person hoped to cut short his brief existence. In a time steeped in sadness, more people died at their own hands than through war or murder. The numbers were astonishing to anyone who thought about them. Pleasure had become as wide as an ocean but as shallow as a pond. Many of the financially and intellectually privileged lived dull, empty lives, isolated in their world. Society afflicted the poor and the well-to-do equally.

The San Pablo jumper was a forty-year-old man with a well-chiseled face, strong eyebrows, taut skin and overgrown well-kept salt-and-pepper hair. His air of sophistication, though, sculpted through long years of study, was now reduced to dust. Of the five languages he spoke, none had helped him understand the language of his internal demons. Drowning in depression, he lived a meaningless life where nothing moved his spirit.

At that moment, only the end of his life seemed to matter. The monstrous phenomenon called death, which seemed so terrifying, was also a magical solution to his tortured soul. He looked upward, as if wishing to redeem himself for his last act, looked at the chasm below and took two quick, careless steps forward. The crowd gasped, fearing he was about to jump.

Some of the onlookers bit their fingernails under the mounting stress. Others didn't dare blink for fear of missing a single detail.

Human beings hate pain but have an extreme attraction to it; they detest misfortune and poverty, but such things seduce the eye. Even knowing that watching the outcome of that tragedy could cost them countless sleepless nights, they still could not look away. Meanwhile, drivers caught in the snarling traffic could not care less about the impending doom above, and leaned impatiently on their horns. Some stuck their heads out the windows and bellowed, 'Jump and get it over with!'

The chief of police followed the firemen to the top of the building, each trying and failing to reason with the would-be jumper. Defeated, the authorities reached out to a renowned psychiatrist, who was hastily called to the scene. The doctor, too, attempted to gain the man's trust, trying to make him see the consequences of his actions — but he couldn't even get close. 'One more step and I'll jump!' the man shouted. He seemed certain that only death would finally silence his thoughts. Audience or no, his decision was made. His mind replayed his misfortunes, his frustrations, feeding the fever of his grief.

Meanwhile, down on the street below, a man tried to make his way through the crowd toward the building. He looked like just another curious on-looker, only more poorly dressed. He wore a wrinkled black blazer over a faded blue shirt, long-sleeved and stained in places. He wasn't wearing a tie. And his wrinkled black pants looked like they hadn't been washed in a week. His longish, uncombed hair was graying at the temples. His full beard had gone untrimmed for some time. Dry skin with prominent wrinkles around his eyes and in the folds of his face showed he sometimes slept out in the open. He was between thirty and forty, but seemed aged beyond his years.

His unstructured appearance contrasted with the delicacy of his gestures. He gently touched people's shoulders, smiling as he passed. They couldn't describe the sensation of being touched by him, but they quickly made room for him.

He approached the crime scene tape but was stopped from going any further. Disregarding the barrier, he stared into the eyes of those blocking his way and said flatly, 'I need to go in. He's waiting for me.'

The firemen looked him up and down and shook their heads. He looked more like someone who needed help rather than someone who could provide it.

'What's your name?' they asked, without blinking.

'That doesn't matter at a time like this,' the mysterious man answered firmly.

'Who called you here?' the firemen asked.

'You'll find out. But if you keep me here any longer, you'll have to prepare for another funeral,' he said, raising his eyes toward the top of the building.

The firemen were starting to get nervous and the mysterious man's last phrase shook them. He hurried past them. 'After all,' they thought, 'maybe he's an eccentric psychiatrist or a relative of the jumper.'

When he got to the top of the building, the stranger was stopped again, this time by the police chief.

'Hold it right there. You can't be here,' adding that he should go back down at once.

But the man stared at them for a moment and answered calmly, 'What do you mean I can't be here? You were the ones who called me.'

The police chief looked at the psychiatrist who looked at the fire chief. They gestured to one another to find out who might have called this man. In that moment of confusion, the stranger hurried past the officer. There was no time to stop him. Any commotion could spook the jumper into carrying out his plan. They bit their lips and waited to see what happened.

This man who had come out of nowhere, uninvited and apparently unshaken by the possibility of this jumper plunging to his death, moved toward the ledge until he was dangerously close, about three feet away. Surprised, the jumper stammered, 'Get away from me or I'll kill myself!'

The stranger didn't flinch. Nonchalantly, he sat down on the ledge, took a sandwich from his coat pocket, and started eating it with gusto. Between bites, he whistled a cheery tune.

The jumper didn't know what to think. He took it as an insult and shouted:

'Stop that whistling! I'm going to jump.'

Annoyed, the stranger turned from his sandwich. 'Could you not interrupt my dinner?' he said and took several more healthy bites of his meal, swinging his legs over the ledge. He then looked at the confused jumper and offered him a bite.

Looking on, the officials were stunned. The police chief's lips trembled, the psychiatrist's eyes widened and the fire chief could only furrow his brow.

The jumper just stared and thought, 'This guy's crazier than me.'

The Introduction

To watch someone enjoy eating a sandwich just inches from a man about to jump to his death was surreal, like something out of a movie. The would-be jumper narrowed his eyes, tightened every muscle in his face and breathed fiercely, not knowing whether to jump, scream or pummel this stranger. Panting, he yelled at the top of his lungs, 'Get out of here, already! I'm going to jump.'

And he came within a hair of falling. This time, to those down below, it seemed, he really would smash into the ground. The crowd buzzed in horror and the police chief covered his eyes, not bearing to watch.

Everyone expected the stranger to pull away. He could have said, as the psychiatrist and the policeman had, 'No, don't do it! I'm leaving,' or simply offered advice like, 'Life is beautiful. You can overcome your problems. You have your whole life ahead of you.' But, to everyone's surprise, especially the man on the ledge, he hopped to his feet and began reciting a poem at the top of his lungs. He spoke toward the sky and pointed at the would-be jumper:

> Let the day this man was born be
> struck from the record of time!
> Let the dew from the grass of that
> morning evaporate!
> Let the clear blue sky that brought joy
> to strollers that afternoon be with-
> held!
> Let the night when this man was con-
> ceived be stolen by suffering!
> Reclaim from that night the glowing
> stars that dotted the heavens!
> Erase from his infancy all his smiles and
> his fears!
> Strike from his childhood his frolicking
> and his adventures!
> Steal from him his dreams and his
> nightmares, his sanity and his mad-
> ness!

When he was done, the stranger let a sadness wash over him. He dropped his voice and his gaze and said softly, 'one,' offering no further explanation. The crowd, amazed, wondered whether it might all be some sort of street theater. Neither did the police officer know how to react: Would it be better to interfere or wait to see where this all led? Hoping for an

12

explanation himself, the fire chief looked at the psychiatrist, who said, confused:

'I don't know a thing about . . . He must be just another nut.'

The jumper was stunned. The stranger's words echoed in his mind. Trying to make sense of it, he lashed out: 'Who are you to try to assassinate my past? What right do you have to destroy my childhood? What gives you the right?'

Even as he said it, the jumper thought, 'Can it be that I'm the one committing this murder?' But he tried to shrug off the thought.

Catching the jumper deep in thought, the stranger provoked him further.

'Be careful. Thinking is dangerous, especially for someone who wants to die. If you want to kill yourself, don't think.'

The man was dumbfounded; the stranger seemed to read his mind. He thought: 'Is this man encouraging me to jump? Is he some kind of sadist? Does he want to see blood?' He shook his head as if to cut short his trance, but thoughts always undermine impulsive desires. Seeing the jumper's mental confusion, the stranger spoke softly, to drive home his point.

'Don't think. Because if you do, you'll realize that whoever kills himself commits multiple homicides: First, he kills himself and then, slowly, he kills those left behind. If he thinks, he'll understand that guilt, mistakes, disappointments and misfortune are the privileges of living. Death has no privileges.' The stranger's personality shifted from confidence to sorrow. He said the word 'four' and shook his head indignantly.

The jumper was paralyzed. He wanted to disregard this stranger's ideas, but they were like a virus infecting his mind. Trying to resist the temptation to think, he instead challenged the stranger.

'And who are you to try antagonizing me instead of saving me? Why don't you treat me like what I am: a sick, pitiful mental case?' He raised his voice. 'Leave me alone! I have nothing left to live for.'

Undaunted, the stranger lost his patience and pressed forward.

'Who says you're this wilting flower? A man who has lost his love of life? Some poor, underprivileged soul who can't bear the weight of his past? To me, you're none of that. To me, you're just a man too proud to be affected by misery greater than your own, a man who has locked his feelings away deep inside.'

The man on the ledge felt as if he had been struck in the chest, unable to breathe.

Angrily, he growled, 'Who are *you* to judge me?'

The stranger had pegged him perfectly. Like a bolt of lightning, his words had pierced the deepest reaches of his memory.

At that moment, the man on the ledge thought about his father, who had crushed his childhood and caused him so much pain — his emotionally distant father, who would never let anyone in. It was extremely difficult for the man to deal with the scars from the past. Rattled by those haunting memories, he said in a softer tone, now with tears in his eyes:

'Shut up! Don't say another word. Let me die in peace.'

Seeing that he had touched a deep wound, the stranger also softened his tone. 'I respect your pain and cannot judge it. Your pain is unique, and you are the only one who can truly feel it. It belongs to you and to no one else.'

These words nearly brought the man to tears. He understood that no one can judge another's suffering. His father's pain was unique and therefore could not be felt or judged by anyone other than his father. He had always blamed his father, but for the first time he began to see him through different eyes. At that moment, to his surprise, the stranger said something that could have been taken as praise or criticism.

'And in my eyes, you're also something else: courageous. Because you're willing to smash your body in exchange for a restful sleep, even if it is inside of a tomb. That is, without a doubt, a beautiful illusion . . . ' And he paused so the man could fully realize the consequences of his actions.

Again, the man wondered about this stranger who showed up just in time with words that cut to the quick. A night of eternal sleep in a tomb? The idea suddenly sickened him. Still, insistent on carrying out his plan, he fought back:

'I don't see any reason to go on with this worthless life,' he argued, vehemently, furrowing his brow, tormented by the thoughts that ran uninvited into his head. The stranger confronted him poignantly:

'Worthless life? You ingrate! Your heart, at this very moment, must be trying to burst from your chest to save itself from being killed.' He pleaded, in the voice of the man's own heart: 'No! No! Have pity on me! I pumped your blood tirelessly, millions of times. I lived only for you. And now you want to silence me, without even giving me the right to defend myself? I was the most faithful of servants. And what is my reward? A ridiculous death! You want to stop my beating only to end your suffering. How can you be this selfish? If only I could pump courage into your selfish veins.' Challenging the man further, he asked, 'Why don't you pay attention to your chest and hear the desperation of your heart?'

The man felt his shirt vibrate. He hadn't noticed that his heart was about to explode. It did in fact seem to be screaming inside his chest. But, just when the man appeared convinced, he mustered one last defense.

'I've already sentenced myself to death. There's no hope.'

'You've sentenced yourself?' the stranger asked. 'Did you know that suicide is the most unjust judgment? Why condemn yourself without defending yourself? Why not give yourself the right to argue with your ghosts, to face your losses? It's much easier to say life isn't worth living . . . You're not being fair to yourself.'

The stranger knew in masterly fashion that those who take their own lives, even those who plan their deaths, can't understand the depth of the pain they cause. He knew that if they could see the despair of their loved ones and the inexplicable consequences of suicide, they would draw back and fight for their lives. He knew that no letter or note could serve as a defense. The man on top of the San Pablo Building had left a message for his only child, trying to explain the unexplainable.

He had also spoken with his psychiatrists and psychologists about his ideas on suicide. He had been analyzed, interpreted, diagnosed, and had listened to countless theories about his metabolic and cerebral deficiencies. And he had been encouraged to overcome his problems by seeing them from a different perspective. But none of it made sense to that rigid intellectual. None of those interventions or explanations could lift him from his emotional quagmire.

The man was inaccessible. But for the first time someone, this stranger at the top of a building, challenged his thinking. The stranger was a specialist in piercing impenetrable minds. His words evoked more noise than tranquillity. He knew that without that noise there is no questioning, and without questioning the gamut of possibilities goes undiscovered. The jumper couldn't stand it any longer, and decided to ask the stranger a question; he had strongly resisted doing so, as he had assumed that he would be entering a minefield. But he stepped into it, regardless.

'Who are you?'

The man was hoping for a short, clear

answer, but none was forthcoming. Instead, he fielded another burst of questions.

'Who am I? How can you ask who I am if you don't know who *you* are? Who are you, who would seek to silence your existence in front of a terrified audience?'

The man answered sarcastically, 'Me? Who am I? I'm a man who in a few short moments will cease to exist. Then I won't know who I am or what I was.'

'Well, I'm different from you. Because you've stopped looking for answers. You've become a god, while every day I ask myself 'Who am I?'' The stranger paused, then asked another question: 'Would you like to know the answer I found?'

Reluctantly, the man nodded.

'I'll answer you if you answer me first,' the stranger said. 'From what philosophical, religious or scientific fountain did you drink to believe that death is the end of existence? Are we living atoms that disintegrate, never again to regain their structure? Are we merely an organized brain or do we have a mind that coexists with the brain and transcends its limits? Does any person know? Do you? What believer can defend his thought without the element of faith? What neuroscientist can defend his arguments without making use of the phenomenon of speculation? What atheist or agnostic can categorically defend his ideas free of uncertainty?'

The stranger seemed to press on with this Socratic method, asking endless questions, challenging every answer, trying to stimulate critical thinking. The man grew dizzy from that explosion of inquiries. He considered himself an atheist, but he discovered that his atheism sprang from a fountain of speculation. Like many 'normal' people, he pontificated about these phenomena without once debating them removed from passion and ideology.

The stranger had turned the questions on himself. But before the man on the ledge could answer, he offered his own response:

'We're both ignorant. The difference between us is that I recognize my ignorance.'

Shaking the Foundation of Faith

While grand ideas were being debated at the top of the building, a few people below walked away without ever knowing what happened. Some couldn't stand to wait to know another man's misfortune. But most remained, eager to see the result.

From the crowd emerged a man named Bartholomew, who was marinated in whiskey and vodka. He, too, was an ordinary man with hidden scars, despite being extremely good-natured — and from time to time brazen. His short, unruly black hair had gone weeks without touching a comb or water. He was over thirty. Clear skin, high eyebrows. A slightly swollen face concealed the scars of his battered existence. He was so drunk that his legs wobbled as he walked. When he bumped into people, instead of thanking them for keeping him on his feet, he complained in a slurred and tongue-tied voice.

'Hey, you knocked me down,' or 'Let me through, pal, I'm in a hurry.'

Bartholomew took a few more steps before tripping against the curb. To avoid crashing into the ground, he grabbed onto an old lady and fell on top of her. The poor woman almost suffered a broken back. She cracked him on the head with her cane as she tried to disentangle herself, yelling, 'Get off me, you pervert!'

He didn't have the strength to move. But hearing the old woman scream, he wouldn't be outdone.

'Help! Somebody help me! This old lady is attacking me.'

People nearby shifted their gaze from the sky to the ground. They pulled the dizzy drunk off the old woman and gave him a hard shove. 'Get moving, you bum.'

Bewildered but petulant Bartholomew stammered, 'Thank you, folks, for the ha . . . the ha . . . ' He was so drunk it took him three tries to thank them for the 'hand.' He tried to brush the dust from his pants and almost fell again.

'You saved me from that — ' he said, pointing at the old woman.

She lifted her cane, menacingly, and he caught himself in time.

' — from that lovely lady.'

He retreated and began to walk away. As he was making his way through the crowd, he asked himself why everyone seemed so intent on staring into the sky. He thought maybe someone had seen a UFO. As if the scene wasn't chaotic enough, he struggled to stare up at the building and started to shout.

'I see him! I see the E.T. Careful, people! He's yellow with awful horns. And he's holding a weapon!'

Bartholomew's drunken mind was hallucinating again. This was not your run-of-the-mill alcoholic. He loved egging people on and making a scene. That's why he called himself Honeymouth. The only thing he loved more than drinking was hearing the sound of his own voice. His closest friends joked that he had CSS — compulsive speech syndrome.

He grabbed those next to him, urging them to see the alien only he could see. But they shoved him aside.

'Man, how rude! Just because I saw the E.T. first they're green with envy,' he slurred.

Meanwhile, atop the San Pablo, the man on the ledge was deep in thought. Maybe what he needed, he thought, was a clear mind. His was a jumble of empty ideas and superficial concepts about life and death. Maybe what he needed was to encourage his ignorance — quite a change for a man who always considered himself an intellectual.

He felt a sudden calm wash over him. And the stranger used that moment to tell the story of a great thinker:

'Why did Darwin, in the waning moments

of his life, when he was suffering unbearable fits of vomiting, cry out 'my God'? Was he weak to call on God when faced with his draining strength? Was he a coward in the face of death? Did he consider it an unnatural phenomenon even though his theory was based on the natural processes of the selection of species? Why was there such a chasm between his existence and his theory? Is death the end or the beginning? In it, do we lose ourselves or find ourselves? Can it be that when we die we are erased from history like actors who never again perform?'

The man swallowed hard. He had never thought about these questions. Though he accepted the theory of evolution, he knew nothing of Darwin the man and his internal conflict. But could Darwin have been weak and confused? 'Could Darwin have ever given up on life? No. It's not possible. He surely was much too much in love with life, more so than I am,' he thought.

This stranger, with his endless piercing questions, had stripped the man bare. His heart quieted and he tried to catch his breath before replying, 'I don't know. I've never thought about those questions.'

The stranger went on:

'We work, we buy, we sell and we build friendships. We discuss politics, economics

24

and science, but deep down we're simply children joking at the dinner table, unable to fathom life's complexities. We write millions of books and store them in immense libraries, but we're still mere infants. We know almost nothing about what we are. We're billions of little children, thoughtlessly at play, on this dazzling planet.'

The man's breathing slowed. And soon, he began to recover who he was. Julio Lambert — that was his name — was the bearer of a sharp, quick, privileged mind. In his promising academic career, he had earned doctoral degrees and become an expert in his field. He reveled in grilling aspiring young graduate students presenting their theses with his incisive, biting critiques. He had always been self-centered, and expected that others would orbit around his brilliance. Now, however, his theories were being picked apart — by a man in rags. He felt like a helpless child realizing his own fears and ignorance. He was being called a boy and didn't react with rage. Instead, for the first time, he took pleasure in recognizing his smallness. He no longer felt like a man reaching the end, but one starting anew.

The Losses

Insanity can only be treated when it drops its disguise. And Julio, who hid behind his eloquence, culture and academic status, was now beginning to remove his mask. But there would be a long road ahead of him.

The sun was low on the horizon. And thoughts of suicide were dissipating atop the San Pablo Building. At that moment, the stranger said the number twenty, and a rush of sadness consumed him momentarily.

'Why do you call out numbers while you talk?' Julio asked.

The stranger did not reply immediately. He stared at the horizon, saw several lights across the city being turned on, others extinguished. He breathed slowly, as if wishing to be able to relight them all. He turned to Julio, looked intently into his eyes and spoke:

'Why do I count numbers? Because in the brief time we've been on the top of this building, twenty people closed their eyes forever. Twenty healthy but desperate people gave up on life. Twenty did not give themselves a chance. People who once played and loved, wept and battled, felt completely defeated . . . Now, they leave a trail of pain for their loved ones in their wake.'

Julio could not understand why this man was so attuned to others' feelings. Who was he? What had he experienced to have these deep sentiments? That's when he noticed the stranger was weeping. It was as if this man were feeling the indescribable pain of children who have lost their parents to suicide and grow up wondering, 'Why didn't they think of me?' Or it was as if he were reading the minds of parents who, having lost their children to suicide, are wracked with guilt and wonder endlessly: 'What more could I have done?' Or perhaps the stranger was simply remembering his own unknown losses.

The fact was that both the stranger's words and his tears completely disarmed Julio. The intellectual began a journey along the path of his own childhood and could not bear it. He allowed himself to break into tears without caring who was watching him. This man who rarely showed his pain was deeply scarred.

'My father used to play with me, kiss me, and call me 'my dear son . . . ''

And, taking a deep breath, he said something he had always thought forbidden to say aloud, something which even his closest colleagues didn't know, something which, though buried deep within his heart, continued to shape his life.

' . . . but he abandoned me when I was a child, without any explanation.' He paused, then added, 'I was watching cartoons in the living room when I heard a loud bang from his bedroom. I rushed in and found him on the floor, bleeding. I was only six years old. I screamed and screamed, begging for help. My mother wasn't home. I ran to the neighbors, but I was so despondent that for a few minutes they couldn't understand what I was saying. I had barely begun my life and had lost my childhood, my innocence. My world collapsed. I came to hate cartoons. I had no brothers or sisters. My mother, a poor widow, had to go back to work and struggled to support me. But she got cancer and died when I was twelve. Relatives raised me. I moved from house to house, always feeling like a stranger. I was a difficult teenager, and hated family gatherings. Sometimes I was treated like a servant and had to keep my mouth shut.'

Julio had developed a rough exterior. He was distant, shy, unyielding. He felt ugly and unloved. He buried himself in his studies, and with little help, got himself into college and became a brilliant student. He worked during the day and went to school at night, studying in the late hours and on weekends. And, now, he vented aloud a deep-seated anger he had never overcome:

'But I showed them. I became more cultured and successful than all those who had ridiculed me. I was an exemplary college student and became a highly respected professor, envied by some and hated by others. I was admired. I married and had a son, John Marcus. I don't think I was either a good husband or a good father. Time went by, and a year ago I fell in love with a student who was fifteen years younger than I. I tried to seduce her, buy her, I took on debts. I ruined my credit, lost everything . . . and in the end she left me. It was as if the earth had opened up and swallowed me whole. My wife discovered the affair and left me, too. When she left, I realized that I still loved her; I couldn't lose her! I tried to win her back, but she was tired of the cold intellectual who had never been affectionate, who was a pessimist, depressed and, on top of everything else, bankrupt. She left me for good.'

At that moment, he allowed himself to cry. He hadn't cried this much since losing his mother. He sobbed and wiped his eyes. Whoever looked at him and saw a rigid professor knew nothing of his scars.

'John Marcus, my son, started using drugs. He was always angry and accused me of being a distant father. He went to rehab several times. Today, he lives in another state and refuses to speak to me. Ever since I was five years old people have been abandoning me. Some through the fault of others, some through my fault,' he said, learning for the first time how to remove his mask.

Pictures of his childhood ran quickly through his head and he remembered the final images of his father, images he had blocked out. He remembered that he had called out to him day and night for weeks after his loss. Julio grew up angry with his father and was convinced he had locked away those injured feelings deep inside.

Now he was reliving all those painful emotions. His notable education was no match for the pain that had been formed in his past. His learning and sophistication could not help him to be flexible and relaxed. He was an intense, rigid man. He never let down his guard before his psychiatrists and psychologists. Instead, he criticized them because he thought their evaluations of him were childish for someone of his intellectual level. Helping this man was a daunting task.

After telling his story openly for the first time, Julio fell silent again, fearing the stranger would offer more of the same glib, useless advice he had often heard before.

Instead, the stranger found a way to joke.

'My friend, you're in a real bind,' the stranger said.

Julio gave a wan smile. He wasn't expecting that response. And the stranger offered none of the empty advice. He couldn't feel Julio's pain, but the stranger was familiar with abandonment.

'I know what loss is. There are moments when our world seems to come crashing down around us and no one else can understand it.'

The stranger wiped tears from his eyes as he spoke. Perhaps his scars were as deep or deeper than Julio's.

Julio, once again moved, said, 'Tell me, who are you.'

The stranger responded with a warm silence.

'Are you a psychiatrist or psychologist?' he asked, believing himself in the presence of an extraordinary professional.

'No, I'm not,' the stranger affirmed with assurance.

'A philosopher?'

'I appreciate the world of ideas, but I'm not a philosopher.'

'Are you the head of some church?' he asked.

'No,' the man replied firmly.

Julio asked impatiently, 'Are you crazy?'

The stranger replied with a slight smile. 'Now, that's more likely,' he said, and Julio couldn't have been more confused.

'Who are you? Tell me.'

He pressed the stranger who was now being watched from below by a confused crowd. The psychiatrist, the fire chief and the police chief strained to hear the conversation, but could only hear murmurs. Seeing that Julio was not going to back down, the stranger spread his arms, raised them to the sky, and said:

'When I think about how briefly our lives pass, about all that has come before me and all that remains to come, that's when I see how truly small I am in the grand scheme of things. When I consider that one day I will fall into eternal silence, swallowed by the passing of time, I realize my limitations. And when I see those limits, I stop trying to be a god and simply see myself as what I am: a mere human being. I go from being the center of the universe to simply a wanderer searching for answers . . . '

The stranger didn't answer the question, but Julio drank in the words. His answer made Julio wonder the same thing as so many who would encounter the stranger: 'Is this man a lunatic or a genius? Or both?' He tried to fathom the depths of the stranger's words, but it was no easy task.

The stranger again looked toward the heavens and began to question God in a way Julio had never heard:

'God, who are you? Why do you remain silent before the insanity of some believers and do nothing to calm the doubts of skeptics? Why do you disguise your will as the laws of physics and conceal your designs as simply random events? Your silence unnerves me.'

Julio was an expert in religion — Christianity, Islam, Buddhism and others — but none of it helped him understand the stranger's mind. He didn't know whether these were the ramblings of a bald-faced atheist or someone who was close friends with God himself. The renowned professor again wondered: What kind of man is this? And where did he come from?

The Calling

People are predictable. Leaders, too. In modern society, most people don't inspire emotion or imagination. But what was lacking in 'normal' people abounded in the mysterious stranger. Julio was so curious about this man's identity that he asked again who he was. Though, this time, he asked knowing full well that he didn't know much about himself, either.

'I don't know who I am. I need to find myself, I know. But please, grant me just this. Who are you?'

The man flashed a thin smile; Julio was finally beginning to speak his language. And feeling that rush of inspiration, the stranger stood up and faced the horizon, spreading his arms to the fading sun, and said confidently, 'I'm a dreamseller.'

Julio was even more confused. The stranger seemed to have plunged from lucidity into lunacy. None of this made any sense to Julio, but it seemed to mean everything to the stranger.

On the street below, Bartholomew's ramblings reached a fever pitch: 'Look, it's the alien leader! He spread his arms and changed colors.'

The dreamseller looked down on the eager masses below and felt a deep, abiding pity for them.

Julio rubbed his face. He couldn't believe his ears.

'A dreamseller? What . . . What is that?' he asked, totally lost for words.

The stranger had seemed so intelligent. He had shown such intrepid thinking, had shattered Julio's preconceptions and helped organize his cluttered mind. And just when he had Julio convinced, this dreamseller had shattered the image with a single word.

The psychiatrist, who was standing about twenty-five yards away, heard the stranger identify himself and quickly sized him up for the police and fire chiefs: 'I knew it. They're both crazy.'

Just then the dreamseller looked to his right and saw a sniper in a nearby building, about a hundred and fifty yards away, aiming a rifle with a silencer at him. The dreamseller quickly pushed Julio to the side and the two fell next to each other on the ledge. Julio had no idea what was going on, and rather than scare him, the dreamseller just said:

'If that fall bothered you, just imagine what

would happen when you hit the ground from this building.'

The crowd below thought the stranger had held the jumper back, but they all misunderstood what had happened. The dreamseller looked toward the horizon and saw that the sniper had left. Was he hallucinating? Who could want such a simple man dead? Then they both stood back up on the ledge and the stranger repeated himself, 'Yes, I'm a dreamseller.'

Julio was still confused and thought maybe the stranger meant he was some kind of traveling salesman.

'Wait, what do you mean? What *products* do you sell?'

'I try to sell courage to the insecure, daring to the timid, joy to those who have lost their zest for life, sense to the reckless, ideas to the thinkers.'

Julio falling back into his staid thinking, told himself, 'This isn't happening. I'm having a nightmare. I must have died and didn't realize it. A while ago, I was ready to kill myself because I couldn't understand the source of my pain. Now I'm even more confused because the man who rescued me claims he sells what can't be sold.' And to his surprise, the stranger added:

'And for those who think of putting a

period to life, I try to sell a comma, just a comma.'

'A comma?' asked Julio.

'Yes, a comma. One small comma, so they can continue to write their story.'

Julio began to sweat. In a kind of sudden enlightenment, he realized that the dreamseller had just sold him a comma, and he had bought it without realizing it. No price, no pressure, no tricks, no haggling. He placed his hands on his head to see if everything that was happening to him was real.

The professor was starting to understand. He looked down and saw the crowd awaiting his decision. Down deep, those people were as lost as he was. They were free to come and go, but they were missing out on the sweetness of life. They didn't feel free to express their own personality.

Julio felt like he was trapped in a movie, floating between the surreal and the concrete. 'Is this guy real, or is my mind playing tricks on me?' he wondered, in a haze of fascination and uncertainty. No one had ever cast a spell on him like this.

Then this stranger made him a very real offer.

'Come, follow me and I will make you a dreamseller.'

Julio's mind was racing, but he was frozen.

His voice was stuck in his throat. He was physically paralyzed, but deep in thought: 'How can I follow a man I've known for less than an hour?' he thought. But at the same time, he was drawn to this calling.

He was tired of academic debates. He was one of the most eloquent intellectuals among his peers, but many of his colleagues, and he himself, lived mired in the mud of envy and endless vanity. He felt that the university where he taught — this temple of learning — lacked the tolerance and creativity to unleash fresh thinking. Some temples of learning had become as inflexible as the most rigid religions. Professors, scientists and thinkers weren't free to explore. They had to conform to their departments' thinking.

Now he stood before a shabbily dressed man with unkempt hair and no social standing, but one who was a thought-provoking adventurer, a dissenter from conventional wisdom, free to chase new thoughts. And this man had made him the craziest and most exciting of proposals: to sell dreams. 'How? To whom? To what end? Will I be praised or mocked?' the intellectual wondered. He also knew that all great thinkers must travel unexplored paths.

Julio had always been sensible and had never made a scene in public — not until he climbed to the top of this building. He knew this time he had caused an uproar. It hadn't been for show; he really was going to end his life. He was afraid of using a gun or taking pills, so he'd come to the top of the San Pablo Building.

But the dreamseller's invitation continued to echo in his mind like a grenade blowing apart all the concepts he held true. A long minute passed. Conflicted, he thought, 'I've tried to live my life sheltered in the life of academia, but it failed me. I tried to challenge my students to think for themselves but instead taught them only to regurgitate information. I tried to contribute to society, but sealed myself off from it. If I manage to sell dreams to a few people, as this stranger has sold to me, maybe my life will have more meaning than it has had until now.'

And so I decided to follow him. I am Julio, this extraordinary stranger's first disciple.

He became my teacher. And I, the first to agree to this unpredictable journey with no set course or destination. Crazy? Maybe. But no crazier than the life I had been living.

The First Step

As soon as we left the scene we were stopped by one of those closely watching us at the top of the building, the police chief. He was a tall man, about six-foot-three, and slightly over-weight, impeccably dressed, graying hair, smooth skin and exuded the air of a man who loved power.

When we stopped in front of him he barely noticed me. He was used to dealing with suicides and considered them weak and damaged. To him, I was just another statistic. I could taste his bitter prejudice and I hated it. After all, I was much more learned than this gun-toting buffoon. My weapons were ideas, which were more powerful and more effective. But I didn't have the strength to defend myself. And I didn't have to. I had a torpedo at my side, the man who had saved me.

The policeman was really interested in grilling the dreamseller. He wanted to know more about this character who fell outside of his statistics. He hadn't been able to hear much of what we said, but the little he heard had amazed him. He studied the dreamseller from head to toe, unable to reconcile the image. The stranger seemed alien to his surroundings. Uneasy, he began his interrogation. I guessed that, like me, the policeman was about to step into a hornet's nest. And he did.

'What's your name?' he asked in an arrogant tone.

The dreamseller studied him for just a second, then said:

'Aren't you happy this man changed his mind? Aren't you simply overwhelmed with joy at knowing this man's life has been saved?' And he gazed at me.

The policeman lost his footing on his pedestal. He hadn't expected his insensitivity to be laid bare in a few short seconds. He stammered, then said in a formal tone, 'Yes, of course I'm happy for him.'

The dreamseller had a way of making any man realize his insensitivity. He made them see how foolish they were acting. And then he launched another torpedo:

'If you're happy, why don't you show your happiness? Why don't you ask him his name and tell him how glad you are? After all, isn't a human life worth more than this building?'

The police chief was stripped naked more quickly than I was, and it was perfect. The dreamseller won back my self-esteem. He was a thought-provoking expert. Watching him rattle the police chief, I started to understand: It's impossible to follow a leader like this man without admiring him. Admiration is stronger than power, charisma more intense than intimidation. And I had begun to greatly admire the charismatic dreamseller.

It made me think about my relationship with my students. I was a vault of information but had never understood that charisma is fundamental to teaching. First you fell in love with the dreamseller's charisma, then you opened to his teachings. I was afflicted with the same disease of most intellectuals: I was boring. I had been dull, critical, demanding. Even I couldn't stand myself.

The police chief, now shamed by the dreamseller, turned quickly to me and, like a child who has been told to apologize, said, 'I'm happy for you, sir.'

In a softer tone, the officer asked for the dreamseller's identification.

The reply was simple: 'I don't have any ID.'

'How can that be? Everybody needs some kind of identification. Without it, you have no . . . identity.'

'My identity is what I am,' the dreamseller said.

'You can be arrested if you don't identify yourself. You could be a terrorist, a public threat, a psychopath. Who are you?' the policeman asked, slipping back into an aggressive tone.

I saw where this was headed. The dreamseller replied:

'I'll answer you if you answer me first. On whose authority should you be able to know my most intimate secrets? What are your credentials for plumbing the depths of my mind?' he said flatly.

The policeman took the bait. He started to raise his voice, not knowing he'd be trapped by his own wit.

'I'm Pedro Alcantara, chief of police of this district,' he said, radiating a proud and self-confident air.

Annoyed, the dreamseller said, 'I didn't ask about your profession, your social status or your activities. I want to know about your essence. Who is the human being beneath that uniform?'

The police officer quickly scratched an eyebrow, revealing a nervous tick he'd hidden away, not knowing how to respond. Lowering his voice, the dreamseller asked another question: 'What is your greatest dream?'

'My greatest dream? Well, I, I . . . ' he stammered, again not knowing how to reply.

Never had anyone using so few words confronted this pillar of authority. He remained motionless. I could look into the dreamseller's eyes and see what he was thinking. The police chief protected 'normal' people but couldn't protect his own emotions.

That's when I began to see myself in him. And what I saw bothered me. How could a person without dreams protect society, unless he was a robot whose sole function was to make arrests? How could someone without dreams mold citizens who dream of being free and united?

Then the dreamseller added, 'Careful. You fight for public safety, but fear and loneliness are the thieves that steal our emotions, and they can be more dangerous than common criminals. Your son doesn't need a chief of police. He needs a shoulder to cry on, a friend with whom he can share secret feelings and who teaches him to think. Live that dream.'

The police chief was speechless. He had been trained to deal with criminals, to arrest them, and had never heard of thieves who invade the mind. He didn't know what to do without his weapon and his badge. Like most 'normal' people, including me, he defined himself through his profession. At home, he didn't know how to be a father, only a police officer. He was unable to separate the two roles. He won medals for bravery, but was wasting away as a human being.

I wondered how the dreamseller knew the chief had a son, or whether he had made a lucky guess. But I saw the police chief squirming, as if handcuffed inside his mind, trying to escape from a prison years in the making.

The psychiatrist couldn't hold back any longer. Seeing the police chief at a loss, he tried to trip up the dreamseller. Using psychiatry, he tried to rattle the dreamseller, saying, 'Anyone who won't reveal his identity is hiding his own frailty.'

'Do you think I'm frail?' asked the dreamseller.

'I don't know,' replied the psychiatrist, hesitating.

'Well, you're right. I *am* frail. I've learned that no one is worthy of being called an expert, including a scientist, especially if he doesn't recognize his own limits, his own frailties. Are you frail?' he shot back. 'Well?'

Seeing the psychiatrist hesitate, the dreamseller asked, 'Which discipline of psychotherapy do you subscribe to?'

That question came as a surprise. I didn't understand where the dreamseller was going with this. But the psychiatrist, who was also a psychotherapist, said proudly, 'I'm a Freudian.'

'Very well. Then answer me this: Which is more complex, a psychological theory, whatever it is, or the mind of a human being?'

The psychiatrist, fearing a trap, didn't answer for a moment. Then he replied indirectly. 'We use theories to decipher the human mind.'

'Fine. Then allow me one more question: You can map out a theory and read every last text on the subject. But can you exhaust the understanding of the human mind?'

'No. But I'm not here to be questioned by you,' he said dismissively, not realizing what the dreamseller was driving at. 'Besides, I'm an expert in the human mind.'

The dreamseller took that opening:

'Mental health professionals are poets of existence, they have a grand mission. However, they can't put a patient into a theoretical text, yet try desperately to put a theoretical text inside of a person. Don't trap your patients between the walls of a theory, or you'll reduce their abilities to grow. Each sickness is unique to the one who's sick. Every sick person has a mind. And every mind is an infinite universe.'

I understood what he was telling the psychiatrist, for I felt in my own skin what he meant. When the psychiatrist approached me, he used techniques and interpretations that I immediately rejected. He dealt with the act of suicide, but not with the ravaged human being inside me. His theory might be useful in predictable situations, especially when the patient seeks help, but not in situations where the patient rejects help or has lost hope. I was resistant. First, I needed to be touched by the psychiatrist the man. And later, by the psychiatrist the professional. Because he had approached me as an illness, and not as a person, I perceived him as an invader and withdrew.

The dreamseller took the opposite approach. He started with the sandwich; he asked me deep questions to know more about who I was, like nourishment that reached down into my bones. Only then did he deal with the act of suicide.

The psychiatrist, though he had been called a poet of existence, didn't like being called out by some shabbily dressed stranger with no credentials. He didn't seem happy at all that I no longer wanted to commit suicide. Damn his envy! I wanted to make him see that he was missing the bigger picture. But then again, I'd done the same thing inside the sacred temple of my classroom.

Then, the dreamseller placed a hand on the shoulder of the young fire chief and told him, 'Thank you, son, for the risks you have taken

47

to save people you don't know. You *are* a dreamseller.'

The dreamseller turned and headed toward the elevator, and I followed him. The psychiatrist turned to the police chief to speak just as the dreamseller turned around to say something himself, and, amazingly, they said the same thing:

'Crazy people understand each other.'

The psychiatrist turned red. He must have asked himself, as I did, 'How could they have been thinking the same thing?'

The dreamseller saw there was time for one final and unforgettable lesson at the top of that building. He told the psychiatrist, 'Some people's craziness is obvious. For others, it's hidden. Which type is yours?'

'Not me, I'm normal!' the psychiatrist snapped.

'Well, mine is visible,' the dreamseller said.

He then turned his back and began to walk, his hands on my shoulders. After three steps, he looked toward the sky and said, 'God save me from 'normal' people!'

Exorcising the Demons

We rode down the elevator silently. I was lost in thought, the dreamseller calmly whistling and staring ahead. We passed through the immense lobby, richly decorated with chandeliers, antique furniture and an enormous reception desk of dark mahogany. Only then did I realize their beauty. Before, my world was colored by my own dark emotions.

Outside, the lights shone brightly, lighting the crowd that was anxiously awaiting news from the top of the building. News that I would do my best not to provide. Truth be told, I wanted to hide, forget the commotion, turn the page and not think about my pain for a second longer. I was ashamed and shrank from the attention. But I couldn't teleport myself out of there. I had to face the stares of my audience. For a brief moment I was angry with myself. I thought, 'There were other ways I could have faced my demons. Why didn't I choose one of them?' But pain blinds us, and frustration clouds our thinking.

When we left the San Pablo Building and broke through the police tape, I wanted to cover my face and leave quickly, but the huge

49

crowd made it impossible; there was no room to run. The media wanted information. I made my way through this Trail of Tears, eyes downcast.

The dreamseller kept my secret. No one knew what had really happened atop the building; the rich exchange I had with that mystery man remained lodged in my head alone.

As we escaped the media and began walking among the crowd, I was startled. We were treated like celebrities. I was famous, but not in the way I had hoped.

To the dreamseller, society's obsession with worshipping celebrities was the clearest sign that we were losing our minds. As we walked, he asked aloud:

'After all, who deserves more applause, an unknown garbageman or a Hollywood actor? Whose mind is more complex? Whose story is more complex? There is no difference. But 'normals' think this heresy.'

As the crowd kept prodding to know what had happened on top of the building, the dreamseller, seeing me withdraw, changed the topic. Instead of trying to discreetly shift the focus, he raised his arms calling for silence, which came only after a prolonged moment.

I thought: 'Here comes another speech.' But the dreamseller was more eccentric than

I imagined. He asked everyone to form a large circle, which was difficult given the tightly packed crowd. And to everyone's surprise, he went to the center and began dancing an Irish jig. He crouched, kicking his legs into the air and sang euphorically.

I couldn't stop thinking: 'An intellectual wouldn't act like this, and even if he felt the inspiration, he wouldn't have the courage to do it.' Damn my prejudice. A little while ago, I had almost killed myself, but prejudice was still alive and well. I was a 'normal' in disguise.

No one really understood the dreamseller's actions, least of all me, but some started to join in. They couldn't believe that just a few minutes ago they had nearly witnessed a tragedy, and now they were dancing with joy. Joy is contagious, and they had been infected with the dreamseller's euphoria.

The circle widened. Those who knew the dance or those who risked dancing it without knowing the steps began hooking arms and whirling in circles. Those at the edge of the circle eventually got into the spirit and started clapping to the rhythm. But many remained farther away, among them several well-dressed executives. They didn't want to be anywhere near that band of maniacs. Like me, they preferred to hide their madness.

51

People kept jumping in and out of the circle to show off their dance skills, each one leaving to wild applause. I felt just fine on the outside of the circle, protected. But suddenly the dreamseller grabbed my arms and thrust me into the center of the circle.

I was embarrassed and just stood there. The others went on dancing around me and urging me on, but I was paralyzed. A few minutes earlier I was the center of attention, and now I just hoped no one would recognize me — certainly not a colleague or student from the university. I didn't fear death, but I was deathly afraid of being embarrassed. God, I was sicker than I thought.

I was usually discreet, reserved and spoke in measured tones, at least when I wasn't annoyed. I never showed joy in public. I was infected with the virus of most intellectuals: a stiff formality. The crowd waited for me to let loose, but I was paralyzed by my shyness. Suddenly, another surprise. The penniless drunk, Bartholomew, hooked his arm in mine and spun me into a dance.

The man had awful breath and, still drunk, he could barely stay on his feet, much less dance. I had to hold him up. Seeing how stiff I was, he stopped dancing, looked at me — and planted a kiss on my left cheek. 'Lighten up, man. The leader of the E.T.s saved you. This party's for you!'

My pridefulness took a direct hit. Seldom had I seen or heard so much liveliness and spontaneity in so few words. And I started to understand. I thought of the parable of Jesus Christ and the lost sheep. I had read it once, years ago, through the eyes of a scientist and thought it ridiculous to abandon ninety-nine sheep to go looking for a lost one. Socialists sacrificed millions of people for an ideal, but Christ took it a step further. He was wild with grief at losing one soul, and wild with joy when he found it.

I had criticized how Christ romanticized that moment, but now the dreamseller was showing the same joy. Only after the loopy drunk kissed me did I realize the dreamseller was celebrating for me. The drunk was more sober than I was. I was thunderstruck; I had never thought it possible for a stranger to place so much importance on someone he didn't know. I was lost then found, 'dead' then brought back to life. What more could I want? Shouldn't I celebrate, too? I tossed aside my status as an 'intellectual.'

I was 'normal,' and like many normals my madness was hidden, disguised; I needed to be spontaneous. I let go. The dreamseller had emphasized that the heart needs no reason to beat. The greatest reason for staying alive is life itself. At the university, I had forgotten that the great philosophers often discussed the meaning of life, the pursuit of happiness and the art of beauty. It was the first time I had ever danced without a head full of whiskey. It had been years since I'd felt this good.

The 'normals' were so starved for joy that when this dreamseller gave them permission, they frolicked like children. Everyone was dancing. Men in ties. Women in long dresses and miniskirts. Children and teenagers joined in.

A little old lady danced by with her cane. It was the same woman Bartholomew had fallen on. Her name was Jurema. She had lived eighty good years. Anyone who thought she should be hobbling around at her age was in for a surprise. She was in better shape than me, though she showed a slight shiver of Parkinson's. But she could dance like a star. The dreamseller liked her immediately. They danced together, and I rubbed my eyes to see if it was all real.

Suddenly, she broke loose from the dreamseller's arms and bumped into Bartholomew at the center of the circle. She tapped him on the head with her cane, and joked sweetly, 'You pervert.' I couldn't hold back. I rolled on the ground with laughter. She did what I'd have liked to do when he gave me that smelly kiss on the cheek.

The dreamseller turned to the old woman and said, 'You're a thing of beauty.' Then, taking her by the waist, he spun her around and she danced like a twenty-year-old.

For a moment, I thought the dreamseller had been patronizing her. But then I thought, 'Who's to say she isn't beautiful? What does it really mean to be beautiful, anyway?' Just then, Bartholomew sidled up to the woman and started pouring on the flattery: 'Yes, beautiful! Wonderful! Delightful! Marvelous!'

Then the old woman whacked him with the cane.

'You hopeless pervert! Cheap Don Juan!' she said, feigning anger. Bartholomew ran for cover before he saw she was joking. Her heart melted. It had been fifty years since anyone had called her beautiful or anything of the sort. She took the dizzy drunk by the arms and danced with him, happy as could be. I was in awe. I had known the power of criticism but was new to the power of praise. Could it be that those who use that power could live longer and better lives? My head was spinning. I had never witnessed so much craziness in a single day.

During this short time, the dreamseller had taught me that small gestures can have more impact than great speeches, that our actions and moments of silence can be more effective than all the world's PowerPoint presentations. I knew he had a great many secrets. But I didn't dare ask, worried that he'd again strip me bare with his Socratic method. He had become an expert in making life a celebration, even when there were ample reasons to weep with sorrow.

He would always tell us, 'Those who can laugh at their foolishness have found their fountain of youth.'

I detested fools who gave simple answers, but deep down, wasn't I a fool myself? I had so much to learn about laughing at myself. I had so much to learn about simplifying my life — an unknown art in any university.

How many students had I sent to commencement without teaching them to look at themselves, to detect their own stupidity, to let go, to cry and to love, to take risks and escape the prison of routine? And to dream. I was the most feared of professors. I drowned my students in criticism, but had never taught them to enjoy life. But how could I? No one can teach what he doesn't know himself. My life, to this point, had been worthless.

I was proud of being just and honest, but I realized I had failed to be just and honest with myself. Fortunately, I was beginning to learn how to exorcise the demons that had made me into an unbearable human being.

Strengthened by Challenges

After twenty minutes dancing at the base of the San Pablo Building, the dreamseller again asked for silence. The euphoric crowd eventually calmed down. To our surprise, he recited a poem aloud, as if he were on a mountain top:

> Many dance on the ground,
> But not on the path to self-knowledge.
> They are gods who do not recognize
>   their limits.
> How can they find themselves if they've
>   never been lost?
> How can they be human if they've
>   never known their own humanity?
> Who are you? Yes, tell me, who are
>   you?

The people stared, wide-eyed. After their street fair, the emcee was now asking them whether they were human or divine. Several men in suits, particularly those who hadn't danced and were ready to criticize, were stunned. Every day they were fixated on the exchange rate of the dollar, the stock market

58

index, management techniques, fancy cars and luxurious hotels, but none had traveled the path to self-knowledge.

They led bored, empty lives, clouded in tranquilizers. They would not let themselves be human first. They were gods who died a little every day, gods who denied the internal conflicts that made them human.

Seeing the crowd fall silent, he continued:

'Without thinking in depth about life, they will forever live superficially. They will never perceive that existence is like the sunlight that comes with the dawn and will inevitably disappear with the sunset.' Some applauded without understanding or realizing that their nightfall was fast approaching.

Moments later, to my surprise, he went around greeting people, asking, 'Who are you? What's your great dream?'

Many were confused at first. They didn't know how to answer who they were or what their great dream was. Some, more uninhibited and open, said, 'I don't have any dreams. My life is shit.' Others said, 'I'm swamped with debt. How can I dream?' and still others stated, 'My work is an endless source of stress. My whole body aches. All I ever do is work.' I was impressed with the responses. I realized that the audience watching me on the ledge wasn't that far removed from my own misery. The audience and actor were living the same play.

The dreamseller had no magical solutions for them. What he wanted was for them to rethink their lives. Seeing their desperation, he called out:

'Without dreams, whatever beast it is that chases us, whether in our minds or in society, will eventually catch us. The fundamental purpose of dreams isn't success but to free us from conformity.'

An obese young woman, five-foot-ten and weighing nearly three hundred pounds, was moved by these words. She felt doomed to a life of rejection and unhappiness. She had been taking antidepressants for years. She was negative and overly self-critical. She always put herself down in the presence of other women. She approached the dreamseller and gathered the courage to open up in a voice that only some of us could hear.

'I'm so deeply sad and lonely. Can someone who's unattractive be loved one day? Can someone who's never even been asked out have a chance of finding true love?' She dreamed of being kissed, held, loved, admired, but you could see she had been ridiculed, rejected, called names. Her self-esteem, like mine, had been killed in childhood.

Bartholomew, reeking of alcohol, called out:

'Sexy! Beautiful! If you're looking for your prince, you've found him. Wanna go out with me?' And he spread his arms. I had to hold him to keep him from falling over. She smiled, but the advances of a shameless drunk were not what she had in mind.

The dreamseller looked into her eyes. Moved, he answered:

'It is possible to find true love. But even with true love at your side, you can never be happy if you cannot learn to love yourself.' And he told her: 'Still, to find true love, you must stop being a slave.'

'A slave to what?' she asked, surprised.

'To society's standards for beauty,' he answered.

Some of those listening were encouraged by his words and commented that they dreamed about overcoming their shyness, loneliness, fears. Others yearned to make friends or change jobs because the money they made was never enough to pay their bills. Others said they dreamed of going to college but lacked the resources to do so.

They were hoping for a miracle, but the dreamseller was a vendor of ideas, a merchant of knowledge. Knowledge was better than gold and silver, more enchanting than diamonds and pearls. That's why he didn't endorse success for its own sake. To him, there were no paths without obstacles, no seas without storms. Looking people in the eye, he said with certainty:

'If your dreams are desires and not plans for living, you will surely take your problems to the grave. Dreams without plans produce frustrated people, servants of the system.'

He fell silent and let us reflect on his words. In a world consumed with wants, no one plans to have friends, no one plans to be tolerant, to conquer phobias, to have a great love.

'If chance is our god and accidents our demons, we will be as children,' he said finally.

I was startled to look around me and realize how society had damaged all of us. Quite a few people consumed a lot but were like robots, living without purpose, without meaning, without goals. They were experts at following orders and not at thinking. I asked myself, as an educator, 'Had I trained servants or leaders at the university? Robots or thinkers?' But before answering these questions, I started to feel uneasy about my own situation. I wondered, 'Does being critical free me of servitude?' I knew it didn't. I was a servant to my negativity, to my false independence. Unless I changed, I would take my troubles to my grave.

'Victory without risk is a dream without value. Our defeats, our challenges help nurture our dreams.'

In studying the history of the wealth of nations, I understood the sociological meaning of this latest thought. Many who received inheritances without working for their success could not value their parents' struggles. They squandered their family fortunes as if the money were unlimited. Inheritance bred empty, superficial lives. They were people who lived for the moment, trying to suck the maximum pleasure from the present with no regard for the future.

While I criticized people for not being masters of their own destinies, I suddenly realized I was no different from them. I didn't understand why such simple thoughts were so true. I dreamed of being a happy person but became miserable. I dreamed of living a better life than my father but replicated what I most despised in him. I dreamed of being more sociable than my mother but inherited her bitterness.

I hadn't learned what my struggles had to teach about reaching my dreams. I hadn't dared reach for my dreams if it ever meant risking my reputation, my so-called brilliant academic career. I was barren inside and gave birth to no new ideas. I forgot that great thinkers were also risk-takers. They were called lunatics and heretics, and often became the subject of public scorn.

Even students defending their masters and doctoral theses weren't encouraged to take risks. Some of my colleagues tried to encourage them, but I held them back. Only after meeting the dreamseller did I come to understand that it was often our youth who brought about our greatest discoveries.

Bartholomew's Dream

A man about thirty-five years old, wearing a beige polo shirt, with well-trimmed black hair and a frown, bluntly told the dreamseller, 'My great dream is to strangle my wife.'

He wasn't joking. He actually seemed ready to kill. The dreamseller didn't answer right away, waiting for the man to continue venting his anger. 'Who deserves a wife who betrays her husband?' the man said.

Instead of calming the man down, the dreamseller added fuel to the fire. 'Are you a betrayer, too?'

The man reared back and hit the dreamseller so hard that he knocked him to the ground and bloodied his lip.

Several onlookers came at the man, but the dreamseller quickly calmed them: 'No, don't hurt him!'

The dreamseller dusted himself off and explained to the man, 'We may not betray with our sexual organs, but we betray in thought, in action. If we don't betray those we love, we betray ourselves. We betray our health, our dreams, our peace of mind. You mean to say you've never betrayed another or betrayed yourself?'

The man silently nodded his head, confirming that, yes, he, too, was a betrayer. He betrayed himself daily with thousands of morbid thoughts. His aggressive nature was only the tip of the iceberg. The dreamseller continued:

'Is your wife your property? If not, why do you want to destroy her or destroy yourself because of her? Who said that because she betrayed you she is no longer a human being, a person who has cried, loved, been angered, known frustration? If you're incapable of forgiving her and winning her back, why don't you simply say, 'I'm sorry, it's over'?'

The man walked away dazed. It was hard to tell if he would manage to win his wife back or allow himself to be won back by her, but he would no longer kill her. I was impressed by the dreamseller's approach. It seemed like he provoked the man, so, in hitting the dreamseller, the man would get just a glimpse of what his murderous rage could do. And maybe that opened the man up to considering another alternative. The people nearby stared at the dreamseller as if watching an action film.

As if that incident weren't enough, the dreamseller turned to Bartholomew and asked him what his greatest dream was. I thought it was a bad time to open up such a question. Honeymouth had a way of turning any serious situation into a joke.

He looked at the dreamseller and spoke so enthusiastically that he almost fell to the ground:

'My great dream, chief? Russian vodka! Oh, oh, and to take a bath — ' Everyone appeared heartened at this desire, because he certainly needed it. That is, until he finished. ' — to take a bath in a vat of Scotch whiskey.' Then he fell into a sitting position. He was penniless and seemed in ecstasy at the thought of that singular bath.

I couldn't hold back. I started laughing at the sight of that poor clown and the dreamseller. But I was surprised at my sarcasm, and that deep down, I found pleasure in another's misfortune. I thought to myself, 'Let's see how the dreamseller handles this one.'

Before the dreamseller could answer, Jurema appeared with her cane and threatened to give Bartholomew another whack. She had overheard his dream and was indignant. This time she didn't call him a pervert but a host of other names. 'You inveterate alcoholic! Dreg of society! Insolent wastrel!'

Honeymouth, who apparently had little

67

schooling, thought they were compliments. 'Thanks for the kind words, but a barrel of Brazilian rum or Mexican tequila would also be fine,' he said.

The man was incorrigible. His drinking had been out of control for twenty years. For the last ten he had wandered from bar to bar, street to street, lost in the drink. I was certain that the dreamseller would never be able to teach that drunk anything. I was sure the dreamseller would dismiss him and quickly be done with him. But, to my surprise, he praised the man's sincerity.

'Well, congratulations on your honesty.'

I cleared my ears to make sure I was hearing right. There's no way the dreamseller was praising this drunk. Between the alcohol swimming in Bartholomew's brain and the dreamseller's praise, the man was euphoric. Feeling a self-esteem that he hadn't known in years, he looked around at the mob that was jeering him just minutes earlier and yelled, 'Aha! You see! I'm environmentally friendly. I run on alcohol.'

Then he crossed his fingers and said, 'I'm like *that* with this guy. He's *the man*. Hey, can I take a ride in your spaceship, E.T.?' Then he tripped against a couple of people and almost fell again.

I, who had always been intolerant, thought,

'Ship the guy off to the loony bin.' The dreamseller looked at me, and for a second, I thought he was reading my mind and taking my advice. But, to my amazement, he said something that almost made me fall over. He touched Bartholomew's shoulder and told him in a firm voice, 'Come, follow me. And I'll inebriate you with a drink unlike any you have ever known.'

I was horrified. I shook my head to see if I understood what I'd heard. The drunk, who was weak both from dancing and from years of running on alcohol, immediately replied, 'You say there's a drink I don't know about? I doubt it. Is it high-proof vodka?'

I was embarrassed by the alcoholic's naive irreverence. But the dreamseller, finding it humorous, smiled. He was always able to relax in these tense situations. He looked at me and said, 'Don't worry, I specialize in the complicated ones.'

I thought about running right then and there. Following this social outcast was one thing. Following him side by side with a witless drunk was too much. Who knew what risks lay ahead?

The World Is My Home

The dreamseller, Bartholomew and I turned to begin our journey. As we were leaving, the crowd applauded. Some people even took photos. I had hoped for a discreet escape, but that idiot Honeymouth posed for pictures. I tried to lead him away without causing more of a scene. The last thing I wanted was to babysit a drunk. A few nearby reporters looked on and took notes.

We hadn't walked three blocks before I started wondering, 'What am I doing here? Where are we going?' But my new companion wasn't thinking at all. He was just happy to be part of our merry band of men. Me? I was worried.

I looked ahead and tried to relax. The dreamseller watched me with a half-smile; he seemed to hear my doubts. I imagined we were heading to his humble home. Judging by his clothes, he seemed to be poor, but surely he must have a rented house or apartment. Maybe it wasn't much to look at, but he was so insistent that we join him, I figured there must be enough room for his guests, Bartholomew and me. The thought of sleeping in the same room with that drunkard turned my stomach.

Maybe the room where I'd sleep would be simple but comfortable. Maybe the mattress would be worn but decent. Maybe the sheets would be old, but at least they'd be clean. Maybe his refrigerator wasn't packed, but I imagined there would be something healthy to eat. After all, I was hungry and exhausted. Maybe, maybe, maybe . . . I thought, but I wasn't sure of anything.

Along the way, he waved at children and adults, helped a few people carry heavy bags. Bartholomew said hi to everyone, even trees and lampposts. I waved, too, but only not to seem out of place.

Most people responded with a smile. I wondered how the dreamseller knew all of them. But, of course, he didn't know them. It was just his way. He treated any stranger as an equal. And, in fact, to him, no person was a stranger. He greeted them because it made him happy. I had never seen such a lively, good-natured, sociable person. He didn't just sell dreams, he lived them.

We walked for blocks, then for miles, but never seemed to be any closer to his home. A long while later, when I couldn't walk any further, he stopped at an intersection and I let out a sigh of relief. We're here, I thought to myself. Yes, he said, we had arrived.

I looked to the left and saw a row of identical, white, low-income homes with small porches. I scratched my head and thought, 'The houses look really small. They can't have three bedrooms.'

Then the dreamseller looked down the other street. Behind a bridge was a tall apartment building that looked to have about eight rooms per floor, like a pigeon coop for people. It looked even more cramped than the row houses.

Remembering my own students, I said to myself, 'I'm not going to complain. It'll just be a tough night and that's that.' The dreamseller saw the look on my face and said, 'Don't worry. There's plenty of room.'

Trying to disguise my worry, I asked calmly, 'So what floor is your apartment on?'

'My apartment? My apartment is the world,' he said calmly.

'I like that apartment,' Bartholomew said.

Confused, I asked, 'What do you mean?'

He explained:

'Foxes have their dens, the birds of the sky their nests, but the dreamseller has no fixed address to lay his head.'

If I was nervous before, I really worried when he started quoting Jesus Christ. Did this man think he was the Messiah? Could he be having a psychotic break? Or would he have one later? I mean, he seemed highly intelligent. And he speaks of God in a secular way. But I couldn't help wonder who this man was. And what I was getting myself into.

'Don't worry,' the dreamseller said, 'I'm not Him. I only try to understand Him.'

'You're not who?' I asked, not following.

'I'm not Jesus Christ. Like I said, I'm just the least of his brethren. I just try to understand him,' he replied calmly.

'But who are you?' I repeated anxiously, seeking a fuller explanation that never seemed to come.

He said emphatically, 'I've already told you who I am. Don't you believe in me?'

Bartholomew should have kept quiet just then, but he didn't have it in him. He tried to correct me by saying, 'You don't believe he's the alien commander.'

This time I couldn't hold back.

'Shut up, *Trashmouth*,' I shouted.

'Trashmouth? You second-rate snob!' he shouted and struck a karate pose. This would be the first of many arguments among the dreamseller's ragtag band of disciples.

The dreamseller gently corrected me, that warm smile and calm demeanor more effective than any physical punishment.

'Julio, you're a smart man, so you know

that no artist owns his work. It's he who interprets the art who gives it meaning. If Bartholomew thinks I'm the leader of an alien race, so be it. You shouldn't worry. Generosity, not obedience, is what I want. Be generous to yourself.'

Back then, I thought he mis-spoke and meant that I should be generous to Bartholomew. But during this journey I would discover that a man who isn't generous to himself can never be generous to others. One who demands much of himself is a tyrant to others.

Generosity was one of the most important dreams that he wanted to share with the world. The 'normals' living in their cages, isolated in their own little worlds, had lost the indescribable joy that comes from giving, embracing, offering a second chance. Generosity was a word found in dictionaries but rarely in mankind. I knew how to compete but not how to be generous. I knew how to point out the ignorance and shortcomings of others, but not how to accept them. Seeing others fail pleased me more than my own successes. I was no different from a politician who wanted to see the ruling party fail.

After that careful lesson, I calmed down. But there was still the question of where we would be staying. Then the dreamseller pointed to the shade beneath the bridge and said, 'This is our home.'

I felt dizzy. Suddenly I began to miss the San Pablo Building. There were several torn mattresses strewn under the overpass and only filthy rags to cover us. There was one jug of water and we all would have to drink straight from the bottle. I had never seen such poverty. I thought, 'This is the man who saved me?'

It all looked so destitute that even Bartholomew protested. Now I was starting to like the guy. He scratched his head, rubbed his eyes to make sure he wasn't hallucinating and said, 'Chief, you sure this is your house?'

The alcohol was wearing off and Bartholomew had begun to see reality. Even he had slept in better places. He slept in a friend's tiny efficiency, in the back of bars and even in homeless shelters, but never under a bridge.

'Yes, Bartholomew, this is my house. And we have a long night ahead of us.'

Because everything the dreamseller said had another meaning, he wasn't predicting a bad night's sleep. We were in for more of the dreamseller's eye-opening world.

For dinner there was some stale bread and old crackers. I had hated fast-food hamburgers, but now I started to fantasize about them. After taking a few bites of the crackers,

I decided to lie down. Maybe tomorrow I would wake up and find it was all a nightmare. I lay down on the lumpy mattress, rolled a piece of cardboard into a pillow, and rested my head — but not my racing mind.

Trying to relax, I told myself, 'OK, stay calm. You're a sociologist. You *like* to study eccentric groups, don't you? Now you're part of one. It'll be good for your academic career. At the very least, you'll have one hell of a story to tell. Remember, 'Victory without risk is a dream without value.''

Still, I couldn't imagine what I was getting myself into. I had left the safe microcosm of a college classroom to live in the underbelly of society, a place completely foreign to a theoretical sociologist like me. My spinning mind wouldn't let me sleep.

But then I tried something else. I started remembering all the lessons I had learned next to the dreamseller, reliving each experience. I tried to think about everything that had happened hours earlier. The experience of following this stranger was so powerful that I thought less about the top of the building and more about my home under the bridge, less about suicide and more about my journey.

And then it hit me. Everyone should set out like this, without a goal or a destination, at least for a day, searching for the lost pieces of themselves. These thoughts relaxed me, the anxiety passed and sleep approached.

I learned that night that what determines how soft a bed feels depends on the anxiety inside our heads. One only sleeps well when he can find peace within. I was beginning to think like the dreamseller. I ignored whatever worry lay ahead. For the moment, that tattered lump became the most comfortable of mattresses.

A Band of Misfits

It was four in the morning, cold and windy, when I awoke to a desperate cry.

'The bridge is gonna collapse! It's gonna collapse!' Bartholomew screamed. He was panting, terrified.

My heart was racing. I had never been so afraid. I leaped up, trying to run.

But the dreamseller took my arm and urged me to stay calm.

'Calm, how? We could die!' I said, looking at the construction and seeing old cracks, in the darkness, as if they were new.

Calmly, he told me, 'Bartholomew is going through alcohol withdrawal.'

My survival instinct had kicked in, even though a few hours earlier I had wanted to end my life. My drunken companion had led me to one of the greatest discoveries of my life: Even those who plan their death don't want to die; they want to kill their pain. I took a deep breath, tried to relax, but my heart was racing. I looked at Bartholomew, who was in a state of terror.

He was in a state of delirium tremens. Because he was addicted, and his body craved alcohol, he was suffering shortness of breath, accelerated heart rate and excessive sweating. The worst part was that his already confused mind shut down, and he was starting to hallucinate.

After imagining that the bridge was falling, he started having other wild visions. He saw spiders and rats the size of automobiles scurrying along the ground, threatening to devour him. His face was dripping with sweat, his hands shaking. His entire body was hot with fever. As the dreamseller always said, you can run from the monsters outside but not those within. And it's incredible how the human mind tries to create phantoms to frighten away those demons. Even in our digital world, these primitive feelings still exist.

Bartholomew tried to fight the beasts attacking him from within. He screamed in agony, 'Chief, help me! Help me!'

We tried to calm him and sat him down on an old crate. But he jumped to his feet with a new nightmare, and, another time, he ran down the street in fear. There were millions of alcoholics in this country, but I never imagined how much they suffered. I just thought they were happy drunks. Fearing Bartholomew would be run over, the dreamseller suggested we take him to a public hospital three blocks away.

That's the day I began to give a little of myself to others without asking anything in return. Of course, there's always self-interest in the things we do, but as the dreamseller said, there are interests that go beyond financial gain and public recognition, such as those linked to the fulfillment of contributing to the well-being of others. It was a system of trade unforeseen by capitalism or socialism, a world alien to me.

I began to understand that selfish people live in a prison of their worries. But those who work to ease the pain of others ease their own pain. I don't know if I'll regret taking this path, I don't know what awaits me, but selling dreams, even with its risks, is an excellent 'business' in the marketplace of emotion. Bartholomew's suffering was so great that, at least for the time being, it made the countless issues in my life, the worry in my mind, seem smaller.

I thought of all the trouble the dreamseller went through to rescue me. He hadn't asked for money, recognition or praise, afterward. But what he received was an immeasurable dose of joy. He was so happy that he danced in public. All he asked of me was that I do the same.

Helping Bartholomew was my first experience in contributing humbly to someone's wellness. A difficult task for a selfish intellectual.

Getting Bartholomew admitted into the hospital was a struggle. We had to convince the night crew that our friend was in mortal danger. His raving alcohol-induced madness wasn't enough to convince them immediately. General hospitals weren't prepared for accidents involving the human psyche. The body they could deal with. But they either didn't know or didn't care about how to deal with an injured mind. By the time we succeeded in getting him admitted, Bartholomew was less agitated. They gave him a strong sedative and carried him, asleep, to his room.

We went to visit him in the afternoon. Bartholomew was much better. He was no longer having hallucinations and was released. He asked us to tell him everything that had happened and how we'd met. His memory was cloudy. The dreamseller signaled to me. I tried to explain the incomprehensible. When I began to speak, the dreamseller left. He didn't like to be praised.

I spoke about the dreamseller, how I'd met him, how he'd helped save me, how we met at the foot of the building, the dancing, the question about Bartholomew's great dream, how he'd called him, the bridge, the night terrors, everything. Bartholomew paid close attention and nodded his head, muttering, 'hmm.' Everything seemed so unreal that I felt like a fool explaining something I didn't even understand. The poor man was as good-natured as the dreamseller.

'You don't know who he is or what his name is? Buddy, I think I need a drink to figure this all out,' he joked. 'I've always wanted to follow somebody crazier than me.'

And that's how I became part of this band of misfits. My sociological experiment was widening. I only hoped I wouldn't run into anyone I knew. I'd rather anyone from my former life think I was dead or had left the country. Bartholomew whistled in a carefree manner. The dreamseller walked beside us with unabashed joy. Suddenly, he started singing a beautiful and rousing song he had composed, with lyrics that portrayed the story of his life. Little by little, the song became the central theme of our journey.

I'm just a wanderer
Who lost the fear of getting lost
I'm certain of my own imperfection
You may say I'm crazy
You may mock my ideas
It doesn't matter!
What matters is I'm a wanderer

Who sells dreams to passersby
I've no compass or appointment book
I have nothing, yet I have everything
I'm just a wanderer
In search of myself.

On the walk home, or rather, to the bridge, we ran into another strange character. His name was Dimas de Melo, nicknamed 'Angel Hand.' His nickname should have been 'Devil Hand,' because he was a con man and a thief. He was twenty-eight with blond hair that fell over his brow, a long, pointed nose and Asian features.

Angel Hand was caught stealing a portable DVD player from a department store. He had already stolen countless other more valuable things without getting caught. But this time a camera had filmed him in the act. Of course he had slyly checked out all the cameras when he placed the machine in his large bag, but hadn't seen there was a hidden one, and he landed in jail.

At the police station, he asked for a lawyer before detectives could question him. He told his lawyer he didn't have money for bail. The lawyer said, 'No money; no freedom.'

Whenever the thief felt nervous, he began to stutter badly. He argued, 'Hold on a minute . . . I'm, I'm gonna get out of this without pa ... paying a thing. Just f ... follow my lead.' The lawyer didn't understand what he had in mind. They went into the office of the impatient police chief.

When the chief asked the prisoner's name, Dimas, acting like he had mental problems, twiddled his lips with his index finger and smacked his forehead three times. The chief got mad and again asked his name. And Dimas repeated the gesture.

'Are you playing with me, son? Because I'll lock you in that holding cell and throw away the key.'

The chief tried asking for Dimas's address and employer, but Dimas just repeated the same gesture, twiddling his lips like a monkey and slapping his forehead three times. He wanted to look like someone out of his mind, someone who couldn't possibly have known what he was doing when he put that DVD player into his bag. The chief insisted on asking more questions and Dimas just deflected them like an imbecile. The chief cursed, banged the table, threatened, but Dimas wouldn't break. He should've won an Academy Award for his acting. The lawyer was enjoying his client's cleverness.

'There's no use. This guy's nuts!' the chief shouted.

The lawyer took over and told him, 'Sir, I

didn't say anything about my client's mental handicap because I knew you wouldn't believe me. But you can see for yourself he has no idea what he's doing.'

Not wanting to waste any more time, the chief let the crook go. Outside, the lawyer shook Angel Hand's hand and praised his cunning.

'That was unbelievable! I've never seen such a clever con man,' the lawyer said, congratulating him. He quickly asked for his fee so he could be on his way to see another client.

Angel Hand stared blankly into the lawyer's eyes and twiddled his lips, slapping his forehead three times. The lawyer laughed out loud, but said he didn't have time to joke around. Dimas repeated the gesture. We were on the other side of the street, watching this all go on.

'OK, enough! Let's settle up,' shouted the lawyer.

Angel Hand repeated his ritual once again. The lawyer became irritated, but Dimas just repeated his act. Nothing could dissuade that scoundrel. The lawyer threatened him in every possible way. He even threatened to call the cops. But how could he? He had told the police chief that his client was mentally ill; if he recanted, it could cause him problems with the bar. It was the first time in the history of jurisprudence that a con artist had tricked the police and his lawyer in the space of fifteen minutes.

The lawyer left fuming and Angel Hand said aloud, 'One more sucker.'

The dreamseller was paying close attention to the thief. I couldn't really understand why. But I thought maybe he wanted to sell him the dream of honesty. Maybe he wanted to reprimand him, deliver one of his sermons. Maybe he wanted to tell us to have nothing to do with a guy like this, who could ruin our path to self-discovery.

He crossed the street and approached the thief. We followed apprehensively, worried that this crook might be armed. Dimas saw him coming and immediately asked who he was and what he wanted. To our surprise, the dreamseller pulled no punches.

'Your dream is to get rich and you don't care how you have to do it,' the dreamseller said.

I liked how the dreamseller put him in his place. But what he said next took me by surprise and sent Bartholomew's head spinning — without vodka. He told Angel Hand, 'Those who steal for a living are terrible money managers. They run from poverty, but it always catches up with them.'

The con man was taken aback. He didn't know how to invest what he stole and lived in poverty. He detested it, begged for the scarcity to go away, but like a faithful companion it insisted on staying. And then, the dreamseller brought the crook's world crashing down: 'The worst swindler isn't he who deceives others but he who deceives himself.'

Angel Hand took two steps back. He wasn't much for thinking, but what he heard rocked his mind. He began to ask himself: 'Am I maybe the world's worst swindler? I'm a pro at cheating people, but maybe I've cheated myself. Who is this character who's stealing my peace of mind?'

Then the dreamseller did what we never expected.

'Come, follow me and I will show you a treasure called knowledge, much more valuable than silver and gold,' he said. The dreamseller had a pointed, seductive way of selling his dreams.

But the con man looked the dreamseller from head to toe, saw his ragged clothes and empty pockets and snickered. He thought about that treasure of knowledge and understood nothing. And he started to stutter again.

'What . . . tre . . . treasure do you mean?

What mo . . . money?' he asked suspiciously.

Without offering an explanation, the dreamseller merely stated confidently, 'You'll find out.'

And he walked away without saying another word. The crook followed us. Initially, he followed out of curiosity. Maybe he thought the dreamseller was an eccentric millionaire. The fact is that the dreamseller's ideas attracted people, especially those on the edge of society, like a moth to a flame.

Bartholomew, many years ago when he had money, had undergone psychotherapy, but it didn't work. In fact, it had left him worse off. He had driven some of his therapists crazy, and they needed therapy themselves after they began to treat him. The guy was hopeless but brilliant. He discovered that pridefulness was my weakness. When we made our first trek toward the bridge, after the San Pablo dance, he nicknamed me Superego, unknowingly misusing Freud's term. He now called me aside and whispered in my ear:

'Superego, putting up with you isn't easy, but having to deal with this crook is impossible.'

'Look who's talking,' I started to say, but then I thought he might be right. This new member of our family could be dangerous. I had never imagined myself associating with a common criminal.

Even more quietly, I told Bartholomew, 'Putting up with an alcoholic like you is complicated, but that crook's too much. Count me out of this.'

I thought about abandoning the sociological experiment for the second time. But then I remembered that I, too, had been lost and was found. I looked at the dreamseller's calm expression and decided to hold out a while longer. I, too, was curious about where this journey would lead me. It could surely be the subject of many future theses.

The dreamseller's new disciple had a disarming voice, but he was an expert in taking advantage of others. He sold counterfeit winning lottery tickets. He stole women's credit cards and snatched purses from little old ladies after graciously helping them cross the street. The problem is that every schemer is overconfident. Dimas thought he could never be caught — until he encountered someone wilier than him. He didn't realize that by accompanying the dreamseller he would be entering the biggest ambush of his life.

We sat down on a bench in the square to rest. The dreamseller suggested that Bartholomew and I explain the project to Dimas. Not an easy task. The young man didn't look very smart and I thought it might be just the right time to scare him off. Bartholomew exaggerated everything that had happened to us.

'Dude, the chief is a genius. I think he's from another planet. He hypnotizes people. He's called on us to set people on fire with dreams.'

Drunk, Bartholomew hallucinated about monsters; sober, he had delusions of grandeur. Unfortunately Dimas liked what he was hearing. These two, living at the edge of society, they spoke the same language. I thought to myself, 'Now I'm living at the edge of society *and* I'm alone. I'm worse off than both of these wretches.'

We knew whatever explanation we gave Dimas about this journey wouldn't satisfy him — we were as confused as he was. But to someone lost in the desert, a mirage of an oasis brings hope. I was hoping to scare off this con man, but he was now determined to follow us. Thus, our band of misfits was born.

The Brave Little Swallows

Later that day, we passed by a news-stand in the square and saw our photo on the front page of the newspaper under the headline 'A Small Band of Misfits Stirs Up the City.' In the foreground was the dreamseller with Bartholomew and me at his side. I bought the paper with the few coins in my pocket.

I was shaken, perplexed. I knew I had caused a scene when I tried to kill myself, but I had hoped it was buried. I just wanted to forget the matter and return to my quiet life in academia. Now my name was on everyone's tongue. The article described my suicide attempt and my rescue by a stranger whose name no one knew.

Dimas and Bartholomew saw one out-of-control intellectual reading that paper. They were accustomed to being insulted. I wasn't. My social image was carefully protected. 'I'll be a laughing-stock, especially to my enemies at the university,' I thought.

What a fool I'd been. I wanted to die without attracting attention, but I went about it all wrong. Instead, I had become infamous. I wanted to grab all the papers and burn them. I wanted to protest the unauthorized use of my photograph. I wanted to sue the journalist for that slanderous reporting. The article called me an attention-seeking mental case. And it also said that the psychiatrist who'd been at the top of the building diagnosed the dreamseller as a dangerous psychopath who could be a public hazard. The way the article read, I hadn't been rescued by a hero; rather, we had been the villains in a Hollywood film.

The dreamseller sat on a nearby bench along with his other followers. Respecting my pain, he merely observed me. He was waiting for my temper to subside before he intervened. But it didn't diminish. My mind raced out of control. I imagined all my colleagues and students reading the story. I was the chairman of a sociology department and had never bowed to any professor or student. I appeared unbeatable, detested stupid minds, but never saw my own stupidity. I had always been skilled at cultivating enemies and rotten at making friends.

'And what will they think of me now?' I thought. 'What will they think of a jumper saved by a crazy man? And what's worse, what will they think of that jumper who, after being rescued, danced merrily in a crowd of strangers? Obviously, they'll say I've gone stark raving mad. They'll say I have an advanced degree in insanity.'

It was everything that Mario Vargas, Antonio Freitas and other malcontents dreamed of, sullying my image. Without realizing it, I sold the dream they most desired, the dream of stomping on my image. Defeated, I concluded that I was through in the academic world, done at the university. Never again would I face the same silence when I wove social criticism, or respect when I debated ideas or corrected someone.

I began to feel angry toward the journalist who had written the article. I fumed, 'Why don't journalists, as part of their training, take a workshop simulating the public destruction of their reputation? Maybe then they'd learn to investigate all the facts and put themselves in other people's shoes before trashing someone else's name.'

To the journalist I was just another story. But to me it was my personal struggle: everything that I have and am, even if it is a twisted, troubling tale. A few minutes can change a life story. How could I go back to my old life? If I returned, I'd never be the same to the others. All I had left was to follow a man who proposes a revolutionary plan without the slightest intellectual, social or financial basis. And, moreover, he calls as his followers people who I normally would never associate with.

I had been protected inside the university for many years. And now, the first time I had left the protection of my notable degrees and become a simple mortal, I had been tossed about. I was outraged.

But just as my anger had reached a fever pitch, my mind suddenly shifted and I saw things from a different point of view.

I glanced at the dreamseller and realized that the 'comma' he had sold me allowed me to feel all of this, even though it was unpleasant. Whatever negative effects that article might have brought, it also came with something positive: The living *feel* frustration. The dead feel nothing. And I was alive.

I had almost died that day. I should be celebrating life. But the conflicts wedged deep in my unconscious, though weakened, were not dead. I wanted to live a simple, calm life, instead of worrying about my public reputation. But I was a man ruled by anxiety.

Now I understand why the father of a colleague of mine, a seventy-year-old man, arrogant, aggressive, prejudiced, who had been kidnapped for six months, hadn't changed at all after his long captivity. When he was released, everyone thought he would be a gentle, generous, altruistic individual, but after his rescue he was more unbearable than ever.

My love of power had always been hidden beneath the cloak of my intellect. It was not eradicated, even by the threat of suicide. I thought this business of selling dreams wouldn't easily change a selfish man like me. It isn't pain that changes us, but the intellect to use that pain. I realized that if I didn't use that pain, I would continue being simply a hollow human being with a vast intellect but stunted emotions.

As I wrestled with these thoughts, I sensed the dreamseller at my side. He seemed to have entered the whirlwind of my ideas. I could see the concern on his face. He seemed to read my thoughts. In an effort to calm the turbulent waters of my emotions, he said:

'Don't fear criticism from the outside. Fear your own thoughts, for only they can penetrate into your essence and destroy it.'

As I pondered his words, he continued:

'Someone can bruise your body without your permission, but he can never invade your mind unless you allow it. Don't let yourself be invaded. We are what we are.' Then he challenged me more than I could have imagined: 'The cost of selling dreams is high, but you're under no obligation to pay.

You're always free to leave.'

The dreamseller had dragged me to a crossroads. I had the chance to turn my back and go anywhere in the world. But to quit now? Me? I had always been stubborn, fighting for what I wanted. I was wracked with doubt in a way I never had been before. I recalled a sociological study I had read about the relationship between Jesus and his disciples, and I began to understand psychological and social truths that I had never analyzed.

I began to think about the indescribable power of Jesus' words and actions. They were enough to convince young Jews, in the flower of youth, wild for adventure, some even with established families and businesses, to abandon everything and follow him. What madness! They blindly followed a man with no known political power and no visible identity. He didn't promise them money or riches or an earthly kingdom. What a risk they took! What internal turmoil they must have felt!

They lost everything, and in the end, lost the man who taught them to love, crucified on a wooden cross. He died humbly, loving as he breathed his last, forgiving as he perished. After his death, the group might have faded away, but they had been invaded by an indescribable force. They became stronger after that chaos. They spread His message throughout the world.

They gave their tears, their health, their lives — everything they had — to humanity. They loved strangers and devoted themselves to others. Countless societies across the world, from Europe to Africa to Asia to the Americas, were founded on these very principles, as well as the basis for basic human rights.

Centuries passed and that life became 'normal.' Churches became excellent temples to conformity. These days, hundreds of millions of people across the world enter these temples to recall a sanitized version of Christmas, the Passion, and other milestones of Christ's life without ever imagining what it's like to sleep out in the open, to be branded a lunatic, and to feel society's scorn. Over the millennia, they have lost the ability to imagine the intense pressure those young men endured to follow that enigmatic master, Jesus.

I imagined the lumpy straw beds they slept on under the open sky. I reflected on the pain they suffered in trying to explain the unexplainable to family and friends in Galilee. They couldn't say they had learned to love a man, lest they be stoned. They couldn't point to this master plan they were helping unfold because the plan was intangible. They couldn't say they were following a powerful man, the Messiah, for he demanded anonymity. What courage they must have had to summon to answer his call. And just like that, Bartholomew brought me back from my deepest of thoughts with a shot. I don't know whether he was praising me or attacking me.

'Hey, Superego, if you're too scared to stick around, we'll still respect you. But you're important to the team.'

I took a deep breath. I thought about the man who had stopped my suicide and brought me to sleep under a bridge. He's not Christ, he has no messianic calling. He doesn't perform miracles. He doesn't promise the kingdom of heaven, or an earthly realm, and he doesn't even provide us safety in society. He had nowhere to live, he's broke, had no car, no health insurance. But he had an incredibly magnetic personality. He was the definition of solidarity, he dreamed of opening people's minds, of fighting the system and confronting selfishness.

Wouldn't it be less dangerous to just let society go on being an insanity factory? Wouldn't it be better to let people wallow in their own selfishness? Wouldn't it be easier to let obtuse minds go on thinking only about the superficial mysteries of shopping centers, computers and fashion instead of the mysteries of existence? We're too small to do anything against the powerful system, anyway. We could be arrested, injured and continue to have our names dragged through the mud.

While this circus was playing in my mind, the dreamseller was still in the center ring performing wondrous feats. Patience was his number one virtue. Seeing my worry, he called the three of us together and told us a simple parable that touched the depths of my fears.

'There was once a flood in an immense forest. The weeping clouds that should have promoted life this time predicted death. The larger animals fled, leaving even their offspring behind. In their stampede, they devastated everything in their path. The smaller animals followed their steps. Suddenly, a small swallow, completely soaked, flew in the opposite direction, looking for someone to save.

'The hyenas, seeing this, were astonished. They said, 'You're insane. What can you possibly do with that fragile little body?' The vultures groused, 'Just look at how tiny you are.' Wherever the fragile swallow flew, it was ridiculed. But it continued seeking someone to rescue. Its wings were fluttering wearily when it spied a baby hummingbird thrashing in the water, ready to give up. Despite never having learned to swim, the swallow plunged into the water and, struggling terribly, grabbed the tiny bird by its left wing. It flew off, carrying the infant in its beak.

'When it returned, it encountered other hyenas, who quickly declared, 'This is crazy! You're just trying to be a hero!' But the swallow didn't stop, despite its fatigue, until it had deposited the little hummingbird in a safe place. Hours later, it found the hyenas in a shady spot. Looking them in the eyes, it told them, 'I only feel worthy of my wings if I make use of them so others can fly.''

The dreamseller let this story marinate in our minds, then told us:

'There are many hyenas and vultures in society. Don't expect much from the large animals. Rather, expect a lack of understanding, rejection, ridicule and a sick need for power. I don't call you to be great heroes, to have your feats recorded in the annals of history, but to be small swallows who fly anonymously throughout society, loving strangers and doing for them whatever you can. Be worthy of your wings. It is in insignificance that great significance is achieved, and in smallness that great acts are realized.'

The dreamseller's parable at once moved

me and wounded me deeply. I thought, 'I have to admit I've acted like a hyena or a vulture on many occasions in my life; now I need to learn how to act like a brave little swallow.'

The Most Lucid Place in Society

'Normals' always get out of bed the same way. They complain the same way. Get irritated the same way. They curse using the same words. They greet their friends in the same fashion. Give the same answers to the same problems. They express the same humor at home and at work. They have the same reactions to the same circumstances. Give presents on the same days. In short, they have a tiring and predictable routine, which becomes an excellent source of anxiety, anguish, emptiness and boredom.

The system has blocked people's imagination, corroded their creativity. They rarely give presents on unexpected days. Rarely react differently in tense situations. They are prisoners and don't know it.

'Normal' parents, when they correct or advise their children, are interrupted midway through. Their children can't stand hearing the same arguments anymore. They say, 'I know that already . . . ' And they really do. 'Normals' don't know how to relate their own experiences in order to stimulate the thinking of others.

I was always predictable in my relationship with students, and I only discovered this when I began my journey with the dreamseller. I taught class in a single tone of voice. I criticized and admonished in the same manner. I varied the verbs and nouns, but not the form or the content. The students were fed up with a professor who seemed more like an Egyptian mummy than a human being. They couldn't stand hearing over and over that they'd be losers in life if they didn't study.

On the other hand, the dreamseller continually sold the dream of enchantment. How can someone who has nothing on the exterior be so captivating? How can a man without any kind of teaching background so effectively engage our imagination? Walking with him was an invitation to innovative thinking. He saw ordinary situations from different angles. We seemed to travel without a destination or purpose. But deep down, he knew very well what he wanted and where he wanted to go. He was training us to find an unimaginable freedom. Each day was like a garden full of surprises, some of them pleasant, others not.

The next morning, after meditating silently on his own worries, the dreamseller rose, took several deep breaths of the polluted city air from under the bridge and gave thanks to God in an unusual way.

'God, you exist in every space in time. You are infinitely distant and infinitely near, but I know that your eyes are upon me. Let me capture your feelings. Thank you for granting us one more show in this surprising existence.'

Honeymouth, who loved country music, said, 'What show are we gonna see, chief?' And he expressed an early-morning enthusiasm that I had seldom seen.

'Show? Each day is a show, each day is a spectacle,' the dreamseller answered, roused with excitement. 'Only he who's mortally wounded by tedium doesn't discover it. Drama and comedy are in our minds. All we need to do is decide to release them.'

Bartholomew had to be drunk to free himself of his sorrow, to rid himself of his boredom. Now he, as well as Dimas and I, were discovering another world, another stage. The dreamseller set off, and we followed. We climbed a hill, walked three blocks, turned to the right, then walked four more blocks. We exchanged glances, questioning one another, trying to guess where the dreamseller was headed.

After walking for forty minutes, Dimas, who still had not been sufficiently astonished by the dreamseller's words, asked, 'Where are we going?'

The dreamseller stopped, looked him in the eye and said, 'Those who sell dreams are like the wind: You hear your voice but don't know where it comes from or where it's going. What matters isn't the route but the journey.'

Dimas understood almost nothing, but he began exercising his rusty mind. And we continued to walk. Fifteen minutes later, the dreamseller stopped in front of a gathering and headed toward it. We slowed our pace, and let him go on about twenty feet ahead of us. Dimas looked at me and said, apprehensively, 'This is a funeral home. I'm not going in there.'

'I'm with you. I don't think the dreamseller knows what he's getting into,' I said.

It was a family wake, the only place where strangers are both unwelcome and have no desire to enter. But the irreverent Honeymouth, trying to maintain his poise, prodded me, saying, 'Come on, Superego. Get over yourself. Let's go to the wake.'

Just then I felt like slapping him. I don't know whether he was humoring the dreamseller or truly following his heart. But since we were close to the wake, a place of respect, I contained my anger. The atmosphere was riddled with pain. There was a crowd mourning a man who had died of a rapidly growing cancer, leaving an only son, twelve years old.

The area where the dead were mourned was grand and ostentatious, decorated with several rounded, marble-covered arches and lit by chandeliers. It was a physically beautiful place to house so much sadness. Fear of causing a scene in a place where silence should reign made us slow our pace even more. We distanced ourselves from the dreamseller, remaining about fifty feet behind him. Looking back, he saw our apprehension and approached his timid disciples.

'What is the most clear-thinking place in the great madhouse of our society?' he asked. 'The courts? Editorial rooms of large newspapers? The politician's pulpit? The universities?'

'The bars,' Honeymouth tried to joke, then quickly apologized. 'Just kidding, chief.'

The dreamseller answered:

'It's here, at wakes. They are the most lucid places in society. Here we disarm ourselves, strip away our vanities, remove our makeup. Here we are who we are. If we can't be ourselves here, then we are sicker than we can possibly imagine. For those closest to the deceased, a wake is a source of despair. For those a bit more removed, it's a place to reflect. But for both, the truth is stark: We fall into the silence of our crypts not as doctors, intellectuals, politicians or celebrities, but as mere mortals.'

These words made me see that it was at wakes where we ceased to be gods and truly came in contact with our humanity, realizing our frailty and accepting our mortality. At wakes, we, the normal, engaged in an intuitive group therapy.

Some said, 'Poor man, he died so young.' These were the ones who could empathize with the deceased and started to wonder whether they, themselves, could live a kinder life. Others said, 'Life is full of risks. In the end, death comes to us all.' These saw the urgency of relaxing, slowing down their lives. Still others commented, 'He worked so hard, and just as he was about to enjoy the fruits of his labors, he died.' These discovered that life passes like a shadow, that, in their search for riches, they neglected their own health. And they realized that they needed to change their unhealthy lifestyles.

People at wakes were trying desperately to buy dreams, to remember the reasons for being alive, but the system steam-rolls them in a matter of hours or days. Everything returns to 'normal.' They didn't understand that dreams will last only if they're woven with fine thread in the secret places of the mind. I had always tried to make myself immune to these feelings. To me, the misery of others was like a movie, nothing more than fiction trying to take root in my mind, but never finding fertile ground.

'Don't expect to see flowers growing in a place where seeds haven't died first,' the dreamseller said. 'Don't be worried. Let's go.' And he smiled.

To him, these words were enough. To us, they merely took the edge off our hesitation. Death is worrisome, but so is life. The former extinguishes courage, but the latter can choke it out. What could the dreamseller offer in a setting where words fail? What could he say in a venue where all arguments fade away? What could he possibly say at a moment when people are disinclined to listen and taste only the bitterness of suffering in the face of their loss? What words would offer them relief — especially coming from a stranger?

We knew the dreamseller would not behave like just another mourner; that was a problem. We also knew he would not stay quiet and stand idly by. And that was a greater problem still.

A Solemn Homage

I went through the same ordeal when I lost my mother. The expressions of sympathy, the prefabricated advice, nothing helped ease the pain. All the comforting words didn't make a dent in the bars that imprisoned me. I would have preferred the silence of embraces or just a few tears shed at my side.

The dreamseller asked to be let through the crowd, and we followed. The closer we came to the coffin, the more the people seemed to be suffering. Then we saw a young man, near forty, with thinning black hair, a drawn and anguished face, lying motionless in the coffin.

His wife was inconsolable. Relatives and close friends were all drying their tears. The son was lost in despair. I saw myself in him and felt his pain more than my companions could. He had barely begun his life and had already begun losing a great deal. I had only just started to understand life when my father ended his, and then I lost my mother, too. I dined with loneliness and slept in my own sealed-off world, plagued by unanswered questions. God ignored me, I thought. I felt bitter toward him in my adolescence. Finally, in adult life, he became a mirage and I an atheist, a specialist in pessimism. Realizing the emptiness in this young boy, I couldn't hold back the tears.

The dreamseller, seeing the boy's despair, hugged him and asked his name and his father's. Then, to our amazement, he turned to those present and in his deep voice offered words that shook them, words that could provoke an uproar: 'Why are all of you grieving so hopelessly? Marco Aurelio isn't dead.'

Immediately, Bartholomew, Dimas and I tried to distance ourselves. We did not want to be recognized as his disciples. The people had different reactions to his claim. Some went from tears to mockery, albeit well contained. They secretly laughed at the crazy man. Others were extremely curious. They thought he was some eccentric spiritual leader invited to officiate the funeral. Still others wanted him thrown out, outraged at the invasion of privacy and disrespect for other people's feelings. Some of these grabbed him by the arms in an effort to usher him out.

But the dreamseller wasn't upset. He said in a strong, firm voice:

'I'm not asking you to silence your pain,

only your despair. I don't expect you to stanch your tears, only the depth of your anguish. The emptiness never goes away, but despair can be alleviated, for it does no honor to the departed.'

Those grasping him released their grip and began to understand that the strangely dressed man with a heavy beard might be eccentric, but he was intelligent. The deceased's widow, Sofia, and his son, Antonio, stared at him.

Then, with an air of serenity difficult to describe, he added:

'Marco Aurelio experienced incredible moments. He cried, he loved, he fell in love, he won, he lost. The reason all of you are sad — thrust into an existential vacuum because of his absence — is because you're letting him die in the only place where he must remain alive: inside you.'

Seeing the people more introspective, he resumed his penetrating Socratic method: 'What scars did Marco Aurelio leave on your emotions? Where did he influence your paths? How did his actions and words color your way of looking at life?'

After offering these words, the dreamseller said something that shocked everyone, including us. Once again we were ashamed of our lack of wisdom and sensitivity. He repeated the question that had shaken his audience: 'Is this man alive or dead inside of you?'

The mourners answered that he was alive. Immediately, he made a comment that lifted them out of their despair and soothed their spirits:

'Shortly before Jesus was killed, a woman named Mary, who loved him, poured the most expensive of perfumes over his feet. It was all she had. By anointing him with her perfume, she was praising him for all he had done and experienced, and he was so moved that he praised her magnanimous gesture, while the disciples scolded her because she had wasted an extremely valuable perfume that could have been used for other purposes. Scolding his disciples, Jesus told them that he was preparing them for his death, and that wherever his message was spread her gesture would be recounted as a timeless homage.'

The mourners pondered his words. The ones who couldn't hear clearly squeezed closer to him. Then he concluded:

'Jesus wanted to demonstrate that a wake may be a place of tears, but it should, above all else, be an atmosphere flooded with praise and solemn remembrance. Mourning should be a perfume, an homage to the departed. A setting for recounting his life and his words. A word of praise can be said about any person. Please, tell me of this man's deeds. Tell me how he impacted your lives. His silence should give wing to our voices.'

At first the mourners just looked at one another. Then what happened was incredible. Many of them began relating unique stories that they had experienced with him. They spoke of the legacy he had left. His kindness. His loyalty. His capacity to deal with failure. His unyielding affection. His friendship.

Others, now more at ease, joked about his mannerisms. There were those who said he loved nature. One friend said, 'I never met anyone as stubborn and obstinate.' And in a setting where usually no one smiles, people laughed at the memory, including Antonio and the widow, because they knew how stubborn he could be. A friend added, 'But he taught me that we must never give up on what we love.'

There were twenty incredible minutes of heartfelt memories. People didn't know how to describe the fascinating emotional experience they had had. Marco Aurelio was alive. At that moment, the dreamseller looked at us, his disciples, and said, whether joking or serious I don't know, 'When I die, don't despair. Instead, speak of my dreams and my wild desires.'

Some people laughed at the strange and amusing man who had lifted them from the valley of despair to the peak of serenity. As incredible as it seems, even young Antonio smiled. There, in that room where so many lavished praise on the deceased, the dreamseller sold a dream to the young boy who had lost his father.

'Antonio, look what a brilliant human being your father was, despite his shortcomings. Don't hold back your tears. Weep as many times as you desire, but don't let his loss make you lose hope. Just the opposite. Honor your father by living maturely. Honor him by confronting your fears. Praise him by being generous, creative, affectionate, sincere. Live wisely. I believe that if your father could use my voice at this moment to say something to you, he would implore you: 'Son, go forward! Don't be afraid of the journey. Be afraid of missing out on life.''

Antonio felt his spirits lift. That was all he needed to hear. He would still cry. Longing would beat mercilessly in his chest. But he would know how to put commas instead of periods in his life when he encountered loneliness, when he came upon sorrow. His life would take on new dimensions.

The dreamseller prepared to leave, but first he left the mourners with his final thoughts, the same questions that had shaken me atop the San Pablo Building.

'Are we living atoms that disintegrate and never again become what they were? What is existence or nonexistence? What mortal can know? Who has dissected death to expose its true essence? Is death the end or the beginning?'

Enraptured, people approached me and asked, 'Who is that man? Where does he come from?' What could I answer? I didn't know either. They asked the same of Bartholomew and, unfortunately, he found himself answering the questions. Honeymouth enjoyed weaving theories about things he didn't know. Puffing out his chest, he replied:

'Who's the chief? He's from another world. And if you need anything, I'm his adviser on international affairs.'

Dimas, the newest member of our group, stunned by everything he'd heard, replied honestly. 'I don't know who he is. All I know is he dresses like a pauper but he seems to be very rich, indeed.'

Sofia, Antonio's mother, was deeply grateful and bursting with curiosity. When she saw him about to leave without saying anything more, she asked, 'Who are you? What religion do you preach? Where do you learn these teachings?'

He looked at her and calmly answered:

'I'm not a priest, a theologian or a philosopher. I'm just a wanderer trying to understand who I am. A traveler who once doubted God, but, after crossing a great desert, has discovered that he is the architect of all existence.'

Upon hearing him, I again fell deep in thought. I didn't know that the dreamseller had been an atheist like me. But something had changed in him. His relationship with God troubled me; it wasn't based on religion, tradition or self-pity, but was rooted in an incomprehensible friendship. Who is he, then? What desert had he crossed? Could he have cried more than the people at the wake? Where had he lived, where was he born? Before more questions could bubble up in my mind, he started to leave. Sofia extended both hands to him and wordlessly declared her gratitude. Antonio couldn't contain himself. He gave the dreamseller a long embrace that moved everyone and asked, 'Where can I find you again? Where do you live?'

'My home is the world,' the dreamseller replied. 'You can find me in some avenue of existence.'

And he left, leaving everyone astonished. We, his disciples, were speechless. For the moment, at least, he quieted our uncertainties. We were beginning to believe it was worthwhile to follow him, little knowing the storms that awaited us.

We made our way slowly through the gathering. The people wanted to meet him, speak with him, open up some chapters of their lives, but he humbly passed them by. He wasn't fond of praise. We, on the other hand, were starting to feel important. Dimas and Bartholomew, who had always lived at the edge of society, felt their egos swell, attacked by a virus I knew all too well.

The Eager Miracle Worker

The day would have been perfect if not for the surprise awaiting us just around the corner. The funeral home was large, and there were several enormous rooms, each separate from the others so several families could mourn their loved ones at once. When we left the hall where Marco Aurelio was being mourned, we passed through another wake, that of a seventy-five-year-old woman.

But a man who walked by caught the dreamseller's attention. He was a young man of about thirty, curly hair, short, navy blue suit and a white shirt. He was good-looking, with a well-modulated voice, imposing. The dreamseller quietly followed him.

The man approached the old woman's coffin confidently. Apparently he was some sort of priest. To me, he seemed harmless, but the dreamseller didn't see it that way. The man positioned himself at the foot of the coffin and made a gesture of reverence. Little by little he revealed his face, and we soon saw his true intentions.

His name was Edson, but people called him the Miracle Worker. Edson had a penchant for 'performing' miracles. Oh, he wanted to help others. But there was always a motive behind his aid: He loved attention. Edson wasn't the spiritual leader charged with offering words of consolation at the funeral. He was there out of self-interest.

Incredible as it seems, the Miracle Worker desired to resurrect the old woman. He wanted to put on a dazzling show capable of making the spectators bow at his feet; he actually hoped to awaken the elderly woman from death and be recognized as the bearer of a supernatural gift. Just as Caligula used his power to be hailed as a god on earth, Edson hoped to use his knowledge of the Bible to invoke the supernatural and be treated like a demigod himself — although he never would have admitted it.

As a sociologist I had learned that there is no power as complete as religion. Dictators, politicians, intellectuals, psychiatrists and psychologists fail to penetrate the minds of others like certain religious figures. Because they represent a deity, these men can achieve a status the likes of which Napoleon or Hitler never could.

In our wanderings, the dreamseller would tell us that spiritual leaders who represented an altruistic, generous God contributed to the good of humanity. But those who represented a controlling, vengeful God — in effect, a God created in their own image — caused disasters, destroyed freedom and controlled people. The dreamseller always warned us that it's easy to construct a manipulative God in our mind. He seemed to want to keep us in touch with our humanity.

But this charlatan we saw at the wake had mixed intentions. At certain times he wanted to contribute to the good of his fellow man and was sincere and caring. At other times he seemed swollen with pridefulness.

But this Miracle Worker, though ambitious, was no fool. He wanted to create a spectacle but not a scene. He wanted to resurrect the old woman but tried to guard against insulting anyone. Many thoughts swirled in his brain. 'What if she doesn't come to life? What if I tell her to rise and she just lies there? My reputation will be lost.'

The dreamseller watched him closely, like a leopard scrutinizing the landscape. We knew the dreamseller took pleasure in dealing with extremely complicated people, but we didn't understand his true intention that day. Little by little we began to see the kind of show the Miracle Worker was hoping to put on.

After a moment of reverence, the Miracle Worker approached the dead woman and whispered in an almost inaudible voice,

'Rise.' He hoped not to be heard in case his faith failed him.

The old woman showed no sign of life. Immediately, he repeated in that low voice, 'Rise.'

If she were to have moved in the slightest, Edson would have shouted to the heavens and proclaimed himself a true miracle worker. It would be his most glorious moment. Countless people hungering for supernatural acts would follow him.

But nothing happened. The deceased remained motionless. Bartholomew, Dimas and I, who were far from saints, were indignant with the Miracle Worker's trickery. What an arrogant jerk, we thought.

But he didn't give up. He filled his lungs and in a louder voice, but speaking between his teeth so no one could understand clearly what he was saying, he declared, 'Rise, woman. I command you!'

The unimaginable happened. The woman moved. But not because of the Miracle Worker. An older man, reeking of alcohol the way Bartholomew did the day I met him, bumped the coffin. But the Miracle Worker, wrapped up in himself and in looking for any signs of life from the old woman, didn't notice when the deceased's nephew came staggering in and smacked the coffin, causing the old woman's hands, gently resting on her chest, to change position.

The Miracle Worker's heart leaped with emotion. He thought his moment of glory had arrived, that his supernatural abilities had finally revealed themselves. Overcome with joy, and desperate to take credit for his 'miracle,' he yelled out and proclaimed to the mourners:

'Rise, woman! I command you!'

This time, everyone heard and was startled by his command. He expected the woman to sit up in her coffin and the crowd to acknowledge his tremendous power. But the old woman showed no further signs of life.

He figured all he needed was just a little more faith to make the coffin move again. And this time, he gave the order to the body again, glancing at the crowd: 'Rise, woman!' he begged the corpse, which would not respond to his appeal.

The longer the woman remained motionless, the weaker his knees became. He broke into a cold sweat, his mouth dried out and his heart raced. Half dazed, he finally saw the drunk trying to regain his balance by steadying himself on the coffin. The Miracle Worker knew he had made a fool of himself. He felt like a wounded deer amid a pride of lions. But this Miracle Worker still had a few tricks up his sleeve. He raised his voice again and said firmly:

'Woman! If you won't rise to live in this evil world, then rest in peace!'

Several 'normals' answered in chorus, 'Amen!'

The Miracle Worker ended his performance by taking out a handkerchief to dry invisible tears and said solemnly, 'Poor, *poor* woman. She was *such* a good person.'

A Very Complicated Disciple

All signs pointed to this being just another con for the Miracle Worker: He used his supposed spirituality to take advantage of others' naivete. 'Normals' have a strong tendency to listen to leaders without questioning them. After watching the Miracle Worker's scheme, I looked at Dimas and thought, 'Not even Angel Hand would do something that low.' In turn, Angel Hand, knowing something of my nature through Bartholomew thought, 'Not even this arrogant intellectual would manipulate other people like that.' Bartholomew, more honest than either of us, said out loud, 'Only after two bottles of vodka could I hallucinate like that guy.'

As soon as my friends and I criticized the Miracle Worker, our legs trembled. We looked at one another and had the same thought: 'Why is the dreamseller so interested in this character? Could he be interested in calling him to join the group?' The thought rattled us so much that we said, simultaneously, 'I'll leave!'

This worried us. We watched the dreamseller's actions carefully, hoping he would turn and leave, but he went up to the man who had captured his attention. Our hearts pounded. The Miracle Worker met the dreamseller's gaze and, to our relief, our leader said nothing, merely shaking his head in disapproval.

The dreamseller may have had his faults, but he never set out to manipulate another person. To him, a person's conscience was sacred. Freedom of choice should always prevail. His strongest criticism of society was that it surreptitiously sold a non-existent freedom, a freedom found in the pages of democracy but not in the pages of history. Too many had been enslaved by their troubled minds.

After disapproving silently, but without exposing the Miracle Worker publicly, the dreamseller made two statements and two conclusions:

'Miracles don't convince people. If they did, Judas would never have betrayed Jesus. Miracles can change the body, but not the mind. If they could, Peter never would have denied knowing Jesus.'

Edson remained silent. He didn't know how to reply because he had never considered that. Then came the bombshell that rocked me as a professor.

'The man you claim to follow never used

his power in order to control people,' the dreamseller said. 'Jesus never used his power to seduce audiences and win over followers. That's why he, unlike politicians, told his followers, 'Don't tell anyone!' Unless they followed him out of the spontaneous emotion of an unfathomable love, he didn't want followers. He wanted friends, not servants.'

These words got me to thinking about our own history. I remembered that in centuries past, atrocities were committed in the name of Christ: People killed, tortured, waged war, conquered, wounded, excluded in his name. They ignored the gentleness of Jesus, who never manipulated anyone, who would not hear of servants. Centuries of opposition and hatred toward Muslims followed, an animosity whose roots are perpetuated even today. In traveling with the dreamseller, I had begun to suspect I wasn't the confirmed atheist I thought I was. Deep down, my disgust was with organized religion.

The Miracle Worker was dumbstruck: Never had anyone corrected him without scolding him. The dreamseller, having said all he needed to say, turned and left, leaving several who witnessed the confrontation confused. We were immensely relieved. For how long? We didn't know.

The next day, a newspaper report on the

recent events appeared in *The Times*, under the headline, 'A Stranger Turns a Wake into a Garden.' A photo taken secretly as we left the wake was on the front page of one section. The reporting wasn't an attack; instead, it contained many interesting facts. It said that a bold stranger wanted to change the dynamic of wakes, to transform them from settings of despair into platforms for paying homage to the dead.

The journalist had interviewed people who had heard the dreamseller speak. Some said they planned to write their families to say that, when they died, they didn't want a funeral marked by despair, loss and self-pity, but one highlighting their best moments. Mourners should instead be revelers, recalling the deceased's acts of love and kindness, their words, their dreams, their friendships — even their foolish moments. They wanted those saying good-bye to remember that day joyfully, despite the pain.

The article said that the stranger was the same one who had caused a flurry near the San Pablo Building. And it ended with two questions: Are we witnessing one of the greatest atheists ever, or a man with incomprehensible spirituality? Are we witness to a modern-day prophet, or a lunatic?

When we awoke the next morning, we

found the dreamseller off by himself, deep in conversation. It was the second time we'd seen him carrying on this monologue. He gestured as if he were having hallucinations or questioning his own reasoning. Ten minutes later, he came to us relaxed. He seemed to have cleansed his mind of the day-to-day noise.

The sky was darkening, threatening a heavy rain. Lightning ripped across the sky. Dimas didn't fear the police or jail time, but he was terrified of lightning storms. We were walking along a wide street when the thunder made our usually unflappable friend cower.

I tried to calm him by telling him that by the time we heard the thunder, the lightning — and the danger — had already passed. But the mind is riddled with traps; he understood my words but they could not calm his irrational fears. I couldn't criticize him, though. I was no different. I had always valued logic over emotion, but it was no consolation from the esoteric pain of my past. It haunted me.

The rain soon began to fall. We quickly sought shelter in a large shopping mall. At the entrance was a vast department store. As we went inside, we heard the earsplitting crack of lightning strike. Dimas dove beneath the first table he found. He was like a child who had seen a ghost. I thought to myself, 'The dreamseller is right. There are no heroes. Eventually, every giant encounters obstacles that transform him into a child. All you have to do is wait.'

The last lightning bolt overloaded the mall's grounding system and the electricity pulsed down the walls of the building. Two painters, cousins, were repainting the store. One of them, who had a stammer worse than Dimas, was working on the walls. When he was nervous, his voice shut down and he couldn't say a word. The other was on top of a six-foot ladder, happily retouching the steel window frames.

When the lightning bolt hit, it coursed through the walls and bounced into the window, striking one painter. The noise was deafening. The painter fell off the ladder, writhing in pain. His cousin, terrified, rushed to his aid. We started forward, but before we could get there, someone rushed past us, looking to be a hero. I don't know where the man came from, but he seemed familiar. When I looked closer, I realized it was the Miracle Worker from the wake.

Edson saw the painter lying on the floor, moaning in pain and holding his right ankle. He saw that the man's foot was deformed. He concluded immediately that it was because of the lightning. Wasting no time, he told the other painter, who was attending the injured man, 'It's OK, I've got him. I'm an expert in this kind of thing.'

He rushed over to the man and tried to straighten out his foot but couldn't. He sat down on the man's leg and began yelling an order at the ankle, trying to call on his supernatural powers.

'Heal! Repair! Align your bones!'

But the ankle didn't repair itself. The painter, now in agony, moaned again. The Miracle Worker applied still more force. In his mind, he couldn't leave such a simple case unresolved. It wasn't possible, he must have thought, for his moral standing with God to be so low. The painter howled in pain. The crowd gathered and buzzed, which only made the 'Good Samaritan' Miracle Worker try harder to show his supernatural powers.

Many of those watching the Miracle Worker thought he was a doctor doing some kind of procedure to alleviate the painter's suffering. The stammering cousin seemed to want to say something to Edson, who instead was distracted by the man's pestering. Losing his patience, he told the painter standing over him, 'Calm down! I am *going* to fix this man's leg.'

And he did. Two agonizing minutes later,

the Miracle Worker completed his task. Wiping sweat from his brow, he told the audience, 'There, the ankle is as good as new.' But the man's pain was worse than ever.

The painter looked at his ankle and appeared more desperate. We thought he was still in shock.

Just as the crowd was beginning to applaud the Miracle Worker, the painter's cousin finally managed to untie his tongue. He came swinging at Edson, shouting, 'Get away from him, you butcher! You worthless liar!'

No one understood what was happening, not even the dreamseller. We all thought the stuttering painter was being ungrateful. Then, stammering, he explained:

'My cousin's crippled. He's had a limp for thirty years, but he's never had surgery to correct it. Now this bastard comes along and fixes it — without anesthesia.'

A crowd, that only seconds earlier was ready to applaud the Miracle Worker, was now growing into a mob ready to pummel him. But the dreamseller stopped them. With one question he tamed an angry mob and rescued the man who loved power:

'Wait! Why do you want to hurt this man? What matters most, his actions or his intent?'

Tempers cooled and people began to disperse. Bartholomew, still confused, said,

'Chief, you need to explain to me what you just said.'

Calmly, with the Miracle Worker still shrinking from the crowd, the dreamseller explained:

'A man's actions may warrant our outrage. His methods can be criticized. But what we should focus on are a person's intentions.'

For the first time in his life, Edson had performed a real miracle — and had almost been lynched for it. We had criticized his attitude, looking only at his actions. Unlike the dreamseller, we hadn't seen the altruistic reasons for what he had done; we simply wanted him as far away as possible from us and our little sociological experiment. But before we could say a word, the dreamseller did what we feared most. He looked at the Miracle Worker and casually told him:

'Come, follow me and I will show you miracles unlike any you've ever known, miracles that can cure our ailing society.'

When we heard the dreamseller's call, my two friends and I embraced one another. Some might have thought we were moved, but actually we were disappointed in ourselves. In that moment, we realized how easy it is to fall under the spell of prejudice. We had accepted scoundrels, drunks and stupidly prideful people into our group, but we had discriminated against the religious types, especially so-called miracle workers. We had to adjust our thinking to the dream-seller's will with a heavy dose of patience and tolerance.

Edson was euphoric about being called. He didn't understand it, but knew that this dreamseller, however strange, possessed great powers of persuasion. He thought that if he learned the dreamseller's techniques, he could use them to go far. He couldn't imagine the depths of the journey he was about to begin. He couldn't imagine the bitter pain he would suffer curing himself of his obsession with power. Deep down, he was as addicted to power as Honeymouth was to alcohol, as I was to my ego, as Angel Hand was to the art of the con. We were addicts, all of us.

An Obsessive Dream

We were no sect, no political party. We were not part of a foundation or any official organization. We didn't rely on public welfare, didn't even know where we'd sleep or what we'd eat. We depended on spontaneous donations from people, and sometimes we bathed in public shelters. We were a band of dreamers who wanted to change the world, or at least our world. Still, we had no guarantee whether we would change anything or cause more confusion. But I was beginning to love this lifestyle, a pleasant sociological experiment, albeit one full of unknowns.

Some were starting to recognize the dreamseller from the news. They would interrupt his walk, feeling the need to tell him their problems. He enjoyed listening to them. After minutes or hours of hearing them vent, he would encourage them to make choices and understand that every choice comes with frustrations and not merely gains.

Gradually, the dreamseller acquired more disciples, each more interesting than the last. The swallows were learning to fly within a system that threatened to clip their wings. But we also learned not to make grand plans for the future. The future didn't belong to us. Life was a celebration, even though the wine always eventually ran out.

We learned to kiss old people and feel the markings of time. We learned to pay attention to children and delight in their innocence. We learned to talk to beggars and journey through their incredible worlds. Priests, nuns, pastors, Muslims, Buddhists, would-be suicides, depressives, neurotics . . . there were so many beautiful and interesting people around us who were ignored by society.

I was starting to develop a new sensitivity to others, an empathy. Even though my pridefulness was dormant, it wasn't yet dead. I recalled action films I had seen. How many countless extras were killed in movies, faceless people who, in the real world, had entire life stories, complete with fear and love, bravery and cowardice. To the dream-seller, there were no extras in society. He praised the poor, calling them to be his closest friends. He cared deeply for those who lived at society's margins.

Just when I thought my sensitivity was at its height, one of those supporting actors came into my life and made me see that I was still only just a beginner. We were on

Kennedy Avenue when we saw a young man of about twenty, close to six feet tall, curly hair, dark skin. His name was Solomon Salles. He had these wild gestures that made even children flinch. He would wink uncontrollably and move his neck restlessly, flexing his trapezius muscles. Before going through a door he would jump three times, believing that if he skipped the routine even once, someone in his family would die. He had severe obsessive-compulsive disorder.

Besides all these bizarre compulsive rituals, the oddest thing of all was that Solomon couldn't see a hole, whether in walls, the ground or furniture, without feeling the urge to stick his right index finger into it. As we were watching him, he was crouching, sticking his finger in various small openings in the sidewalk.

Passersby made fun of him. To tell the truth, we couldn't hold back either, though we tried to disguise our laughter. We thought we'd finally found someone more messed up than any of us. But the dreamseller was upset at our reactions.

'Is this young man more fragile than we are, or stronger?' he asked us pointedly. 'What price does he pay for having to live with his tics in public? Is he weak or gifted with unusual courage? I don't know about

136

you, but beyond a doubt he's a stronger man than me.'

We fell silent, but he went on:

'How often do you think this young man has felt he was in the center ring of a circus, as he is now? How many sleepless nights has he spent thinking about the laughter of others? How many times has he felt the white-hot sting of prejudice?' And so we would truly feel the burn of our discrimination, he concluded, 'Criticism injures a person, but prejudice annihilates him.'

Whenever the dreamseller analyzed one of us, he stripped us, leaving us 'naked.' I discovered that people like me, who always defended human rights, are grossly prejudiced in some areas, even if this barbarity is subtly manifested in a hypocritical smile or in indifferent silence. We're worse than vampires. We kill without extracting blood. He continued:

'If you want to sell the dream of unity, you have to perceive the suffering of others. You have to learn to dry the tears never shed, the anguish never verbalized, the fears hidden below an impassive face. The ones who don't develop such characteristics will have traces of psychopathy even if they live in unsuspecting settings, like the temples of universities or the temples of business, politics or religion.

They'll pressure, wound, coerce, without feeling the pain of others. Is that you?' he asked us.

I tried taking a deep breath to see if I could get oxygen to my brain. Could I have traces of psychopathy? Classic psychopaths are easily discerned, but those with subtle traces of psychopathy can disguise their insensitivity behind their academic titles, their ethics or their spirituality. I wore a disguise.

I never sought out my son to ask him about his fears, his frustrations. I imposed rules on John Marcus, pointed out his mistakes, but I never sold him the most important dream: That I wanted to know him, to love him and to be loved by him. I never sought out a student who looked sad, irritable or indifferent. I never lent my shoulder for another professor to cry on. To me, professors were technicians and not people. My arrogance turned against me like a boomerang.

When I was ready to give up on life, my colleagues and students had no idea of my emotional state. An intellectual like me couldn't declare his pain. To them, depression was something that happened to weak people. No one noticed the suffering secretly drawn on my face. Were they blind or was I incapable of showing my feelings? I still don't know.

As the dreamseller always advised us, no one is a hundred percent villain or a hundred percent victim. I was insensitive but also surrounded by people with low levels of sensitivity. I didn't need applause or praise. What I needed was just a shoulder to cry on, to feel the support of people saying, 'I'm here. You can count on me.'

When the dreamseller made us see the courage and greatness of the young man with OCD, he offered us a challenge: 'Are you going to sell dreams to him?' He said nothing more, awaiting our reaction.

We remained silent. After endless seconds with a lump in our throats, we felt lost. It was an odd reaction for a group of supposedly experienced people. We didn't know what to say. We didn't know what he would think of us. Just a few minutes earlier we had branded him a lunatic, and now we were afraid of being branded lunatics by him. Isn't that what insanity is? We went from one extreme to the other.

The dreamseller remained silent and made us uncomfortable. We knew how to ridicule the misfortune of others but not how to alleviate it. We were creative when it came to exclusion but helpless in matters of inclusion. If someone asked the Miracle Worker to deliver a long, bombastic speech to the young man, it would be an easy task, but asking him to sell dreams paralyzed him. If Bartholomew were under the influence and was asked to make friends with the stranger, it would be no problem. But sober, it was much more complicated. If someone asked Angel Hand to steal his wallet then give it back to win his admiration, it would be easy. But charming someone with words was an almost impossible task for him.

If they asked me to teach a class to demonstrate my sophistication, I'd have no problem. But for me to win over a stranger, my fellow man, without using the power of information, was a hellish task. I knew how to address large audiences but not how to engage a man alone. I had been trained to speak about Kant, Hegel, Auguste Comte, Marx, but not about myself. The system had made a mockery of our humanity. And I had nurtured it.

Since there was no instruction manual for selling dreams to an obsessive, and since the dreamseller refused to offer guidance, I shyly tried my hand. I, the most urbane of the group, was also the most unbending. Honeymouth, worn down by life, crouched down and tried to stick his hands in the holes in an effort to initiate contact. But the young man just laughed at him. Bartholomew felt like a fool, and the young man went on with his compulsion.

Edson couldn't stand watching it. He turned his back and covered his mouth, trying helplessly to stifle his laughter. Suddenly, the obsessive young man stood up and saw the opening in the Miracle Worker's Dumbo-like right ear. He rushed over and stuck his finger in Edson's ear, making the Miracle Worker leap to the heavens and shout, 'Away with you, demon, this body doesn't belong to you!'

Solomon was startled at the Miracle Worker's rudeness. Edson put his hands on his head, realizing that once again he had displayed his weakness for the supernatural. This time, however, he'd gone too far. He had wanted to cast out the mental illness lodged in the man's brain. But Solomon looked wounded.

'I've been called crazy, psychotic, mad, demented, insane, bonkers, off my rocker, but possessed by demons is a first,' he said.

Edson saw how deeply he had hurt the young man. He realized that deep down, he had trouble accepting people who were different, and, in effect, was selling nightmares instead of dreams.

'Forgive me. Please, forgive me,' Edson said solemnly. 'I was stupid and unjust and

141

superficial. I actually think you're much stronger than me. You put up with mockery while I look for applause.'

Edson's honest and courageous words fascinated us. He had begun to achieve one of the most difficult miracles, that of humility. Like him, I had never asked for anyone's forgiveness. We were small gods, I in the temple of knowledge, Edson in the temple of spirituality. We were beginning to understand that we only became strong when we allow ourselves to be fragile.

That moment of honesty broke the ice. We introduced ourselves to the young man and began to become part of his life. He had attempted to study psychology but had to give it up because his professors said an obsessive couldn't treat the mentally ill. He tried law school but had to give it up because his professors said an obsessive with such wild obsessions wouldn't be taken seriously by his clients, much less when presenting arguments in court.

He hadn't lasted three months at any job. No one wanted to hire a person seemingly unable to control his behavior. He didn't have a girlfriend because no one wanted to be with someone who was constantly being insulted. His whole existence was based on exclusion. Nevertheless, he was a very strong human being, as the dreamseller had imagined. Despite those mounting difficulties he hadn't become depressed or thought about taking his own life, as I had. He had serious issues, to be sure. But despite those moments when he felt rejected, he had learned to enjoy life. He lived better than the disciples. We were the ones who needed to buy dreams from him, and he knew it.

Entering that young man's world was a marvelous journey. We discovered a fantastic human being hidden behind society's ridicule. And we were proud to have him along when the dreamseller called him to be a seller of dreams.

The dreamseller led us to an open green space and began to tell us the story of another Solomon, the great king of Israel. The dreamseller explained that King Solomon had had an excellent start in life. He didn't want gold, silver or political power; he wanted that most coveted of treasures, wisdom. Every day, he breathed and drank wisdom. His kingdom progressed prodigiously, becoming one of the first ancient empires, and its relationship with neighboring nations was marked by peace.

But time passed, and power corrupted him. He abandoned wisdom and sought out the pleasures of the physical world. Soon, nothing satisfied him. He became profoundly depressed and was honest enough to admit that he was bored with his life. That vain existence robbed him of life's joys.

'The great king had hundreds of wives, chariots, palaces, servants, armies, golden garments, honors and victories like few kings before him,' the dreamseller said, 'but he neglected to love a woman and to regard the delicate lilies of the field, which represent friendship and so many other fundamental things.'

As he was about to elaborate on the last lesson, my unpredictable companion chimed in and once more made everyone burst with laughter.

'Chief, may I say something?' asked Honeymouth.

'Of course, Bartholomew,' he said patiently.

'Maybe Solomon got depressed because he had hundreds of mothers-in-law?'

The dreamseller laughed and offered, 'I don't know, but I do know there are some mothers-in-law more lovable than many mothers.' And he concluded with this lesson: 'Success is more difficult to deal with than failure. As Solomon learned, the danger in being successful is that the person can turn into a workaholic, forgetting to savor the small things in life and missing out on that which only dreams can achieve. The sight of an idyllic country landscape, of a flower garden, of a painting, can evoke more emotion in the man who seeks to behold it than in the man who seeks to own it. God gave us all equal access to life's greatest pleasures. Rich are those who seek out that treasure, poor are those who seek to possess them.'

Placing his hands on Solomon, the newest disciple, the dreamseller said, 'Great human beings are at the margins of society. Here is someone who has very little and yet has everything. Thank you for selling us your dreams.'

Looking for Life
Among the Dead

The next day, the sun's first rays broke over the horizon and shone down on our makeshift beds, inviting us to a new day of discovery. As always, Bartholomew was the last to get up. I imagine that if he were in a comfortable bed he'd sleep the entire day.

Before we headed out, the dreamseller extended an unusual invitation, one that would become an integral part of our story. He invited us to one of the most important tasks of the mind: to do nothing, merely experience the art of observation.

He led us to a busy tree-lined avenue. There he handed each of us a crumpled sheet of white paper and pens and asked us to write down all the sounds and images that excited us. Anything man-made didn't count. The traffic noise was deafening, the air polluted, the commotion intense. What could excite us if not the colorful stores, the stylish cars, the shape of a stranger? And what does that have to do with changing human thinking? What does the art of observation have to do with selling dreams? To me, it was a boring exercise with no intellectual appeal.

It wasn't long before the dreamseller prodded us.

'Anyone who doesn't develop the art of observation is missing the fullness of life. He may be a warehouse of information, but he will never construct great ideas.'

I remembered that the day before I hadn't seen the complex human being hidden behind Solomon's rituals. I was a terrible observer. I saw what every 'normal' person acknowledged. Edson and Dimas also didn't know what to write. Bartholomew hummed to summon up inspiration, but none came. He looked up, then to the sides, and remained inert. Minutes passed without our observing anything interesting. Solomon was the only exception. He calmed his compulsions and began writing ceaselessly. He was excited, saying frequently, 'Hmm . . . Wow, amazing . . . Fantastic . . . '

He was writing, and I was stumped. The dreamseller gave me a nudge.

'You will develop the art of observation only if you learn the most difficult art of the human intellect.' And he didn't provide the answer.

'What is it?' I thought.

'The art of calming the mind,' he said

eventually. 'Minds that once were brilliant have lived a mediocre life because they didn't calm their thoughts. Great writers, notable scientists, magnificent artists have shattered their inspiration because they had a cluttered mind. The thoughts, mental images and fantasies that can make our creativity take flight can also clip its wings, if excessive, robbing us of our intuition and ingenuity.'

'That's my problem,' I thought. My mind was a dark cavern of disturbance. Thinking foolish thoughts was my specialty. Silence was always my enemy. But for the dreamseller, I tried to silence the voices within. It wasn't easy; I was inundated with images racing through my mind faster than the cars on this street. My thoughts were choked by intellectual pollution.

My friends were also lost. But little by little we entered the infinite world of silence. Starting at that moment, our perception was heightened. I began to make out the sharp songs of a bird. It strummed a beautiful melody with unbelievable fervor. I jotted it down. Then another bird sang a mournful song. Moments later, a dove performed a courtship ritual with a female.

I observed more than ten extraordinary birdsongs. They had little reason to rejoice in that concrete jungle, I thought, but unlike me they were celebrating life. I observed and noted the resilience of the weathered tree trunks, which, despite the impermeability of the soil and a shortage of water, survived in an inhospitable setting — bravery that I never had shown. More than ten million people had passed by those trees since they were planted, and maybe ten, at the most, had actually stopped to observe them in detail. I was beginning to feel like a privileged person in a societal desert.

Bartholomew, who wouldn't normally notice an elephant in front of his nose, also began to have more luck. He contemplated five multicolored butterflies dancing across the sky. Unlike them, he noted, he only danced when drunk. Edson noted various types of sounds produced by leaves rustling in the wind, humbly applauding passers-by, unlike him, who sought applause. Dimas analyzed insects that worked tirelessly preparing for winter, something he had never done. He stole and, like all thieves, was a terrible manager, believing that life was an eternal springtime.

After this gratifying exercise, we spoke one of our favorite phrases: 'How I love this life!' Never had doing so little meant so much. I had never imagined that nature was present in such a meaningful way, right here, in the middle of the city. How could a specialist in society never have done this exercise? For the first time, I truly loved silence, and in that silence I discovered that I had not had a childhood.

I don't remember any pleasant experiences as a child. Maybe I've become a rigid adult because I didn't know how to relax as a child. Maybe I've grown into a paranoid man because I'd never experienced the innocence of childhood. Maybe I was a chronically depressive and ill-tempered grown-up because I hadn't lived my first years of life joyfully. The losses in my life made me into an adult very early, a young man who thought a lot, but felt nothing.

As I was recalling my childhood, the dreamseller seemed to be studying me. Taking a deep breath, he commented on the death of childhood in our time, one of the things that bothered him the most.

'The Internet, video games, computers — they're all useful, but they've destroyed something invaluable: childhood. Where is the pleasure of silence? Where is the fun of playing outside? Where is innocence? It pains me so deeply that the system is creating unhappy, restless children — better suited for psychiatric care than happy, carefree lives.'

All of a sudden, the dreamseller acted in a way I'd never seen before. He turned to watch as several parents passed us, taking their seven- and eight-year-old children shopping. The children were dressed at the height of fashion, every accessory matching their outfits, and they were each carrying cell phones. But they were clearly disillusioned with life. Some whined and complained and caused a scene for a new dress or a gadget. To simply keep them quiet, the parents gave in.

The dreamseller looked furious and he confronted those parents.

'What are you doing to your children? Take them to know the forests. Have them remove their shoes and let them walk barefoot on the ground. Let them climb trees, and encourage them to invent their own games. The human species has shut itself inside a bell jar of selfishness and materialism. Instead, teach them about animals and let them learn a new way to behave.' And he paraphrased Jesus' words: 'Children do not live by shopping centers alone, but by all the adventures of childhood.'

I was impressed by his boldness in the face of strangers. Some of the parents considered his words. Others reacted brashly. One said, 'Isn't that the crazy guy we saw in the papers?'

Another, an intellectual and probably, like me, seething with pridefulness, was more arrogant: 'I'm a professor with a doctorate in psychology and I won't stand for this invasion of privacy. Let me worry about my children.' Looking us up and down he told his friends, loud enough for us to hear, 'What a boorish bunch.'

Honeymouth heard the insult and couldn't stifle his compulsive urge to talk. He seconded the dreamseller:

'Listen, pal, I'm not a 'doctorate' of anything,' he told the professor. 'But let your children be immersed in nature. Let them play and get dirty. That way, none of them will turn out to be a crazy no-good drunk like me.' He made a gesture, asking for patience and added, 'But I'm getting better, chief.'

He turned to the children and said, 'Anybody who wants to fly like a butterfly, raise your hand.'

Three children raised their hands, two remained indifferent and three hid behind their parents and answered, 'I'm afraid of butterflies.'

Offended by the forwardness of the strangers, several parents called the security guards at the entrance to the large Megasoft department store they were about to enter. The guards quickly ushered us out.

'Get out of here, you bums.'

But, before leaving, the dreamseller turned

to the parents who had argued with him and said, 'I ask your forgiveness for my actions and hope that one day you won't have to ask your children's forgiveness for yours.'

For some of the parents, the dreamseller's ideas didn't fall on barren ground. Some, even while angry, began to realize they needed to work on their relationship with their children. Their children had received the best possible educations under the existing system; they had become experts in consuming products and using computers, but they were perpetually dissatisfied. They didn't know how to observe, feel and draw conclusions. These parents realized that nature may not be as important to the mental survival of the human race as it was to its emotional survival. They began to frequent forests, zoos and urban gardens.

Nature is a more invaluable teacher than all the other educational theories for expanding the mind's horizons.

I was moved at seeing the dreamseller's and Bartholomew's tenderness with children. I had never thought too much about them. I was too busy criticizing society in the classroom. I didn't understand that the true educational material was the student and not the information. I was only concerned that they keep quiet and pay attention in class.

That same afternoon, we passed through a residential district. We came upon a large, gloomy building. The garden was overgrown with tall grass. Enormous trees cast looming shadows, preventing the low plants from flourishing. The old building with its arches was beautiful, but its paint had faded. The wooden window frames were rotting and seemed painted in the green moss. Plaster was peeling from the filthy white walls. It was a nursing home, but definitely not a pleasant place to live out the last years of one's life.

Many elderly people went there not because their families had abandoned them, but simply because they had no close relatives. The majority of those residents had only one child or at most two. When an only child died or moved to a different city or couldn't physically or financially care for his aging parents, the elderly were sent to these institutions for their medical and daily care. They fled from the suffocating trap of loneliness to these nursing homes.

Looking at the building, the dreamseller told us, 'Behold a good setting for dreams. Go and bring joy to the people who live there.'

In our 'holy' prejudice we thought, 'Dreams? In a nursing home? Those people are bored and depressed. What could possibly excite them anymore?' We had been in the world of children, and now we were entering the world of the elderly. Worlds so far apart yet so alike. The problem was that the dreamseller took a step back. We were waiting for him to at least guide us with some instruction, but he simply said he was going for a walk. Before the dreamseller left, Dimas, who began stuttering and blinking uncontrollably, expressed his uncertainty:

'Make . . . the . . . the old folks hap . . . happy? How, dreamseller? They ha . . . have one foot in the grave.' He knew how to pick old people's pockets, how to worry them half to death, but he had never cheered up or had a deep conversation with one of them.

'Dimas, prejudice will age you more than the passing of time. Inside, you're older than many of them,' the dreamseller said.

'If it were up to me, I could solve their problems in about two minutes,' Bartholomew added. 'I'd give 'em a couple quarts of booze and get the party started.'

He immediately apologized. Edson and Solomon also didn't know how to achieve the miracle of happiness. We were all at a loss.

Before we realized it, the dreamseller had already set off for some unknown destination. The group gathered, each one explained his

155

ideas, we formulated a strategy and went in search of materials, returning two hours later.

Honeymouth was wearing a long wig and dark glasses and was chewing gum. Excited, he told us, 'Guys, I've got it! We'll pretend we're normal.' We all burst out laughing.

We headed for the nursing home. Before I could say anything, Bartholomew again took the lead. He made up what sounded like a pretty good story to get us in.

'OK, here's the deal. We're a professional band of musicians and we want to put on a show for the people here. For free. We don't need money but any donations are welcome.'

When he mentioned donations, I poked him. That wasn't in the script. Dimas was wearing a red hat and dark Ray-Ban-type glasses. I had on a long pigtail wig. Solomon sported thick sideburns like Elvis Presley's. Edson had a red ribbon on his head and a long collarless T-shirt. We borrowed the outfits saying we were putting on a fund-raiser and had promised to return them afterward.

The nursing home staff looked suspiciously at our costumes, but since young people rarely came to visit the elderly, the staff wanted to see what we had in store. I said to myself, 'What are you doing here? This isn't going to work.' An impromptu audience was arranged. More than a hundred retirees sat down quietly in front of our so-called band.

We had two battered guitars. The Miracle Worker, who claimed to have learned to play in his church band, played way out of tune. And Solomon, who had the other, wasn't much better. I blew into a sax, trying to recall the handful of notes I had learned in a few classes with my grandfather. Dimas had a double bass and didn't know what to do with it. Honeymouth was — what else? — on lead vocals. But he assured us that he could carry a tune and said he used to sing in nightclubs when he was more or less sober.

We played our first piece of music, a rock ballad. But we were nervous and stiff. Honeymouth's voice was a disaster; he couldn't keep up with the music and it probably would have been better if he had just danced along — not that he realized how awful he was. Our audience just watched us. We thought maybe things should be livelier. We stopped halfway through the first song and broke into a heavy metal jam. Oh, what a ruckus we made. We were really worked up, shaking our hips, jumping around the stage, but from the old folks? Nothing. Not even Honeymouth's verbal gymnastics with that off-key voice drew a laugh.

I thought: 'We're toast. We've just made these people's depression worse.' Bartholomew broke into his anthem, a samba, and we just tried to keep up: '*I drink, yes I do, I'm livin', there's folks who don't drink and are dyin', I drink, yes I do.*'

And he repeated the refrain, looking at the old people, believing a little alcohol in some form would get them moving.

But no one sang. Or clapped. Or smiled. Or so much as moved. Instead of selling dreams, we were selling embarrassment. We looked at the nursing staff and saw that they were motionless, too. Like us, they thought the elderly had one foot in the grave and were just waiting for death. Just when the afternoon was looking like one of the worst since we started following the dreamseller, he returned. When they saw him, several of the old men and women rushed to hug him passionately. That was when we realized that he was a frequent visitor here.

The dreamseller handed out our instruments to the audience, though they could barely hold them. We thought they wouldn't even realize what a guitar, saxophone or double bass were, much less be able to play them. To our surprise, three of the men, Mr. Lauro, Mr. Michel and Mr. Lucio, took the two guitars and the double bass, positioned them correctly, and began to play in tune. The sound that emerged made us tingle. We couldn't believe what we were hearing.

A woman picked up the saxophone and put on a show. I was speechless. 'Wait,' I thought, 'isn't this supposed to be a warehouse for old people awaiting death?' We were shocked — and humbled — to realize this place was a prison for full, rich, gifted people with incredible repressed potential.

The dreamseller delighted in hearing them. Then he took Bartholomew's microphone, and gave it to a much older gentleman, who could barely walk. But when he breathed into the microphone, his voice was unrivaled even by Frank Sinatra.

Then the dreamseller called the elderly who could still move about to the floor and began to dance with them. Even I started to dance. It was a riot. These old folks turned that nursing home upside down. Smiles sprang onto their faces and they felt like people once again. Of course they had looked at us like we were idiots. We had underestimated them and given them our worst, thinking that just because they were old — that their muscles were weak, their memory failing — they would swallow whatever pathetic show we put on.

Many of them had enjoyed a wonderful childhood, much better than mine. And now, the child within awakened from its slumber. Later, the dreamseller would tell us he had sent us to the nursing home not with the intention of our selling them dreams but so we could buy dreams from them. He showed us there is no such thing as a person without worth, only someone who is grossly undervalued.

Upon hearing these words, I realized another mistake I had made. My grandfather, Paulo, was fun and sociable. He died almost fifteen years after my mother, but I never let myself into his world. I had felt rejected by my uncles and cousins, and so I ended up rejecting my grandfather. Every victim bears the scars of a hostage. I had admired my grandfather's ability to play instruments, but had never asked about his tears and his fears. I never valued his great sense of humor and his lifetime of experiences. I missed out on enjoying such a surprising human being.

That day, the dreamseller wove together thoughts that still echo in my mind:

'The time between youth and old age is shorter than you can imagine. Whoever doesn't delight in reaching old age isn't worthy of his youth. Don't fool yourselves: A person doesn't die when his heart stops beating. He dies when the world tells him he's no longer of any value.'

The Temple of Electronics

The event that occurred in the nursing home came to light not because a journalist was present but because a nurse photographed it and gave the information to a newspaper. Ever since our visit to the nursing home, our days were filled with commotion. As the days went by, our group became ever stronger. We formed close ties despite our bickering. We held lively outdoor round tables to discuss our own stories and what we'd seen in society.

At least once a week the dreamseller invited new people — bricklayers, painters, sculptors, gas station attendants, mechanics, garbage collectors — into our expansive 'home' to sit on fruit crates and tell us about their lives. They were delighted at the invitation. And we had never had as good a time communing with our fellow man, listening to stories of their real difficulties and expectations, dreams and nightmares, passions and disillusionments. It was a unique sociological experience, a magical apprenticeship.

Meanwhile, the dreamseller's fame was

growing. He had become a mythic figure in the city. People in cars would point at him and tell one another, 'Isn't that the guy who stopped traffic near the San Pablo Building?' 'Isn't that the same one who shook up an old folks' home and a wake?' Judging by how 'normals' like a spectacle, they'd soon be saying he raised the dead.

One day, a man of about sixty with a serious and tormented expression recognized the dreamseller on the street. He called to the dreamseller and hurried to catch up to us.

'Master,' he said. 'For thirty years I worked for the same company. I truly started to come into my own as a manager and distinguished myself among my peers. But my boss didn't like it and started finding all sorts of ways of making my life hell for years until he finally fired me. I gave that company my all, but I was tossed aside like trash. I became depressed. I felt betrayed and didn't have the courage to start all over again with a new company. Besides, they prefer young employees who'll take less pay. I hate my old boss with all my heart. What can I do?'

The man's lips trembled. He appeared to be looking for some kind of relief amid the agony. The dreamseller looked first at us, then at him, and stated:

'Envy and revenge are phenomena exclusive to the human race. No other species has them. He envied you because you had something he didn't. But there's a way to exact revenge on him.'

I was confused. 'What kind of man am I following?' I thought. 'Isn't he the master of forgiveness?'

Bartholomew liked the dreamseller's attitude. Echoing his words, he said, 'That's right. An eye for an eye, a tooth for a tooth. Give the guy a good punch in the mouth.'

Dimas puffed out his chest. 'If you need somebody to get your back, you found him,' he said and began making karate gestures.

Honeymouth was emboldened. He began to shout and make disjointed karate chops like he was some kind of sensei. The two started play-fighting and Dimas, without meaning to, popped Honeymouth upside the head and dropped him like a bad habit. He went out cold and was slow to get up. When we rushed to his side, he rubbed his head and told Dimas, 'Are you mad at me?'

Bartholomew realized this eye-for-an-eye was a dangerous business. The fired manager, watching this, didn't know whether to laugh or cry.

'How should I get even?' he asked the dreamseller.

'By killing him,' the dreamseller replied flatly.

My legs buckled. I never thought I'd hear those words come out of the dreamseller's mouth. My heart was pounding and I even thought about leaving the group that very moment. Then, dripping hatred, the man bared his true intent.

'You're right. That's what I'm going to do. That son of bitch doesn't deserve to live.' But before the man could leave, the dreamseller searched for the root of his hate.

'The greatest revenge you can take against any enemy is to forgive him. Kill him inside yourself.'

'How do I do that?' the man asked, surprised.

'The weak kill their enemies' body; the strong kill how they regard their enemies. Those who kill the body are murderers. Those who kill what they represent are wise.'

The man started to feel light-headed. We had to grab him and lean him against the closest wall. The dreamseller went up to him again, looked him straight in the eyes and said:

'Take your revenge by reclaiming your peace of mind and by shining even more in your next job. Otherwise, he will haunt you for the rest of your life.'

The man stood paralyzed for several seconds. Then he regained his composure and realized that he couldn't behave like a victim, like a poor fool who only fuels his anger. He should take action, but a different kind. He gave the dreamseller a long embrace, the way a son hugs his father. And when he left, he was clearly headed down a different path.

That's when I noticed the revolver bulging under his shirt. I was flabbergasted. The man really was ready to commit murder. Only then did I understand the dreamseller's shocking attitude. No gentle words would have dissuaded this man, just like when I tried to commit suicide. The dreamseller hadn't wiped out his desire for vengeance; he had just redirected it.

'What kind of therapy is this?' I wondered.

Days later, the Consumer Electronics Show, the greatest consumer electronics fair in the world, was taking place in the wealthiest part of the city. More than 2,500 companies were participating and some 140,000 visitors from more than 130 countries were expected. Even in a down economy, end-users and retailers eagerly flocked to the event, which proved the industry had experienced uninterrupted growth.

The dreamseller turned his attention toward the big event; he wanted to stand in the temple of electronics. We couldn't understand why he was so interested in the event since it looked like he had never even used a computer. But he simply said, 'Let's go to the fair.'

Skittish, we followed him. The event was way too upscale for people like us. After all, we were unkempt in torn shirts and frayed and patched jeans. We weren't part of any corporation, and of course, didn't have an invitation. We looked as if we had teleported from some rural area of the 1900s into the peak of the twenty-first century.

Bartholomew, trying to put us at ease, repeated his famous phrase: 'Guys! Let's pretend we're 'normals.'' Immediately, our posture improved, we tried to smooth our hair and walked upright and confident.

As we approached the doors, Dimas put his arm around Solomon's shoulder and tried to keep his nervous tics under wraps. Pulling away from him, Solomon joked, 'Watch it, Nimble Fingers. I'm all man, here!'

'Hey, it's Angel Hand or Saint's Hand, to you,' Dimas said.

'More like Devil's Hand,' Bartholomew joked.

Dimas didn't like the joke and his eyes grew wide and angry.

'In the old days, Dimas. In the old days

— many hours ago,' he joked again, and ran away, afraid of retaliation.

Our group was impossible; I swear we were like children, sometimes. But our sense of humor faded as soon as we set foot in the fair. Seeing the apprehension on our faces, the dreamseller told us:

'Does rejection still frighten you? Do these tense settings still threaten you? Haven't you learned that someone can injure your body but not your mind, unless you let him?'

His words just fueled our anxiety. The entrance hall alone intimated us: a beautiful patio with a multicolored water fountain. Dozens of vases with roses, hibiscuses, daisies and tulips decorated the place.

Endless panels of illuminated ads for the major corporations glowed at the entrance. A red carpet led visitors inside. But to get in, besides showing an invitation and ID, guests had to submit to a full-body scan and a metal detector. It's a dangerous world and a man's word apparently was worth little.

In that moment, I realized that I, the intellectual of the group, was the most insecure of all. I drifted behind the others. The dreamseller didn't actually want to go into the fair, he wanted to stand in the entrance hall and watch people. But Bartholomew, demonstrating uncommon boldness, tried to get in. But two security officers quickly intercepted him. One of them asked him to spread his arms and ran a security wand over every part of his body. When the guard began to touch his private parts, Bartholomew jumped: 'Easy, there, buddy!'

We went to his aid. The dreamseller tried to calm him and asked the rest of us to hang back. When several other security officers approached, they took one look at our band of misfits and asked to see invitations. Since we had none, they started scanning us with their machines and frisking us as they'd done to Bartholomew. The guards got angry when Solomon said he was ticklish and wouldn't let himself be searched. They tried to throw us out of a public area.

Then, one of the guards recognized Angel Hand from his past life. He gave him a hard shove and said, 'Get outta here, you crook.'

As he fell, he stole the guard's wallet in a moment of weakness. But he regretted it before he even hit the floor and returned the wallet. The dreamseller was pleased, but it only made the guards more suspicious.

Edson was fuming. I felt if he actually had supernatural powers, he would have rained down fire on those guards. But the dreamseller displayed a disquieting calm, like he had fully expected that situation.

While pushing us toward the door, the guards began mocking us.

'Maybe these guys are the clowns the fair hired as entertainment,' one of the guards said as they followed us to the door. And they all laughed. In fact, we did look like something out of a comedy — or a horror film. Another guard shoved the dreamseller, who almost fell.

'Why do you attack me when I didn't attack you? What have I done to incur your wrath?' the dreamseller said, regaining his balance.

One of them said what the other guards were thinking. 'Get lost, you lousy bunch of con artists.'

Suddenly, I said something I never imagined I'd ever say: 'How I'd love to be a millionaire so I could give those guys a swift kick in the ass.'

I spoke before I realized what I'd said. For the first time, I had expressed a love of money. The power of money had subtly seduced me, but I had never admitted it, not even to myself. I loved luxurious cars, cruises and summer homes. It was a secret love. I criticized the petty bourgeoisie who traveled first class in planes, but deep down I envied them. I detested flying coach class, where we were packed in like sardines.

Since we couldn't go inside the fair, we stayed outside in the reception hall. Undaunted, the dreamseller told us, 'Let's approach people as they enter and leave the event. After all, our stage is the world.'

'Approach people? But I thought we were here to see computers,' I said to myself. Angel Hand wondered aloud whether any kind of dream could be sold in a place like this.

But then I noticed something odd. What looked like a businessman, dressed impeccably in a suit and tie, examined us from head to toe as he walked by and into the event. His badge read Megasoft Group, one of the world's largest computer companies. I looked out of the corner of my eye and saw him stop to talk to other men in suits, who we later learned were undercover anti-terrorism agents. He pointed at us as he spoke.

The agents quickly approached, and one of them again asked the dreamseller to identity himself. They ignored the rest of us. When he couldn't produce any kind of identification, they acted fast: One of them punched him unexpectedly in the face, dropping him to the floor with an awful thud. They pounced on him, shouting 'terrorist!' and quickly overpowered him. It all happened so fast that for a few seconds we stood paralyzed. When we tried to protect the dreamseller, we were also attacked.

Honeymouth again feigned his karate pose but was knocked out by a single blow. I'd never seen such violence. In the confusion, one of the agents drew his gun, ready to shoot the dreamseller. He might have been shot dead on the spot if not for two local police officers who had been driving by in their patrol car and ran toward the commotion. Staring at the supposed criminal, one of the police officers drew his gun and shouted at the agents.

'Drop your weapons! I'm the police chief of this district,' he said. The agents lowered their guns. 'I know this man. He's no terrorist.'

'Yeah? Well, where's his ID? Who is he?' the head agent asked.

The cop searched for a plausible answer. 'He's, uh . . . a salesman. A traveling salesman. And if you don't leave him alone, I'm going to arrest you for using excessive force,' the chief threatened.

The police chief was the same one from the top of the San Pablo Building. Since that day, he had not been able to get the dreamseller out of his mind. He had spent several sleepless nights after the dreamseller's comments about his relationship with his son, and had since followed the dreamseller's 'minis-try' in the papers.

I was overjoyed and felt my faith in the police restored.

Though he was bleeding, the dreamseller tried to play down the situation and told the chief, 'These are good men. There was just a misunderstanding.'

It was only then that Bartholomew started to regain consciousness and asked, 'Where am I?'

Remembering he'd been knocked out but realizing the situation was under control, he jumped back up in a karate pose:

'Oh, now these guys are in trouble! I'm a black belt in judo, karate, kung fu and lots of other stuff. Hold me back or things are gonna get ugly.'

Instead of holding him back, we let him go. Honeymouth leaped up in a bound and seeing that the agents were eyeing him again, told them, 'Yeah, well, I'm calm now . . . '

The agents moved on, and so did the police officer, but not before the chief thanked the dreamseller for the few words on that rooftop.

'My son would like to meet you,' the chief said.

'Someday. Tell him to have many dreams and to fight for them,' the dreamseller answered.

The dreamseller's right eye was swollen, and blood was dripping from the left side of his lip, but he didn't complain. We knew that following him meant running the risk of mockery and scorn, but now we realized we were also risking our lives.

I was shocked to see how quickly people could snap from tranquillity to brutality. What shook me most was that the specter of aggression was also inside me. I knew about my pridefulness, but not about the latent violence.

I was beginning to believe in the concept of harmony and solidarity, but I felt like attacking anyone who hurt the gentle dreamseller. I never imagined that love and aggression could live so close to each other. I never thought that peace and war could inhabit the same person. Mild-mannered people, as it turned out, also harbor monsters in the recesses of their minds.

Living Longer in a Shorter Time

Things had been too intense at the electronics fair. We thought the dreamseller should see a doctor right away and then rest. We lifted him up under his arms and started to carry him outside. But instead he climbed onto a low wall surrounding a multicolored fountain and courageously started inviting people to hear about the latest innovations at the fair.

We couldn't believe our eyes. Some began to approach us because they recognized the rabble-rouser described in the newspapers. Controversial as ever, he continued provoking the participants and exhibitors of the Consumer Electronics Show.

'The most vulnerable child has a more complex mind than all the computers in the world strung together. But where is more money and research invested, in helping children or in building machines?'

Paying attention only to the first part of the question, a scientist addressed the dreamseller:

'You don't know anything about artificial intelligence. In a few years we'll have machines superior to the human brain. They'll have the programming of the human mind, but with superior memory. It'll be the greatest invention. Just wait and see!'

The dreamseller accepted the challenge:

'Well, I disagree. Computers will forever be condemned to the sleep of unawareness. They will never know conflicts. Never be disturbed by the search for their origins and their purpose. Never produce philosophy or religion. They will always be slaves to their programming.'

I thought: 'Where did the dreamseller learn that information? How does he manage to confidently discuss controversial matters?' On the other side, the computer engineers and programmers listening to him seemed at a loss.

'Can it be that computers will never know they exist?' the scientists asked.

'Our conflicts speak to our complexity. If we're not capable of being happy because we have computers, at least we should admire them as the fruits of our ingenuity,' the dreamseller said.

I looked at some of the members of our group and realized that they understood nothing. Bartholomew, in particular, was lost. But I bit my tongue, and later he surprised me by reading my mind and whispering,

'Hey, Superego, I've always been a deeply complex person, but I just can't stand hearing all your back talk.'

Bartholomew was always giving me a hard time when he knew I couldn't answer back. I wanted to crush him with my intellect, but I needed to work on something I'd never had: patience. I, who was never religious, asked, 'God, grant me the patience to not lose my temper with this *deeply complicated* character.'

Meanwhile, the dreamseller, after criticizing blind faith in machines, turned his guns on the Internet.

'The system produced the Internet and cell phones, sparking a revolution in communications the likes of which history had never seen. People lost their inhibitions to technology, and felt more comfortable dealing with machines than with other people. Not to engage others is a tolerable act, but to not engage oneself is indefensible.'

Now I understood why the dreamseller often isolated himself. When I first saw him talking to himself, I found it extremely odd. To me, such behavior had always been a sign of madness. But he turned the concept upside down, considering it a clear sign of sanity.

More and more people gathered, forcing him to speak louder. They had come to the magnificent fair to see the newest innovations in computers and instead discovered the latest news about their own mental 'computers.' The dreamseller made an argument bolstered by numbers unknown to me to shine a light into the audience's mind:

'Millions of people have never had an encounter with their own being. Their tombs will hold foreigners who never found their true home,' he said.

The people meditated on these words as if they were a prayer. At that moment, Honeymouth raised his hand. He should have kept his mouth shut to not spoil the mood. But he was even more addicted to the sound of his own voice than he was to alcohol. He said, 'Chief, I think we're in worse shape than everyone else here.'

'Why, Bartholomew?' he asked patiently.

'Because we don't even have an address. We live under a bridge.'

The crowd roared with laughter and Bartholomew realized what a blunder he'd made. But the dreamseller just smiled at his disciple's spontaneity. Honeymouth was a hyperactive, mischievous child. And to the dreamseller, freedom grew in that spontaneous terrain. Most people killed their spontaneity in school, church, at work, even here, at this electronics fair; they're robots admiring other machines. They don't say what they think. At that moment, I looked within myself and realized that I was no exception. In the name of discretion, I was formal, deliberate, guarded. I didn't know myself or let others know me. I was an expert in pretending everything was fine. It wasn't easy to admit that Honeymouth had an advantage over me.

Calmly, the dreamseller said, 'Yes, Bartholomew. We have no home, but we seek the best home of all. Remember our song.'

And once again he startled a crowd with his eccentricity. He interrupted his speech to sing his song, even making the gestures of a conductor. We joined in. During the first verse I was stiff. Honeymouth and Dimas went all out. We left the hilltops of reflection to revel in a relaxing waterfall of fun.

I'm just a wanderer
Who lost the fear of getting lost
I'm certain of my own imperfection
You may say I'm crazy
You may mock my ideas
It doesn't matter!
What matters is I'm a wanderer
Who sells dreams to passersby
I've no compass or appointment book
I have nothing, yet I have everything

I'm just a wanderer
In search of myself

Hearing that song, some of the listeners were completely stunned. They asked, 'What kind of group is this? Where did they come from? Who's this conductor? Could he be a speaker from some corporation in disguise as some sort of publicity stunt?' Others loosened up, followed the beat and began to sing with us. They lost their fear of getting lost, lost the fear of letting go, discovering for a few moments that they were not researchers, engineers or businessmen, just wanderers themselves. And still others moved away from the audience muttering, 'That guy's stark raving mad!' Whatever their reactions, it was impossible to remain indifferent to the dreamseller's words. He penetrated the most intimate reaches of loneliness.

We looked around us and saw that several people were moved, especially two well-dressed female executives. Despite being surrounded by people, they felt crushingly alone. They were successful professionally, but they were unhappy with their lives.

Seeing the crowd become reflective, the dreamseller touched on another matter. He asked something apparently obvious: 'Do people live longer today or in the past?'

One person, taking the initiative, answered, 'Today, beyond the shadow of a doubt!'

But the dreamseller, looking at his disciples, particularly at me, turned to challenge the crowd: 'No! We die younger today than in the past!'

Many jeered the dreamseller. I thought this time he had it all wrong. One scientist couldn't resist. Laughing, he said confrontationally, 'This is nonsense! Even the poorest student knows that average life expectancy has expanded because of new sanitation methods and vaccines.'

The dreamseller was no fool and knew what he was saying. Addressing the scientist, he replied:

'In Roman times the average life expectancy was barely forty years. In the Middle Ages, forty-five. Today we're nearing eighty. But I'm referring to the average life of the mind. In our minds, we die earlier. Doesn't it seem you went to sleep and woke up at your present age, ladies and gentlemen?'

And, raising his voice, he declared:

'Technology and science have their upsides. They have produced vaccines, antibiotics, water treatment plants and sewers, agricultural techniques, preservation of food; all of which have led to a longer average physical life. But the same system that has made us free has imprisoned our minds with its excesses. Do you understand me?'

We didn't understand, at least not fully. He was often sparing with his words, speaking almost in code. We didn't know what he meant by 'excesses' of the system. To clarify, he once again did what he loved to do: He told a story.

'In 1928, the Scottish bacteriologist Alexander Fleming was analyzing a fearsome bacteria in his lab,' the dreamseller said. 'Distracted, like any good scientist beset by an overload of activities, he left the door open when he went home. A fungus found its way into the Petri dish, producing a mold. What seemed to be a disaster generated a notable discovery: The mold killed the bacteria. From that discovery came the first antibiotic, penicillin. Millions of lives were saved. But penicillin came to be used excessively and indiscriminately. The result? A disaster. The excessive use of antibiotics has produced resistant bacteria which are now much more dangerous. Penicillin, one of medicine's greatest gifts to humanity, stands accused today of creating so-called superbugs. By the same token, the system that expanded average physical life, through its excesses, is burying us mentally earlier than in the days of smallpox.'

Pausing to take a breath, he concluded his story:

'We live longer physically than in the past, but time seems to pass so much faster. The months rush by, the years fly by. Many are in the infancy of their mental development but look at themselves and discover their bodies are seventy or eighty. Nowadays, eighty-year-olds have the mentality of history's twenty-year-olds. And what about all of you? What are the excesses that have damaged you?' he asked his listeners. They shouted out answers:

'Excess of commitments.'

'Excess of information.'

'Excess of social pressures . . . excess competition . . . goals . . . demands . . . the need to keep up.'

We were the society of excesses, even an excess of insanity.

Bartholomew wasn't about to be left out. Fortunately, he was on target.

'Excess of drinking,' he said. And because he never let anyone have the upper hand, he looked at each of us and added, 'Excess of ego, of crookedness, of religiousness.'

We pinched him playfully.

People were beginning to see how excess had invaded our lives. They needed to buy dreams. And the dreamseller wanted to sell them.

'How do we turn back this eccentric, stress-filled life?' asked a worried man of about sixty.

The dreamseller was direct and to the point:

'Cut out the excesses, even if it means losing money and status. If you don't want to be old people complaining about your lost youth, you have to find the courage to make cuts. There are no cuts without pain.'

I started thinking, 'Had the dreamseller found the courage to make such cuts in his own life, or was he one of those theorists who talk about something they haven't experienced? Can a person without experience open up the mind of others?' He made me see that my own life was passing me by. I was mired in the quagmire of excess. Excess of classes, worries, thoughts, depression, complaints, debts. I had created 'superbugs' that were infecting my mind.

Besides talking about cuts in lifestyle, he sold the art of observation that we did weekly. And he concluded his ideas by saying:

'Life passes quickly in this small interval of time. To live it slowly and meaningfully is the great challenge of mortal men.'

These words made me remember that in the past, the days sped by so rapidly that I didn't notice. Now, with this uncommon family, my days stretched long and lavishly. We lived intensely.

Just as he was speaking, the dreamseller began to feel dizzy. The stress of the beating and the strain of the speech had drained him. We helped him down from the wall, and Solomon and Dimas took him by the arm and led him outside.

He left to warm applause and went to rest under the Europa Avenue Bridge across the street.

One man caught up to him just to say, 'I've never heard so much craziness in one day. You're a fraud!'

We turned purple with rage. But the dreamseller calmed us and responded: 'I hope my ideas are those of a crazy man and yours are those of a sage.' And he walked away.

People were watching the dreamseller as he left.

'Maybe he wants to found a new society,' one said.

'How will I find the strength to make the necessary cuts in my excesses?' another told a friend.

Some wanted to go live in the countryside, grow orchids and raise animals. Others wanted to make a fresh start in society, change jobs or work as volunteers for children's hospitals or cancer centers. They went home haunted but fueled by the dreamseller's words. None of them slept well, understanding that each needed to lose the fear of getting lost. As it turned out, our teacher wasn't only a seller of dreams but also of insomnia.

As we were leaving the temple to electronics, a well-dressed woman, seeing the dreamseller's weakened condition, approached him. We told her it wasn't the right time, but the dreamseller ignored his dizziness and gave her his attention.

'My wonderful daughter Joana, six years old, has cancer,' she said, on the verge of tears. 'When the doctors said she probably had only three months to live, my world collapsed. I wanted to die in her place. Worse, I can't even stay at home. I'm here because when I look at her I drown in despair, and she's so special that in those moments she tries to console me.'

We were stirred and, once again, ashamed of our insensitivity.

'My dear, I have no supernatural power to help little Joana. But I can say this: Three months lived badly pass like seconds, while three months lived fully are an eternity. Don't bury your daughter in the tomb of your fear. Go home, discover her and let her discover you. Live intensely with her during the time she has left.'

The woman left encouraged, eager to make each minute a unique moment with her daughter. We didn't know if it would help Joana live any longer. But we were certain that in those three months, they would live a richer life than most parents do with their children in a span of thirty years.

I thought about the job I had done as a father. And I felt like running to John Marcus and begging his forgiveness.

The White-Hot Spotlight

As we were helping the dreamseller to a place where he could rest, Bartholomew separated from the group. A reporter wanted to write a story about us, in particular about our mysterious dreamseller and his intentions. Seeing that during his speech Bartholomew had asked a question, the reporter called him aside and asked for an interview. Bartholomew was excited, unaware he was entering dangerous territory.

The journalist wasted no time.

'Is it true that this man called you all to follow him, without promising money or offering the least bit of security?'

'Yes,' he replied simply.

'Is it true that you actually live under a bridge?'

'Not just one,' he answered. 'We live under lots of bridges.'

'Why? Who are you all? Who do you follow?'

Not being able to give any precise answers, Bartholomew, without thinking much about it, said, 'Us? We're a group of artists.'

'Artists? Are you painters, sculptors, a

theater group?' asked the journalist, thinking he was dealing with a bizarre group of performers.

Smiling, Honeymouth replied, 'No, no, nothing like that. We practice the art of complicating life.' And he laughed that distinct laugh that could be heard fifty yards away.

The journalist thought he was being spoken down to. But my friend had been sincere and spontaneous. Then, trying to better explain his thought, he added:

'Throughout history, we've complicated life, but now we're going through a complicated process of *uncomplicating* our lives. It isn't easy, but we'll get there.'

Honeymouth was enthusiastic because it was the first interview he'd ever given. He felt drawn — at least a little — to the white-hot glow of the spotlight.

'But who is this leader of your group? What does he do?' asked the curious reporter.

'I don't know who he is. But I do know that he sells dreams,' Bartholomew said innocently.

'He sells dreams? How does that work? Isn't the guy dangerous? Isn't he crazy?'

The disciple looked all around and said:

'I don't know if he's crazy, but I know he says we're all in a world of madness. And the chief wants to change the world,' he said, making the dreamseller's goals seem fanciful. In reality, the dreamseller wanted to stimulate people to thirst and hunger for change, for only they could be responsible for their transformations.

Puzzled, the interviewer inquired:

'Wait, what? That raggedy character said that *we* live in a world of madness? And *he* wants to change the world? And you people *believe* him?'

'I don't know if he's gonna change the world,' Bartholomew said. 'But he's changing my world.'

'Are you anarchists?' the reporter said, changing directions.

Bartholomew knew nothing about the anarchist movement. He didn't know that Pierre-Joseph Proudon, who inspired that movement in the nineteenth century, defended the idea of building a new society, one capable of expanding individual freedom and liberating the worker from the exploitation of big business. In that social order, constituted by organizing the workers, people would treat their fellow men fairly and develop their potential. Anarchists didn't recognize the governments power, its laws or its institutions. They lived under their own governance. Without the intervention of the state, they

190

thought, humans could live freely.

But the dreamseller disagreed with the central idea of anarchism. To him, without constitution and institutions, human beings could commit atrocities, trounce the rights of others, assassinate, extort, live only for themselves and display unrivaled savagery. Nor did he want to replay the hippie movement, which had emerged in the wake of America's war in Vietnam. Young people's frustration with the war generated disillusionment with institutions, and that had become the seed of a movement of peace and love, but one without social commitments.

The dreamseller's plan to sell dreams, on the other hand, was replete with commitments to society, especially to human rights, freedom and mental health. That's why he recommended to those who would follow him that they not abandon their activities in society. Only a few, maybe the weirdest, were called to his training.

Bartholomew didn't know what to answer. He just scratched his head and replied with philosophical simplicity: 'Look here, my friend, I don't know if we're anarchists or not. What I do know is that until a short time ago I didn't know who I was.'

'And now you do?' the interviewer asked.

But our friend tied his mind in more complex knots.

'Now? I know even less. I don't know who I am or what I am, because what I used to think I was isn't what I am at all. I still don't understand who I am, but I'm searching to find myself. You understand?'

'No!' answered the reporter, completely confused.

'Thank goodness! I thought I was the only one who didn't,' Bartholomew said. 'Look, my friend, I only know that I used to live falling down drunk every day, but now I'm lifting others up.' And, staring at the journalist, he extended a friendly invitation: 'Wouldn't you like to be part of the group?'

'Not me! That's crazy stuff,' the other man scoffed.

At that, Bartholomew countered, 'Now, wait a minute. What do you know about being crazy? Being crazy is a beautiful thing!'

He playfully hopped up, spread his arms and began to dance and sing his favorite song in that unsteady voice: 'I'm going to go crazy, too crazy . . . ' The reporter left without saying good-bye, as Bartholomew sang on: 'Oh, how I love this life!' He shook his hips and sang, 'I'm going to go crazy, too, too crazy . . . ' He was lost in the moment.

The journalist, before interviewing Bartholomew, had already mapped out his article. He merely needed to confirm some facts with Bartholomew. He had let prejudice guide him.

But Bartholomew was so euphoric with his first interview that he lost his way. He decided to celebrate the only way he knew how. He went to a bar and got wasted. It was his third relapse since he was called, except that the first two had been mild. This time he ended up passed out on the sidewalk.

We started to worry when he went missing. The dreamseller set us out to look for him. My friends and I said impatiently to each other, 'Again? The guy's hopeless.' After an hour, we found him, almost unconscious. We tried to lift him to his feet, but he could barely stand, and he just let his body dangle like deadweight. We each took an arm and lifted, while Dimas pushed from behind.

Bartholomew, his voice slurred, complained to Dimas, 'Not so hard, bud. My bumper's a little temperamental . . . '

And he passed gas — often and loudly and noxiously, joking, 'Sorry about the broken tailpipe, guys.'

We all felt like smacking him. I said to myself: 'I left the world of ideas in the academy to listen to the ideas of a drunk.

Unbelievable!' I had never loved my fellow man unless there was something in it for me. Now I was taking care of someone who, besides offering me nothing in return, drew me away from serious reflection and made fun of me. We had to carry him the last hundred feet to the bridge. The hardest part was putting up with his declaration of love for us:

'I love you, guys, I love you so, so, so, so much . . . '

'Shut up, Bartholomew!' sweating and exhausted, we said in chorus. But it was no use. Asking him to keep quiet just made him louder. Twice more on the way to the bridge he loved us. Maybe he was being sincere, maybe his affection was greater than ours. As soon as we got to the bridge, he tried to give us all kisses of gratitude. We dropped him on the ground like a sack of potatoes.

'*Mis amigos*, it's a privilege for you to take me in your arms,' he said.

Impatiently, we complained to the dream-seller. 'What this guy needs is Alcoholics Anonymous.' But without Bartholomew, there was no laughter in our group.

'Send him to a mental institution,' Dimas said.

'Master, how long do we have to put up with this?' the Miracle Worker asked.

We weren't happy with his response.

'It's a privilege to carry him,' the dreamseller said.

Bartholomew, even intoxicated, felt validated. 'You heard the chief. I'm not worthless!' he said almost incomprehensively but clear enough to raise our tempers.

'It's better to carry than to be carried,' the dreamseller said. And he added something that once again flew in the face of my atheism:

'The god constructed by man, the religious god, is merciless, intolerant, elitist and prejudiced. But the god who hides behind the scenes of existence is generous. His capacity to forgive has no limits. It inspires us to carry those who frustrate us as often as necessary.'

While the dreamseller was speaking, I started to doubt him. I remembered my sociological analysis of texts from the Old Testament, which portrayed a rigid, aggressive, intolerant god. 'Where is the generous god, if he accepted only the people of Israel?' I asked myself. As if reading my thoughts, the dreamseller said:

'God's generosity and forgiveness was shown by Jesus when he called Judas his friend, amid the act of betrayal, and when Jesus called out from the cross, 'Father, forgive them, for they know not what they do.' He protected those who hated him, he loved his enemies and that love made him intercede on behalf of his torturers.'

His words exposed my own lack of generosity. I had never known how to forgive. I had never forgiven my son for using drugs. To me, he had taken his excellent upbringing for granted. I had never forgiven my wife for leaving me. To me, she had left one of the best men in the world. I had never forgiven my father for killing himself. To me, he had committed the greatest of crimes in having abandoned me while I was still a child. I had never forgiven my faculty colleagues who betrayed me after they had promised their support.

Now, with the dreamseller's guidance, I had the chance to forgive by carrying a childish, confused, irresponsible alcoholic. How could I do that without complaining? It was incredibly difficult for me. But I was actually coming to love that clown. Bartholomew had what I'd always wanted: authenticity and self-esteem. Sociologically speaking, irresponsible people are happier than responsible people. The problem is that the irresponsible depend on the responsible to carry them.

The next day, we saw the consequence of Bartholomew's interview. Plastered across the front page of the major newspaper was a photo of the dreamseller under the headline: 'Psychotic Calls Society a 'World of Madness.''

The journalist wrote that there was a lunatic who claimed that mankind was on its way to becoming a gigantic worldwide insane asylum. But this time — according to the lunatic — that asylum wasn't some gloomy, ugly, stinking, dark place like the psychiatric hospitals of the past, but a pleasant, colorful setting full of sophisticated machines, a perfect place to indulge our madness without being inconvenienced by it.

He gave speeches in public places, with the intention of changing the mind-set of people. No one knew his origins, but to deceive people he called himself by an attractive name, 'the Dreamseller.'

The article included photos of onlookers hypnotized by him and went on to say the guy was stark raving mad but charismatic and provocative. His power of seduction was unrivaled. Even intelligent businessmen fell into his trap, the article said. A gang of misfits followed him. The story said that the dreamseller didn't work miracles or consider himself a messiah, but not since the time of Jesus had the world seen a lunatic so boldly trying to reproduce his steps.

The reporter made no mention of the dreamseller's provocative ideas. He said nothing about the need to dialogue with one's self, the sleep of unawareness to which computers are eternally condemned, the excesses of society that cause us to die prematurely in our minds. He concluded the piece by saying that the dreamseller's followers were a band of anarchists who put democracy at risk and who might commit terrorist acts.

The article burned our real story to the ground, devastating our project and our true intent. We were profoundly depressed and discouraged. We couldn't go on, I thought. Once again, the dreamseller tried to ease our minds:

'Remember the swallows,' he said, calming us. 'It's not our calling to be myths.

'Never forget that it's impossible to serve two masters: Either we sell dreams or we concern ourselves with our image in society; either we remain loyal to our conscience or we fall prey to what others think and say about us,' he said.

And once again he gave us the option to leave:

'Don't worry about me. You have already brought great joy to me and to many others. I've learned to love you and admire you the way you are. I don't want to put your lives in danger. It's better that you go.'

But where would we go? We wouldn't any longer succeed as 'normals,' servants to a system wracked with tedious social routine, slaves complaining about life as we waited for death. The selfishness of the past still lived inside us, but was slowly losing ground to the pleasure of serving others.

We decided to stay. After all, if the person most defamed by the story felt free, why should we chain ourselves?

That very day, we saw the article had backfired. The story, instead of killing the movement, added fuel to it. People couldn't take more news about murders, accidents, rapes, robberies. In a city marked by sadness, the dreamseller became a social phenomenon.

People were hungry for something new, even if it were clothed in madness. The dreamseller became that novelty, made into a local celebrity, which was precisely what we most feared. From then on, he began to be followed by paparazzi.

Upon realizing his growing fame, he warned us:

'To create a god, all that's needed is a bit of charisma and leadership in a climate of social stress. Be careful, the system gives but also takes away, especially our humanity.'

I understood the dreamseller's warning. The most cultured people on earth, a people who had won Nobel Prizes in the early twentieth century, enthroned Hitler in a period of social crisis. Times of crisis are times of change, for better or for worse. Recalling the risks of power, the dreamseller said:

'The majority of people are unprepared to assume power. Power awakens phantoms — blackmail, vanity and a hunger for power — which are hidden beneath a cloak of humility.

'Power in the hands of a wise man makes him into an apprentice,' he continued, 'but in the hands of a fool turns him into a tyrant. If you acquire great power one day, what demons will you face?'

His question shook me. When I took over as chair of the department, I became hard, inflexible, demanding. I came to understand that we cannot judge a person by the mildness of his voice, the kindness of his acts or the simplicity of his attire, but only after he has been given power and money.

The dreamseller spoke in a way that intrigued me. He gave the impression of someone who had tasted real power. But what power could someone so poor, with no home and no identity, have had?

Some religious people began to hold his ideas in great esteem, but others were concerned about the attention he was gaining; God was their personal property. They were the erudite theologians, experts in divinity. A penniless man who lived under bridges wasn't qualified to talk about God, they said. Some religious radicals wondered, 'Couldn't he be a prophet of evil? The Antichrist foretold centuries ago?' He had become an emblematic figure. He wanted to move about unnoticed, but it was impossible for him to hide.

People began asking for his autograph everywhere we went. But, looking them in the eye, he said to their surprise:

'How can I give an autograph to someone as important or more important than I am? It would take decades to get to know you a bit, to understand some of the pillars of your intelligence and unveil some of the phenomena that make up the construction of your thoughts. I'm the one who feels honored to meet you. Please, give me your autograph.'

They would leave his presence speechless and reflective. And some even bought the dream that there are no celebrities or 'ordinary' people, only complex human beings with different places in society.

The Superiority of Women

In the days that followed, it was all blue skies for us. No social trouble. No rejection. We were enjoying prestige, attention and recognition. Not bad for someone who challenged the powerful system and resided in inhospitable places. But we had no idea what lay ahead.

Just as everything was progressing in perfect harmony, the dreamseller challenged us once again. He invited us to the most charming of all temples, the temple of fashion. In the southern part of the city an exquisite fashion show of famous designers was taking place. The powerful Megasoft Group was again represented by their worldwide chain of feminine apparel called La Femme, which encompassed over ten international designer labels and had two thousand stores in twenty countries.

We found the dreamseller's invitation bizarre. It seemed like a strange place to sell dreams. After all, we believed that at least in that environment self-esteem had found its most fertile ground.

'What's the dreamseller looking for in a

place like that?' we wondered. 'How would he respond to it? Who could he possibly approach?' We were hoping he'd be discreet and not cause a scene, but, at this point, we knew better.

Just getting into the event would be a problem. After all, if we hadn't succeeded in getting into the computer show, how would we get into the fashion show — especially looking the way we did?

That day, the dreamseller was wearing a faded, patched black blazer that he'd gotten in a secondhand store and was a size too large. His faded black pants were hemmed oddly and the back pockets were patched with blue cloth. He was wearing a wrinkled moss-green shirt with a few pen stains.

I was wearing a polo shirt and beige pants that I had been given by a traveler who had found his dreams. We were all disheveled, but Bartholomew's clothes were the funniest and the most ridiculous. A widow who lived near the Europa bridge had given him clothes that belonged to her husband. His yellow pants ended well short of his ankles. His left sock was navy blue and his right sock baby blue. His white T-shirt boasted an eloquent slogan that faithfully reflected his personality: 'Don't follow me. I'm lost, too.' There was no way this ragtag bunch would ever be allowed into the show, I thought.

As we approached the immense hall of the fashion show and carefully watched the exquisitely dressed people, the dreamseller once again scrambled our thinking. He neither gave a speech nor criticized the world of fashion. He said with assurance:

'I'm thinking of calling a few women to sell dreams. How do you feel about that?'

Our roving bachelor pad was rocked. We were an eccentric, admittedly weird group, but we had adapted. We had our differences, but we were adjusting. Our arguments away from the dreamseller were heated but capable of being overcome. Calling women to join our brotherhood seemed like too much. How could it work?

I immediately posed the question: 'A woman? I think it's a bad idea.'

'Why?' he asked.

Luckily, before I could reply, Honeymouth came to my defense. 'They won't be able to bear this lifestyle. How will they stand to sleep under bridges?'

'What bathroom will they use? What mirror will they use to comb their hair?' asked Solomon. But the dreamseller replied:

'Who said they have to leave their own homes to follow us? After all, everyone should sell dreams, whether to himself or to others, wherever he — or she — is.'

For the first time, his words brought us no relief. We didn't believe a woman could participate in the group. We considered ourselves revolutionaries, protagonists of a fantastic sociological experiment. We didn't want to share our macho glory. Infected by discrimination, we thought that women would diminish our boldness.

'Following you, Dreamseller, is for . . . real men, and good ones. Besides, women talk too much and act too little,' Angel Hand said with conviction. Then he realized his arrogance and tried to backpedal. We had taken over the dreamseller's project and given it a masculine feel.

The Miracle Worker also was against the dreamseller's proposal. He used his knowledge of theology in an effort to dissuade him.

'Dreamseller, Buddha, Confucius and Jesus all had men as disciples. Why would you want to call women to follow you? Look at history. It'll never work.'

For the first time, the group was unanimous in showering praise on the Miracle Worker. We began to think he could make interesting contributions. Nevertheless, the dreamseller had an answer for our theologian.

'When Jesus called his disciples, where did

he put them, at the periphery or at the center of his plans?' he asked.

'The center, of course,' the Miracle Worker replied without hesitation.

'And women?' he asked, testing him.

Edson thought, reflected and rubbed his forehead. After a prolonged moment of analysis, he answered shrewdly:

'I can't say at the periphery, because they provided material support, but they weren't at the center of his work, because they weren't active participants in his project.'

Wow,' I thought to myself. I had always thought Edson wasn't much of a logical thinker, but he was proving me wrong.

Then, the dreamseller looked at him and then at all of us.

'Wrong,' he said, then fell silent.

Because I had studied these sacred texts, I thought Edson was right. I waited for the dreamseller's arguments, but suspected this time he wouldn't convince us.

'They were always at the center of the project. First, according to Scripture, God didn't choose a caste of Pharisees, Greek philosophers or priests to raise the young Jesus, but a woman, an adolescent uncontaminated by the ruling class, someone outside the system.'

'Second, the first person who talked about

Jesus was a female, the Samaritan woman. She had lived a promiscuous life, been with many men, but his words were enough to satiate her hunger. She gathered her people and spoke of the man who had moved her.' After uttering these words, he stopped to take a breath and took ours away by adding, 'A prostitute was more noble than the religious leaders of his time.'

Bartholomew came out with a phrase that broke the tension hanging over us. I don't know how he came up with such imagination.

'Chief, I've always thought women were smarter than men. The problem is, the credit card was invented . . . ' And he started laughing. Ironically, he'd given the impression that he was the one who had supported the women in his life. In reality, they had supported him.

The dreamseller, unhappy with our prejudiced masculinity, attacked even further. He asked our acting theologian:

'Tell me, Edson. In the most important moment in Jesus' life, when his body was withering on the cross and his heart was weak, where were the men, at the center or at the periphery of his plan?'

Edson, paling, was slow to answer. And our faces were flushed. In the silence, the dreamseller said:

'His disciples were heroes when he was shaking the world, but they were cowards when the world came crashing down on him; they kept quiet, fled, denied they knew him, betrayed him. But even then, he loved. Men, I say again, are more timid than women.'

'But don't men make war? Bear arms? Don't they start revolutions?' the sociologist in me blurted out.

'The weak use weapons; the strong, their words,' he answered and asked the question we feared most:

'Where were the women when he was dying?'

Humbly, because we were familiar with the Bible, we muttered, 'Near the cross.'

'More than anything, they were at the epicenter of his project. And do you know why? Because women are stronger, more intelligent, more humane, generous, altruistic, supportive, tolerant, faithful and sensible than men. Suffice it to say that ninety percent of violent crimes are committed by men.'

We were stunned by so many favorable adjectives about women. The dreamseller didn't seem like a feminist, nor did he appear to be trying to cast words into the air in an effort to compensate for millennia of discrimination against women. He seemed totally convinced of what he was saying.

To him, the system that controlled humanity was conceived in the hearts of men, although its creators could never imagine that one day they would become the victims of their own creation. It was time for women to come into the picture and sell dreams. Lots and lots of dreams.

The Temple of Fashion

The dreamseller gave us fair warning. He reminded us that the most cultured of Jesus's disciples, Judas, betrayed him. The strongest, Peter, denied knowing him. And the rest, except John, ran in fear. After demonstrating masculine fragility and feminine greatness, the dreamseller revealed why he was in the temple of fashion.

He told us that in the past, the male-dominated system had subjugated women, burning them, stoning them, silencing them. In time, they freed themselves and partially reclaimed their rights. He paused and, out loud, said the number 'one.' This numerical citation in the middle of a speech made me uneasy. I'd seen how that movie ended.

The dreamseller noted that women had begun to vote, to excel in the academic world, to increase their numbers in the corporate sphere, to occupy the most varied social areas. Women had become more and more daring. They began to change vital sectors of society, to introduce tolerance, solidarity, affection and romanticism. But the system was unforgiving about their audacity.

It set for them the most cowardly and underhanded trap. Instead of extolling their intelligence and obvious sensitivity, it began to exalt the female body as never before in history. It was used tirelessly to sell products and services. They started to feel special. It seemed as if modern societies were trying to make up for millennia of rejection and intolerance. The dreamseller paused to take a breath.

Staring at the immense, colorful temple of fashion, he became outraged and in a loud voice began inviting people to talk about what was so great about the latest fashions. Nothing could be odder for someone dressed like him. But, since the fashion world makes room for the eccentric, they all thought he represented some designer rebelling against conventions. We felt out of place seeing such finely dressed people around us. Some of them recognized him.

He quickly began a discourse about his controversial ideas:

'When women came to feel they occupied the throne of the male-dominated system, the fashion world locked in on the most subtle stereotype.' And he recited the number 'two,' deeply saddened.

I didn't know where the dreamseller was heading with this. I knew that stereotypes are a sociological problem. The stereotype of the crazy person, the addict, the corrupt politician, the socialist, the bourgeois, the Jew, the terrorist, the homosexual. We use stereotypes as a vile standard to brand people with certain behaviors. We don't evaluate the content of their character; if they show certain characteristics, we immediately imprison them behind the bars of a stereotype, classifying them as junkies, corrupt, unstable.

But what does the beautiful world of fashion have to do with stereotypes? The women were free to wear whatever they wanted, to buy any clothes they fancied, and have the body they desired. I didn't understand why the dreamseller was so concerned. Nevertheless, the more he spoke, the more I was impressed.

'What a crime that what the fashion world has stereotyped as 'beautiful' is nothing more than a genetic accident.'

Bartholomew wasn't sure what the dreamseller was talking about.

'Chief, is that stereotype expensive?' he asked, thinking it was some kind of clothing. The dreamseller told him:

'Its implications are extremely expensive,' he explained. 'To maximize sales and create an ideal image for women, the fashion world began using the bodies of uncommonly thin young women as the epitome of beauty. One young woman out of ten thousand with a very thin body and exceedingly well-formed face, hips, nose, bust and neck became the stereotype of beauty. What consequences that had for the collective consciousness . . . '

More and more people were gathering around. After a brief pause, he continued:

'The genetic exception became the rule. Children looked to their Barbie dolls for direction, and adolescent girls turned runway models into an unattainable standard of beauty. That process engendered a compulsive quest for the stereotype, as if it were a drug, in hundreds of millions of women. Women, who were always more generous and supportive than men, turned on each other without realizing it. Even Chinese and Japanese women are mutilating their anatomy to come closer to the beauty of Western models. Did you know that?'

I didn't know that, but how could he? How could someone completely outside of fashion be so well informed about it? Suddenly, he interrupted my thoughts by uttering the number 'three,' and a moment of sorrow washed over his face.

He continued by saying that such a distorted model of beauty had sunk into the collective unconscious, imploding women's self-image and committing an act of terrorism against self-esteem. In the past, stereotypes didn't have serious collective consequences because we weren't yet a global village. And just when women thought they liberated themselves, the system clipped their wings with the 'Barbie syndrome.'

A male designer challenged him tensely, 'I don't believe any of that. That's ridiculous.'

'I wish it were. I would love for my ideas to be foolish.' And he spoke the number 'four.'

At that moment, a young woman, confused, asked, 'Why do you count while you speak?'

The dreamseller turned and stared at me silently. It seemed like some great force was dragging him into the hearts of families who were losing their sons and daughters. His eyes swimming with tears at the thought, he turned to the crowd and said:

'Lucia, a shy but lively young woman — creative and an excellent student — weighs just seventy-five pounds, despite being five feet, five inches tall. Her bones stick out under her skin, forming a repulsive image, but she refuses to eat for fear of putting on weight. Marcia, a smiling, extroverted young woman, an enchanting girl, weighs seventy-seven pounds and is five-foot-three. Her cadaverous face drives her parents and friends to despair, but even so she refuses to feed herself. Bernadette weighs less than ninety-five pounds and is five-seven. She used to like to talk to everyone but has isolated herself from her boyfriend, her friends and lives in chat rooms on the Internet. Rafaela weighs one hundred and five pounds and stands six feet tall. She played volleyball and liked going to the beach and running on the sand, but now she's starving to death.'

He paused again, looked attentively at his audience, and said:

'In the time you've been listening to me talk, *four* young women will have developed anorexia. Some will survive their troubles, others will not. And if you ask these young women why they don't eat, they'll answer, 'Because we're obese.' Billions of cells beg them to be fed, but these woman have no compassion for their bodies, which lack the strength to exercise or even walk. This desperation to reach this ideal body type, this stereotype of what is beautiful, has managed to suppress a vital instinct living things have never managed to block out naturally: our instinct to eat.'

And he stated that if those individuals lived in tribes where the stereotype wasn't so powerful, they wouldn't be sick. But they live in modern society, which not only propagates an unhealthy thinness but places excessive value on a certain type of eyes, neck, bust, hips, the shape of a nose — in short, a world that excludes and discriminates against anyone who doesn't measure up to the standard. And the worst part is that all this is done subtly. He emphasized:

'I don't deny that there can be metabolic causes for eating problems, but the social causes are undeniable and unforgivable. There are fifty million anorexics in the world — as many as the number of deaths in World War Two.'

Suddenly the dreamseller put aside his somberness, changed to a more pleasant tone and climbed on top of an armchair beside him and called out:

'The social system is clever: It shouts when it should keep quiet and keeps quiet when it should shout. Nothing against the models and the intelligent and creative designers, but the system forgot to shout that beauty can't be standardized.'

Various people, international models and famous designers who were passing by, were attracted to the eccentric man showcasing his ideas. There were already people across the world fighting those stereotypes in society, but their voices were but a whisper compared to the monstrous system. Drunk with indignation, the dreamseller once more turned to his incisive Socratic method:

'Where are the heavier women in these shows? Where are the young women with less shapely hips? Where are the women with prominent noses? Why, in this temple of so-called beauty, are there no young women with saddlebags or stretch marks? Aren't they human beings? Aren't they beautiful, too? Why is the world of fashion, which came about to promote well-being, destroying women's self-esteem? Isn't that a socially acceptable rape of self-esteem?'

Listening to this indictment, I began to feel disgusted with the system. However, just when the dreamseller had taken us to the heights of reflection, along came Bartholomew to once again wreck the mood. He raised his hand and clumsily attempted to second the dreamseller:

'I'm with you, chief. I don't discriminate when it comes to women. I've dated every type.'

The audience burst into laughter. But we were so nervous already that we hushed Bartholomew.

'Pretend you're normal, Bartholomew!'

The people were split by the dreamseller's ideas. Some were enthralled, their mouths agape; others hated the ideas down to their last thread. Paparazzi began taking photos, eager to record the scandal of the year.

As the buzz from the crowd died down, the dreamseller lowered his voice to make an emotional request:

'I implore you, the brilliant designers, to love women, all of them, to invest in their mental health by using not just these unattainable body types to express your art. You may not make as much money as you otherwise might, but you'll realize immeasurable gains. Sell the dream that every woman has a unique beauty.'

Some people applauded, including three international models to my right. Later we learned that models were exposed to a host of mental conditions. They were ten times more likely to be anorexic than the population as a whole. The system both enthroned and incarcerated them, and after a short career, it discarded them.

Three people booed the dreamseller. One of them threw a plastic water bottle at him, opening a cut over his left eyebrow, which bled profusely. We took him by the arm and asked him to stop talking, but he wasn't intimidated. Wiping away the blood with an old handkerchief, he called for silence and continued. I thought: 'There are many who hide their thinking for the sake of their public image; here's a man who's faithful to his ideas.' Then he offered a proposal that made our skin tingle:

'Most women in modern society don't see themselves as beautiful. So in every clothing store and on every label there should be a warning, like on packs of cigarettes, that reads: 'Every woman is beautiful. Beauty can't be standardized.''

These words got quite a reaction from the press. At the very moment he said them, a paparazzo photographed him from an angle that caught the upper half of his body and, in the background, the logo of the international clothing chain of the Megasoft Group.

His ideas about discrimination in fashion reminded me of when he told us: 'Discrimination can be constructed in a matter of hours, but can take centuries to dismantle. A full century after Abraham Lincoln freed African-Americans from slavery, Martin Luther King Jr. was on the streets of major American cities, still fighting discrimination.' I kept asking myself, 'Who is this man who makes these revolutionary proposals? Where does his knowledge come from?'

The dreamseller told the crowd that our existence can never be standardized. All of us experience life differently, from sex and the taste of food to our appetites, art, even beauty.

'What's the normal frequency for having sexual relations? Every day? Every week? Any classification would generate serious distortions. What's normal if not that which satisfies each person? Isn't being satisfied enough?'

A stunningly beautiful international model named Monica, deeply moved by his speech, interrupted him and had the courage to say publicly:

'My whole life, all I knew how to do was strut, strut, strut down a runway. My world was the runways. I've been photographed by the best international photographers. My body has been on major magazine covers. I was raised to the top by the fashion world, but the same world that praised me cast me aside when I gained ten pounds. Today I have bulimia. I eat compulsively, then feel so guilty about it that I have to make myself throw up. My life is a living hell. I can't even bear the taste of food. I don't know who I am or what I love anymore. I've tried to kill myself three times.'

There were no tears in her eyes, none left to cry. The dreamseller, seeing the model's suffering, took two deep breaths. He thought it better to remain silent, realizing that Monica's experience spoke more eloquently than his words. But first he wanted to see her smile. He switched from reflection to humor.

'When women are in front of the mirror, they say a famous phrase, even unconsciously. What is it?' The women present answered in unison, 'Mirror, mirror on the wall: Who's the fairest of them all?'

'No,' the dreamseller said. 'They all say, 'Mirror, mirror on the wall. Who's got the most defects of them all?''

The crowd smiled. Monica laughed a beautiful laugh; it had been five years since she laughed like that. That was what he wanted: to sell her the dream of happiness. It was an admirable sociological experiment. It was the first time I'd ever seen humor grow out of such despair.

Bartholomew told the dreamseller, 'Chief, I don't see any defects when I look in the mirror. Have I got a problem?'

'No, Bartholomew. You're simply beautiful. Look at your friends. Aren't they marvelous?'

Honeymouth took a long look at the group of disciples.

'Don't push it, chief. The family's kinda shabby.'

We broke into laughter and headed for the door. We'd never felt so beautiful.

Calling a Model and a Revolutionary

When we left, Monica came outside to express her profound gratitude. She hugged the dreamseller affectionately and gave him a kiss on the cheek. The rest of us were green with envy.

The dreamseller looked at her and suddenly took the most extraordinary attitude:

'Monica, you shone on the fashion runways, but I want to invite you to parade down a different runway, one harder to cross, one tougher to keep your balance on, but definitely more interesting to experience. Come sell dreams with us.'

Monica didn't know how to answer. She had read several stories about the dreamseller but had no idea where this would lead. When we heard the call to the enchanting model, we, who had rejected letting women into the team, changed our position immediately. We agreed with the dreamseller that women were not only more intelligent than men, they were also much better to look at.

Noting our enthusiasm, the dreamseller moved on to talk to another person. He left it up to us to explain to the newcomer the fascinating world of selling dreams. We'll surely convince her, we thought. We tried to explain, then explain our explanations. But we stumbled over one another and over our words. We were like a pack of stray dogs in mating season.

Seeing that Monica looked far from convinced, the Miracle Worker withdrew to pray. He didn't want to fall into temptation. Angel Hand was euphoric, unable to articulate his words, but nevertheless he tried to invent a poem to attract the model:

'A life without . . . dreams, is . . . is . . . like a winter without . . . snow, an ocean without . . . waves . . .'

Monica had never seen such a band of lunatics — dirty, poorly dressed, weird — trying to win her over at all costs. She grew more doubtful. After all, we were like a swarm of bees around the queen. While we were speaking, Monica glanced to the side and several times saw the dreamseller listening attentively to the person with whom he was talking. After half an hour, the model looked like she wanted to get out of there. Unfortunately, that was when Honeymouth went into action.

'Monica, hon, selling dreams is the craziest experience I've ever had. Not even when I was soaked in vodka was I so delirious,' he said, scaring the girl.

'Pretend you're normal, Bartholomew!' we all said again.

But he didn't know how to pretend; he was what he was. Then something unexpected happened. When Bartholomew spoke of the craziness of the project, she took heart. She wanted something more exciting than the world of fashion runways. But she was still undecided about this sociological experiment.

When the dreamseller returned, Monica asked him, 'Sir, I know the man you were talking to.'

'Really? He's a fascinating person,' he said effusively.

'He's a deaf-mute and doesn't know sign language,' the model replied, suspicious of the dreamseller's motives. If the deaf man didn't know sign language, it wasn't possible for them to communicate. We fell silent. It was clear she wouldn't follow him.

'I know,' replied the dreamseller. 'That's why it's rare that anyone pays attention to him to free him from his loneliness. I heard the words he didn't say. Have you spent any time trying to understand him?' She fell as silent as the deaf man.

Monica agreed to join the journey, but at the dreamseller's request she would sleep at her own home. She didn't know about the sleepless nights that awaited her.

The next day, the dreamseller was in every major daily newspaper in the city and on all the television morning newscasts. His ideas were spreading. Some papers were already calling him by the name he liked: 'Dreamseller.' They said he had turned the fashion world upside down.

Some journalists, extremely concerned with the eroding self-image of today's youth, wrote about the Barbie syndrome and came to conclusions that expanded on what the dreamseller had said. They said he had shouted that because of the unrealistic standards of the fashion industry many adolescent girls lose a grip on reality and are perpetually dissatisfied with their bodies, finding defects in their faces and constantly complaining that their clothes didn't fit.

Young people who didn't like to read newspapers clamored for the articles. Some took it to school, where it spread from hand to hand. Many boys and girls breathed a sigh of relief when they read the articles because they so often had agonized about the 'anatomical defects' they saw in themselves. Soon they began laughing at their 'paranoia.'

They felt the story covered conflicts almost never discussed at school. From that point on, a rebellious streak started forming within some of the students. They began criticizing the social system and wanted to learn firsthand the ideas of that mysterious dreamseller.

Monica met us that afternoon and told us about the waves the article had created in the fashion world. She said that some of her designer friends as well as some stores had bought into the dreamseller's ideas and were beginning to spread the view that beauty couldn't be standardized.

Seeing the model more enthused, we decided to tell her about the countless adventures we'd had in the last several months. A week later, the dreamseller told us he wanted to invite another woman to the group.

The way Monica looked, we felt he could invite not one or two or three, but ten women. 'How we've changed our stance,' I thought. I, who had always criticized politicians who were enemies one day and the best of friends the next, began to understand that such fluctuation was a sickness inherent to the human mind. It all depended on what was at stake.

Convinced of the wisdom of his new plan,

the dreamseller looked upward and then to the sides, placed his hands on his chin and began moving away from us. He was lost in thought again. I heard him ask himself in a low voice, 'Which woman should I call? What characteristics should she have?'

The dreamseller was about fifty feet away, walking in circles in the lobby of the shopping mall where we met. Just as we were celebrating the proposal of bringing more women into the group, an elderly woman appeared and gave Honeymouth a light tap on the head with her cane. It was Jurema.

'How are you, boys?' she said.

'Just fine, Jurema. How nice to see you again,' we said politely.

Suddenly we looked over at the pensive dreamseller, then back at the little old lady and had a terrible thought: 'She might be the next to be called! We better get her out of here fast.'

The dreamseller, his gaze turned toward the sidewalk opposite where we stood, raised his voice and said to himself, 'Whom to call?' We felt a shiver run down our spines. We tried to hide Jurema. We had to get rid of her.

'The sun is . . . scalding. You could get dehydrated, you're sweating so much. You should . . . go home,' Dimas, the great manipulator of hearts, told the old woman, trying not to stutter. But she insisted on staying.

'The weather's fine, my boy,' she said assuredly.

Edson took her arm politely.

'You look tired. At your age one needs lots of rest,' he told her.

'I feel just great, son. But thanks for your concern,' Jurema said.

I also gave it a shot, trying to remind her of something she might have forgotten — an appointment, a doctor's visit, a bill to pay. But she told me everything was taken care of.

Monica didn't understand our concern over Jurema. She thought we were being a little too nice. Bartholomew, who had always been the most honest of any of us, slipped up again. Seeing that she had no intention of heading home, he appealed. He raised one eyebrow and said:

'My dear, beautiful Jurema,' he said, and she seemed to melt, batting her eyelashes. Just when he'd gotten her attention, he blurted out, 'I'm sorry to tell you that you're as red as a beet. I think you might be having a heart attack. You need to get to a hospital right away.'

Solomon tried to cover Bartholomew's big mouth, but it was too late. Jurema did the job. She hooked his neck with the crook of

228

her cane, yanked him close and said flatly:

'Bartholomew, with your mouth shut you're absolutely perfect.'

We roared with laughter. But Jurema was bothered, realizing we were hiding something from her. To show us she was still strong and full of life, despite being more than eighty years old and having a touch of Alzheimer's, she crouched down and did a few push-ups. She asked us to try and match her, but we couldn't keep up. Then she leaped into a pair of ballet pirouettes and dared us to try. But we all clumsily almost fell on our faces.

'You guys are a bunch of old geezers,' she said. 'I feel younger than any of you and I'm as healthy as a horse. Now, where's that guru of yours?'

Guru? I thought. The dreamseller didn't like even being called master, much less guru. We said he was having some problems . . . had an appointment . . . couldn't talk to her now. We tried to block her view of the dreamseller, but she poked her head between us. By then, Monica had already figured out our little game and I think wondered whether there was any hope of redemption for any of us.

Jurema shouted even louder, 'Where's the guru?'

We cringed when we heard the dream-seller's deep, powerful voice.

'How wonderful to see you again!' he told her, and then said the words we had all dreaded: 'Come with us. Come and help us sell dreams!'

Monica couldn't help laughing and laughing, but we were worried. We wandered off to one side and began to whisper questions to one another. 'What will society think of us, a band of eccentrics followed by an old lady? We'll be a laughing-stock. Oh, the newspapers are going to love this. What'll it be like living with her? We'll probably waste all our time waiting for her to catch up. And that old-lady smell? Does she wear dentures?'

We worried that our journey would suffer with the addition of Jurema. The dreamseller patiently watched our boys-only conference as Monica tried to explain the calling to Jurema. But she was a beginner herself and had trouble making it clear.

Jurema, an honest woman, called us aside and said, 'I've never sold anything in my life. What type of product is it?'

The dreamseller went off to speak with Monica and left us alone to explain the project to Jurema. This gave us a golden opportunity to dissuade the old woman. In the privacy of my thoughts, I wondered whether the dreamseller hadn't seen Jurema first and was testing us again, in an attempt to unveil the subtle prejudices in our minds.

We had had a fantastic experience at the nursing home, where we had discovered the greatness of the elderly, but we insisted on harboring a prejudice against them. We were convinced the old lady wouldn't be able to keep up with the pace of the group. We thought that, with her, the dreamseller would have to be less aggressive with some of his plans.

We spoke honestly with Jurema about the adventure of dreams. After all, even when our interests were thwarted, we were learning to be transparent. But, to dissuade her, we emphasized the dangers we faced, the public shame, the insults, the beating the dreamseller had suffered.

She listened attentively, nodding her head. She arranged her white hair, as if wanting to massage her restless brain. We were sure we were leaving her more uncertain than before. Solomon looked to the heavens and made the sign of the cross. 'I'm getting scared just thinking about the dangers that lie ahead,' he said.

He signaled to Bartholomew to keep quiet for once because we seemed to be making progress. But, not thinking twice, the bungler said in a trembling, horror-movie voice: 'It's very risky to follow this man, Jurema. We could be arrested. We could be kidnapped, beaten, tortured. We could even be killed!'

We thought, for once, he'd managed to say just the right thing. Little did we know his words would be a kind of prophecy. Jurema's right eye widened, her left eye closed. Just when we were sure we had convinced her, it was our turn to be startled.

'Fantastic!' she said. We exchanged dumbstruck glances.

'Fantastic? What do you mean, 'fantastic,' Jurema?' I asked, thinking that her senile mind had somehow misunderstood everything we had said.

'Everything you've told me is fantastic,' she said. 'I'm absolutely ready to be a wanderer and I accept the invitation to join the group! I was always a rebel in my student days, and later as a university professor. But I was punished, subjugated by the educational system. I had to follow an agenda I disagreed with, a curriculum that did nothing to form thinkers.'

Our little brotherhood was shaken. We couldn't breathe. As if the mysterious identity of the dreamseller weren't enough, now we had a mysterious old lady to contend with. Some of us snorted, disturbed by her. I tried to dab the beads of sweat off my face.

'I've always wanted to sell dreams, to stimulate minds, but I was silenced,' she said. 'I get disgusted every day when I think about modern society steamrolling young people's intellect, mashing them all together, crushing their critical thinking and turning them into tape recorders of information. What has society done to our children?'

I asked what her full name was.

'Jurema Alcantara de Mello,' she said flatly.

When I heard the name, I took a step backward, even more shocked than before. That's when I discovered that Jurema was a renowned anthropologist who had been a university professor at the highest level. She had even done postdoctoral work at Harvard. She was internationally known and had written five books in her field of study and they had been published in various languages.

I leaned against a nearby post to steady myself. I remembered having read several journal articles of hers, as well as all her books. She had played an important role in helping me formulate my ideas. I had admired her organized power of reasoning and her boldness. And here, just minutes earlier, I had wanted to kick her out of our group. I thought to myself: 'Damned prejudice! Who will free me from this intellectual cancer? I dream of being a free and open person, but I'm hopelessly stubborn.'

Her ideas were right in line with the dreamseller's. Jurema went on to say that societies, with some exceptions, had become quagmires for conformist minds that were untroubled by the complexity of existence, devoid of great ideas, and they never questioned who they are.

'We need to stimulate people's intelligence,' she said.

The dreamseller smiled in delight. He must have thought: 'I hit the bull's-eye.' Jurema was more of a rebel than all of us. As she aged, she became more determined. She began to challenge us the second she joined us. Since age brings an incurable courage and honesty, she was very outspoken. She started pointing out things that Monica hadn't yet had the courage to say. She confronted the dreamseller and criticized the group's look.

'Being a band of eccentrics that sells dreams is fine, but being a band of filthy ragamuffins is absurd,' she said.

Oh, did we get angry at that. But even after seeing us pout, Jurema didn't back down.

'Calling a group eccentric in order to create a spirit of solidarity is laudable,' she said, 'but not caring whether that group looks shabby and unkempt, that's just wrong-headed.'

The dreamseller remained silent. But Dimas couldn't take it.

'Jurema, sweetie . . . li . . . lighten up,' he stuttered, attempting a familiarity that only Bartholomew could get away with.

She didn't let it slide. She came close to him, took several whiffs of his body and scowled, 'Lighten up? You smell like rotten eggs.'

Bartholomew roared with laughter.

'Didn't I tell you? I'm a saint for putting up with that guy's smell!' Bartholomew said. And he laughed so hard he couldn't hold back and ripped a sonorous thunderclap of his own.

'You should be ashamed of yourself,' she told him. 'If you can't hold it, you should at least do it so no one can hear you.'

We were starting to get worried. We looked at the dreamseller and began to realize that this new member of the family wanted to pour cold water on us — literally. For the first time we saw him scratch his head, without taking action. Jurema was a revolutionary, but she was unbalanced. She turned to the dreamseller and did what we never thought anyone would be bold enough to do: She confronted him.

'And don't give me that story about how Jesus called those who cleansed the outside of their body but forgot to cleanse the inside hypocrites. Yes, we must emphasize the inside, but without ignoring the outside. His disciples bathed in the Jordan and in the houses where they were guests. But look at you. Look at your followers! How long has it been since they've had a real bath?'

We had bathed in public bathrooms, but not as often or as well as we probably should have. The master didn't argue. He simply nodded his head in agreement. He had taught us many lessons, and the greatest one was to have the humility to learn from others.

And if that weren't enough, Jurema turned to Edson and boldly asked him to open his mouth. He did so cautiously. We felt that the dreamseller had to have regretted his choice at this point. But maybe not. 'Wasn't a female disciple with just these characteristics what he was looking for?' I thought.

'Good lord, what a stench! You need to brush your teeth,' she told the Miracle Worker, pinched her nose and told him to close his mouth.

I laughed — but between clenched lips. She noticed it and said, 'What are you laughing at?'

She didn't spare anyone, except Monica,

who hadn't had this much fun in years. She felt that we were a traveling circus.

The dreamseller said Jurema wouldn't sleep under the bridge with us, because of her age. She and Monica would return home and reunite with us the following day.

At the end of the day, Jurema invited us to bathe and eat supper together at her house. The prejudice virus, which was dormant, reawakened. We looked at one another and thought that, given her age, a professor's meager pension and what she had to pay for medicines and doctors, her financial situation couldn't be much better than ours. We probably couldn't even all stand in her house, much less have dinner there. And with the old woman plodding away at the stove, it would be midnight before the meal was ready.

Jurema turned her head up the street and whistled.

When we asked what she was doing, she said she was calling her driver. We thought she must have been suffering some kind of dementia and Dimas said under his breath, 'It must be the bus driver.'

There was no sign of any driver. She whistled again, this time more loudly. Nothing.

'I think 'Driver' is the name of her dog,' Bartholomew said. Jurema shot him a dirty look and wagged her cane, but instead of smacking him, she seemed amused by the joke.

'Just imagine everybody cramming into some old Ford straight out of a museum,' Edson said.

Our group always had some kind of retort. In the few months we had been together, I had enjoyed myself more than I had in my entire life, even when we were making fun of each other. The dreamseller fostered that environment. Monica felt as if she were always at a street fair. In her former life, she had been wealthy, but what she hadn't blown on luxury items, she lost in the stock market. But traveling with the group, she was getting something the free market couldn't sell.

While we were joking, a beautiful white limousine pulled up in front of us, almost running over Bartholomew's foot. An impeccably dressed chauffeur said, 'Sorry, ma'am. It took me a long time because there was traffic.'

Our jaws dropped. And I'm sure we all, conveniently, had the same thought: 'What a great new disciple!'

The Butterflies and the Cocoon

Jurema was the widow of a millionaire. But she never felt a need to flaunt her wealth. Sometimes she bypassed cars, chauffeurs, designer clothes and other benefits that her fortune might have afforded her. She lived modestly. We had never been in such a luxurious vehicle. We were smitten, but the dreamseller, someone who seemed never to have driven a car, remained indifferent. He asked Jurema for the address and said he would walk. He needed to think.

He met us at her house two hours later. The millionaire widow had made a quick stop at a store and bought clothes for all of us. We looked civilized again. We had already taken a bath and were nibbling on delicious cheese and cold cuts. It was all so delicious that it made us remember there are some wonderful things about the system. Honeymouth was so hungry that he used his hands to grab the snacks instead of the metal toothpicks. Solomon didn't talk, making time only to eat. Funny, but I noticed that his tics and quirks had diminished considerably with a filling belly. I didn't know whether it was hunger or a lasting improvement.

Dimas stuffed his mouth with cheese, like a rat, and stared at all the expensive objects on top of a china cabinet and the beautiful paintings hanging on the walls. I think that if he hadn't been called by the dreamseller, he might have returned to clean the place out. Monica ate discreetly. She was so happy about being part of the group that nothing distracted her. I never imagined that such a good-looking person could live such a nightmare.

The dreamseller was led into the main area of the house, which comprised over 5,000 square feet of space, divided into five rooms. Jurema's luxurious mansion barely fazed him and that seemed to make her happy. She was tired of people who fawned over her house but had nothing to say to her. He then went to bathe and was given new clothes.

As all of us were beginning to enjoy a delightful dinner, the dreamseller had a request for her: 'Tell us about your husband.'

She was surprised, for people seldom asked about the dead, not wanting to cause any awkwardness. But she loved to talk about him and had always admired him. She told us about the time when they were young, their courtship, the marriage. Then she spoke of his tenderness, boldness and intellect. Twice, the dreamseller said, 'What a great man. He was also a dreamseller.'

She mentioned that her husband had been CEO of one of the most important companies of the Megasoft Group, which was made up of more than thirty firms. We thought the business world would be of no interest to the dreamseller, but he unexpectedly asked, 'How did he become wealthy?'

To tell the story of her husband's rise, she first had to give us some background on the Megasoft Group's president. She said that the owner of an important firm had died and left a fortune to his twenty-five-year-old son. The young man had an exceptional mind and was endowed with unusual enterprise and leadership ability. He far surpassed his father. He took the company public and, with the money from his booming shares, expanded the business and invested in the most diverse activities in the corporate world. He invested in oil, clothing store chains, communications, computers, electronics and hotels. Within fifteen years he had put together the Megasoft Group, which became one of the ten largest corporations in the world.

She told us that when the company went public, the young president gave all the employees the chance to buy stock, and her husband became a minority stockholder in the company. With the phenomenal growth of the group, he made a lot of money. When I heard Jurema's story, I interjected:

'When you mentioned that young millionaire's enterprising spirit, I remembered that the largest shareholder at my university was precisely the Megasoft Group. After it became the university's biggest booster, there was no shortage of money to underwrite research and theses.'

The dreamseller then asked Jurema a few questions:

'Did you know the young man who expanded that group so explosively? Was he free or a prisoner of the system? Was his philosophy to love money more than life or life more than money? What were his priorities? What values motivated him? Was he conscious of the brevity of life or did he position himself as a god?'

Jurema, caught by surprise, didn't know how to answer, as she had rarely seen the young man personally. He was extremely busy, courted by kings and presidents, while she was simply a professor. But she said that her husband liked him a lot.

'Judging by the comments he made,' she said, 'I believe he was a very good and well-bred person. But after my husband passed seven years ago, I heard little about him, except that some misfortune had struck his family. It appears he had mental problems. They said he passed away, but the press covered up the story. They say that if he were alive today he would have displaced the old magnates and be the richest man on earth.'

The dreamseller looked at us and said:

'My dear Jurema, you were very generous to that millionaire. I, too, have heard of his boldness, his story and his death. But we have the tendency to make the deceased into saints, to exalt their good qualities and conceal their defects. Someone who knew him intimately told me he was ambitious and had no time for anything except increasing his wealth. He forgot what mattered most in his life.'

Sadly, displaying the heavy air of one who disagreed with the path taken by that leader, he added some memorable observations:

'I don't ask you to hate money or material goods. Today we sleep under bridges with the sky as our blanket; tomorrow, who can know? I ask you to understand that money itself doesn't bring happiness, though lack of it can diminish it drastically. Money can't make us crazy, but the love of it can destroy our serenity. The absence of money makes us poor, but its misuse makes us miserable.'

We all fell silent.

'Chief, being broke and happy is fine by me, but with money life's a lot better,' said Bartholomew, drinking coconut water while the rest of us had French and Chilean wine.

The dreamseller smiled. It was difficult for him to have a deep conversation with those street 'philosophers.'

★ ★ ★

As we moved from town to town and people recognized the dreamseller, people wanted to hug him immediately. Their eyes shone when they saw him. Some kissed him. Little by little, he was becoming more famous than society's politicians, and that was stirring envy.

Seeing people gather around him in front of an imposing shopping mall, the dream-seller climbed a few steps leading to the main entrance and began one of his fascinating speeches. He gave a philosophical interpretation of Jesus' most famous homily, the Sermon on the Mount.

He had told us he loved that text and agreed with Mahatma Gandhi that if all the sacred books of the world were banned and only the Sermon on the Mount survived, humanity would not be without light

'Happy are the humble of spirit, for theirs is the kingdom of wisdom,' the dreamseller shouted. 'But where are the truly humble, those who have emptied themselves of themselves? Where are those who recognize their mistakes? Where are those who courageously admit their smallness and fragility to be found? Where are those who struggle daily against pride?'

After speaking these words, he stared attentively at the apprehensive, anxious faces of the crowd. He took a breath and continued:

'Happy are the patient, for they shall inherit the earth. Which earth am I referring to? The earth of tranquillity, the soil of enchantment with life, the terrain of simple love. But where are these gentle souls? Where are the open-minded? Where can we find those who are intimate friends of tolerance? Where are those who temper their irritability and anxiety? Where are those who act calmly in the face of setbacks and frustration? Most people are not gentle even to themselves. They live a pressured life of unending demands and self-inflicted punishment.'

The crowd flowed more and more around him. He raised his eyes to the sky, slowly lowered them and finished his interpretation of the second beatitude, inverting the classical motivational thoughts:

'Stop the neurotic need to change others. No one can change anyone else. Whoever demands more of others than of himself is qualified to work in finance, but not with human beings.'

And he continued:

'Happy are those who mourn, for they shall be comforted. But why do we live in a world where people hide their tears? Where are those who shed tears over the selfishness that blinds our eyes and keeps us from learning what goes on in the minds of those we love? How many hidden fears have never been revealed? How many secret conflicts have never been given voice? How many emotional wounds have we caused and never admitted to?'

As he spoke, the people reflected. Many were lamenting the pitfalls in their personal relationships.

'Happy are the peacemakers, for they shall be called the children of God. But where are those who calm the waters of emotion? Where are the masters at solving interpersonal conflicts? Aren't we all experts at judging others? Where are those who protect, challenge, surrender themselves, reconcile and believe in others? Every society divides its people, and every division implies a subtraction. Peacemaking is not, therefore, teaching the mathematics of addition but understanding the mathematics of subtraction. Whoever fails to understand that is qualified to live with animals and machines, but not with human beings.'

I was speechless. I was schooled in how to be an academic, but was very poorly equipped to live among people. I had owned dogs, and I had no problems with them — or at least they never complained. But dealing with human beings was a constant struggle. I was very demanding. I was qualified to work, but didn't understand the human toll of the mathematics of subtraction. People were free to think, as long as they thought like me. Only then did I begin to comprehend that living well means learning how to lose before learning how to win.

More were congregating to hear the dreamseller speak. Traffic stopped, creating mass confusion. The chaos grew and he quickly had to bring his explanation to an end. That day, the dreamseller chose more disciples, all with particular characteristics. None of them was a saint. None had a calling to be perfect.

Many began to accompany the dreamseller wherever he went. Word had spread on the Internet, and people kept track of where he was and where he was headed. Despite being

The Journey

Three days later, he called a special meeting. Apparently, he was going to tell us about his greatest dream. I could see it burning inside him. He took us to a calm grassy clearing where there was barely any noise or people. He had us sit in a semicircle. It was seven a.m. and dew had settled on the lawn. The first rays of sunlight were glittering on the horizon and lighting the petals of the hibiscuses, forming a kind of arch of gold. Birds were chirping, celebrating the dawning of a new day.

More people were joining the group. Unlike us, the closest group, they had their lives like any other member of society. They had jobs, families, friends, hobbies. That day, there were thirty of us. Among them were manual laborers, managers, doctors, psychologists, social workers. There were Christians, Buddhists, Muslims and people of several other religions.

To our surprise, he started the meeting by telling us something tangible about his mysterious past.

'In the past, I had unimaginable power at

249

my fingertips, a level of control that spanned more than a hundred countries. But there came a period in my life when time stopped. I lost all peace in my life. I cried endlessly and inconsolably. Finally I isolated myself on an island country in the Atlantic Ocean and stayed there for more than three years. The food was good, but I wasn't hungry. I only hungered for knowledge. I devoured books. I had access to one of the most spectacular libraries. I read day and night, like an asthmatic gasping for breath. I read more than a dozen books a month, almost a hundred and fifty a year. Books on philosophy, neuroscience, theology, history, sociology, psychology. I read while eating, sitting down, standing, walking. My mind was like a machine that photographed page after page of knowledge. All that knowledge helped me understand my past and deal with all I had been through. That's how I became the human being you see, a small and imperfect seller of dreams.'

He offered no further explanation. His words gave me the wings to fly far off into the heavens of my mind. I saw that while he told his story, some of my friends looked lost. But I can't say my mind was any better at fitting the puzzle together. 'How can he say that his power was so great? What power is he

250

referring to: financial, political, intellectual, spiritual? He seems so fragile, so docile, so poor. He eats with paupers. There are times when he's tense, but he knows how to control his tension. He demands nothing. He sleeps anywhere. Puts up with aggression. Protects those who oppose him. How can someone who once had so much live so meagerly? Could that power be a figment of his imagination?' Interrupting my thoughts, he elaborated some important recommendations:

'The project to sell dreams doesn't conflict with your religion, culture or beliefs. In fact, respect your beliefs, value your culture, appreciate your nation's past and the traditions of your people. I only ask that you change one thing . . . '

He paused for a long time, as if slowly moving toward his fundamental goal.

'I ask you to expand your horizons. To value and, above all else, respect your condition as human beings. My greatest dream is that we can form a network of people without borders, in every nation, among all peoples, all religions, all scientific environments. A network of people to rescue human nature, the instincts our species has lost. Humanity lives in a pressure cooker of stress because of the ruthless way in which we compete, because of our lack of respect for the international rules of commerce, because of social conflicts, because of the devastation to the environment. The French Revolution took place over two centuries ago, but we speak of it as if it had occurred yesterday. Yet, when we look to the future we have no guarantee that our species will survive one or two more centuries.'

Then he spoke of his model. He said that Jesus repeated more than seventy times in the New Testament that he was the son of man. 'Throughout history, few have understood what he meant. He revealed that he was for all mankind. By insisting he was the son of man he wanted it known that he was the son of humanity — the first human being completely without borders. His culture, his race, his nationality were important, but his humanity was much more so. His passion for his fellow man was at a level that theology doesn't understand and psychology can't reach. Only a human without borders could say that prostitutes should enter heaven before illustrious Pharisee theologians. His limitless love was a scandal during his time, and still is in our own.' And the dreamseller added solemnly:

'I have thousands of shortcomings. I've made more mistakes than any of you can imagine, but Jesus' philosophy and psychology is my model.' And he proposed founding a society of human beings without borders, based on just four principles:

To go beyond race, culture and nationality and position ourselves as humans without borders, with a vital commitment to protect man and the environment;

To fight discrimination in all its forms and support all forms of inclusion;

To respect the differences that make us unique;

And to promote interaction among people of different cultures and beliefs.

The dreamseller knew that his proposals shared the principles of the French Revolution, the United Nations Declaration of Human Rights and the Magna Carta of many nations. But the difference was that he dreamed of taking pages from those charters and printing that text within the hearts and minds of humans without borders.

'It's too utopian,' I muttered to myself. But the dreamseller read my lips.

'You're right. Nothing could be more Utopian, imaginary, romantic. But take away the dream of utopia and we are left as machines. Take away hope and we are left as slaves. Take away dreams and we are left as robots. If business and political leaders thought in terms of humanity, two-thirds of the world's problems would be solved in a month. And that's no dream.'

I nodded my head, recognizing that he was right. I remembered all the times I had felt like a teaching machine whirring steadily for students who became learning machines.

The dreamseller seemed more fixated than ever. He measured his tone more than he normally did. Anyone could see this was a special day for him. And he seemed to have something important left to say. Then he told us the parable of the cocoon.

'Two caterpillars each spun a cocoon. In that protected atmosphere they were transformed into beautiful butterflies. Just when they were ready to fly free, their fears gripped them. One butterfly, being so fragile, thought to herself: 'Life outside has so many dangers. I can be torn to bits and eaten by a bird. If a predator doesn't kill me, I might be torn apart in a storm. A lightning bolt could strike me dead. The rain could weigh on my wings and send me crashing to the ground. Besides, spring is ending. What if the nectar runs out? Who will help me?' The risks were in fact many, and the little butterfly had reason to be scared. Frightened, she decided not to leave. She remained in her protected cocoon, but, having no means to survive, she died a sad death, starved, dehydrated and, worst of all, walled in by the world she had spun.

'The other butterfly,' he continued, 'was also apprehensive. She was afraid of the world outside, knowing that many butterflies didn't last a day outside the cocoon. But she loved freedom more than she feared the dangers that could befall her. And so she set off, flying in the direction of all the dangers. She chose to be a wanderer in search of the only thing that defined her essence.'

When he finished telling the parable, the dreamseller unveiled his intentions. He paused briefly to listen to the exquisitely beautiful birdsongs that seemed to be sung in his honor and made a series of simple yet profound requests. There were so many that I found it hard to take notes:

'I called you here so early because for two days I'd like you to go out and live the principles of being 'a human being without borders.' I'm sending you out in pairs into the social landscape. Take with you neither purses, money, checks, credit cards, nor food — nothing that provides survival support, only medicines and personal hygiene products. Eat whatever you're offered. Sleep in the beds prepared for you. Discriminate against no one. If someone rejects you, don't resist, treat him with gentleness. Act like social therapists. Give and receive. Don't feel the need to win people over. Don't defend your beliefs, don't impose your ideas. Instead, emanate humanity. Ask those you meet on the road how you can be of help to them. Talk to people, get to know their hidden stories, uncover dazzling human beings among the anonymous. Don't look at them through your eyes but through theirs. Don't invade their privacy, don't try to control them, go only as far as they allow. Listen to them humbly, even those who are thinking of ending their lives, and encourage them to listen to themselves. If they manage only to listen to themselves instead of you, you have succeeded. Remember that the kingdom of the wise belongs to the humble.'

He paused and seemed concerned when he warned us:

'We're living in the third millennium. Selling the dream of being a human without borders in a society that has reached the pinnacle of selfishness seems like the absurdity of all absurdities. Being true, generous and considerate when others ask it of us already seems like going beyond extraordinary; just imagine how difficult it will be to teach others to be this way when no one asks it of them. You'll be called fanatics, lunatics, proselytizers. But if they accepted me, they'll also accept you.'

Other than that, he offered no rules about how to approach people or whom to look for: rich or poor, educated or illiterate, city dwellers or those in rural towns. He gave us no map, only the inspiration to continue the journey. His hair blew in the wind, and we were dripping sweat. We were all scared of what awaited us. I thought to myself, 'This isn't going to work. We'll be misunderstood, maybe even reviled. And what if I run into one of my colleagues from the university? What will they say about me?' The dream-seller added:

'There are many ways to contribute to the good of humanity, but none of them is easy, and none of them come with applause. People will be suspicious of your motives. You may be famous in the morning, and infamous by nightfall. You may be heralded one moment and treated like the dregs of society the next. The consequences are unpredict-able. But I guarantee you that if you overcome these obstacles, you'll emerge much more human, much stronger, and able to understand what books can never teach you. You'll understand, to some small degree, what millions of Jews experienced at the hands of the Nazis, Christians in the Colosseum, Muslims in Palestine . . . You'll begin to understand the kind of oppression that homosexuals, blacks, prostitutes, the deeply religious and women have suffered throughout history.'

I thought to myself, 'Letting Bartholomew and Dimas loose to represent the dreamseller without monitoring could be a disaster. It's not that different from letting a medical student perform surgery without a supervisor.'

What the dreamseller was asking of us was to create a social laboratory unlike any I had studied in sociology. He didn't want us to do charity work in Africa with financial backing, or give philanthropically to some institution, or to support a religion or a political party. He wanted us to return to our roots. We could take nothing with us, not even our prestige in society. We would have to be merely human beings connecting with other human beings.

He insisted that we had a right to choose.

'I encourage you to leave the cocoon at least this one time, but no one is obligated to do so. There are many risks, and the consequences are unforeseeable. The choice is yours, yours alone.'

The group shook with tension, but no one backed down from the dreamseller's challenge, not even a pair of eighteen-year-olds near the front. Youth yearns for adventure, and they were ready to experience the journey.

Sending Forth the Disciples

When the meeting was over, he sent us off for our two-day journey. Each took the person who'd been sitting on his right as his partner. He gave the women the option to sleep at home, but they all declined.

'We want the full experience. We choose to leave our cocoons for those two days,' Jurema said, speaking for the women. Four other people asked to be excused, though they promised to return on the appointed day.

Our results couldn't have been more mixed. We were taken for thieves and kidnappers. We were rejected, ridiculed, threatened. Several pairs had to explain themselves at the police station. But in spite of everything, we had spectacular experiences. We enjoyed ourselves and learned so much. It seemed as if we were traveling in another society, that we had entered a completely different world, the world of 'the other person.' Everyone said they felt totally insecure without money or credit cards. Sometimes we felt like a wandering people with no home, no country and no protection, wondering how we would survive from day to day. We were just humans and nothing more. The dreamseller's sociological experiment proved that we were concealing our true humanity behind concepts like ethics, morality, titles, status and power.

Honeymouth, with Dimas as his partner, set off to sell dreams in the places he knew best, bars and nightclubs. He was met with countless hassles. Some threw vodka in his face, others humiliated him, some cursed him, and still others simply threw him out. 'Get outta here, you drunk!' He lost his patience five times and threatened to punch two alcoholics. He began to realize just how difficult a calling this would be.

Despite the setbacks, he helped alcoholics to their feet, listened to rambling conversations and consoled them. Many told him they drank to drown out the pain of losses, betrayals, financial crises and deaths in the family. He had no magic solution, but he lent his ear. At the end of the first day, he went up to a middle-aged man sitting by himself at a table and said, 'Sir, I don't mean to bother you. I'd just like to know how I can be of service.'

The answer was swift: 'Get me another shot of whiskey.'

He said he had no money. The alcoholic shoved him rudely.

'Then get out of here or I'm calling the police.'

Bartholomew was a husky man. He grabbed the alcoholic by the collar and was about to shake him when he remembered the dreamseller's counsel.

'Oh, if this had happened a couple of months ago . . . ' he said angrily. Dimas was also indignant.

The drunk put his hand on his head, quickly regaining his composure. Even with his judgment impaired, he saw he had been rude. He apologized and asked them to sit with him. Then, without explanation, he sobbed for twenty solid seconds.

When he regained his composure, he introduced himself. He said his name was Lucas and he was a failed surgeon. He had made a mistake that didn't threaten his patient's life, but the patient's lawyer used that mistake to take him to the cleaners. He was sued and lost everything he had built up in twenty years of practicing medicine. Deep in debt, he couldn't make his mortgage payment and was about to be evicted. He couldn't meet the monthly payment on his car, and that was about to be repossessed soon, too.

'Don't cry, my friend. You can live under bridges,' said Bartholomew, which only depressed the man even more.

Dimas jumped in. In an effort to console the doctor, he told part of his story, a story Bartholomew didn't know. He said his father had served twenty-five years for armed robbery. His mother soon took up with another man and abandoned the boy, just five years old at the time, and his two-year-old sister. They were sent to separate orphanages. She was adopted and they never saw each other again. Dimas wasn't adopted and grew up without a father, without a mother, without a sister, without schooling, without friends and without love, until he aged out of the system.

Bartholomew tried to console his friend:

'*Mi amigo*, I always thought you were just a crook and a cheat. I didn't really know you,' he said, putting his arm on Dimas's shoulder. 'You're the most normal one in the whole crazy group.'

Dr. Lucas was moved by his story. The effects of the alcohol had started to wear off. They became friends, chatting for more than three hours. They left arm in arm and singing, 'For Lucas is a jolly good fellow, for Lucas is a jolly good fellow . . . ' They felt the pleasure of a true friendship. They understood that living outside the cocoon has its undeniable risks but also irrefutable charm.

Bartholomew and Dimas slept in a guest room at the doctor's house. His wife had heard of the social movement of 'dreams,' and she made them a delicious spaghetti dinner. The next day, she thanked them. It had been six months since she'd seen her husband motivated to face his life.

Dimas and Bartholomew continued their journey. At the end of the afternoon of the second day, they found another alcoholic in a pitiful situation, slumped over the counter of the bar. Bartholomew appeared to know him. When he turned his head, he recognized him immediately. It was Barnabas, his best friend from bars and nightlife. He was well under six feet tall and weighed 242 pounds. He was always boozing and eating. Alcohol hadn't succeeded in taking away his appetite. They called him the 'Mayor,' as he loved to give speeches, argue about politics and come up with fanciful solutions to society's problems. He and Bartholomew were two peas in a pod.

'Honeymouth?' Barnabas yelled, almost in code because of how badly he slurred his words.

'Mayor, how good to see you!' And they embraced.

Dimas and Bartholomew took him to a park near the bar. They stayed together for hours until the alcohol had worn off. After

Barnabas became a bit more lucid, he told Bartholomew:

'I've seen you in the papers. You're famous now. You're tending bar. No, no, sorry, you're playing Santa Claus, distributing free gifts, right? Cool,' he said, his voice slurring. 'You're one of the good guys, now. Not one of us sloppy bohemians.'

'I am still the same. I just slightly changed my way of looking at things,' Bartholomew said. And he took advantage of being among friends to tell a story of his own. Like Dimas, he had been in an orphanage in childhood, but for different reasons.

'My father died when I was seven, and cancer claimed my mother two years later. I was taken to an orphanage on the outskirts of the city. I stayed there till I was eighteen, then I ran away,' he said.

Dimas looked at Bartholomew in surprise and said:

'Wait, don't tell me you're 'Goldfoot.'' That was Bartholomew's nickname at the orphanage because he was such a great soccer player. Bartholomew hadn't heard that name in a long time. He really looked at Dimas and recognized him, too. They both had felt they knew the other from someplace but could never quite place the face. As children, they had known each other for a year, and now, twenty years later, they had found each other again.

'That's great. A family reunion. I guess I'm the only one who doesn't have anybody,' said Barnabas, feeling suddenly dizzy and holding his head in his hands, his elbows on the table.

Bartholomew felt sorry for his friend. He looked at the clock and saw they were late for the meeting with the dreamseller. He asked Dimas to go on ahead. He wanted to chat a bit with Barnabas about the new family.

Jurema and I went to speak to students in a university across town from mine. I tried to challenge their thinking. I urged them to develop the Socratic method, to develop their own social experiment and to expand the world of ideas. Everyone was impressed by Jurema's eloquence. She had more vigor and drive than they did. The students were weary, apathetic, discouraged.

Suddenly I saw two professors I recognized coming toward me, and my face immediately flushed. They were colleagues from my university who were teaching a course in that same building. They approached us, laughing. I could read their lips, saying to each other that the authoritative head of the sociology department had lost his mind.

Jurema told me, 'It's time to face them. It's time to leave the cocoon.'

That was the price I had to pay for being such a tyrant. One of the professors who hadn't kept up to date, a guy I thought had been a terrible teacher and thought I was too hard on him, didn't hesitate to open with, 'So, how goes the life of a crazy person?'

I wanted to turn and run. But Jurema took me by the arms and tried to ease my mind.

I got myself under control, looked him in the eye, and replied:

'I'm trying to understand my madness. When I used to hide behind intellect, I thought I was completely healthy, but since now I'm a wanderer in search of myself, I know I'm sicker than I ever imagined.'

They were astonished. They saw that I still had my rapid power of reasoning, but they had never seen me acknowledge an error, never seen me with any semblance of humility. They began to sheathe their swords.

I tried to explain myself, not really expecting anyone would understand.

'Do you know the essence of who you are? How many moments of real pleasure have you had today? Have you had time to relax? Have you invested in your personal projects or have you buried them? Have you behaved like intellectual giants isolated in your brilliance, or have you been men without borders who know how to share your pain?

Have you been teaching machines or have you been agents who mold thinkers?'

They felt the crazy man who had wanted to commit suicide had become a better debater than the professor they had once known. One of them, Marco Antonio, a professor of sociology who was the most erudite in the department, but whose teaching methods I had always criticized, praised me:

'Julio, I've been following your work through the press and through our students. I am truly impressed by the courage it must have taken to break from your life and to reorganize it. Sooner or later everyone should take such a break to try to find himself, to rethink his story.'

I told them about the dreams project. I said that it wasn't a motivational, self-help project, but one of forming humane thinkers. It was a project to mold 'a man without borders.'

Professor Marco Antonio thought for a long time and confessed that he was bored with social conformity and weary of the pernicious paradox of 'personal isolation versus mass interaction.' I asked him to explain the paradox, as I didn't understand the full extent of his idea.

'Human beings choose to live on islands when they should be on continents. And other times, they are on continents, when

268

they should be on islands. In other words, they should be sharing ideas and experiences to help everyone overcome frustrations. But we should be islands — individuals — when it comes to taste, lifestyle, art and culture. Television, fast food, the fashion industry all have served to homogenize our tastes and styles. We've lost our sense of individuality.'

I thought to myself, 'This professor's thoughts are very close to the dreamseller's.' Then, he asked us how he could get acquainted with the sociological experiment of being a person without borders. And I was happy to tell him.

All the pairs returned flushed with enthusiasm. They had encountered unforeseeable tribulations but had experienced notable deeds. Deeds that did nothing to increase our bank account or our social standing but brought us back to our origins.

Some of the pairs brought with them friends whom they'd met along the way. Monica brought five model friends of hers. They were excited about parading on unfamiliar runways. Jurema and I brought two professors and two students. Dimas brought Dr. Lucas and his wife. Solomon brought his old psychiatrist, who specialized in anxiety disorders but was constantly depressed. He had been infected by his patient's happiness and wanted a dose of this social antidepressant.

Everyone spoke to each other about their simple but meaningful experiences. They spoke euphorically about the joy it had brought them to really know people who might otherwise have been just anonymous extras in the movie of life. They discovered the indescribable pleasure of contributing to someone else's story and the anonymous solidarity that came with it.

All told, thirty-eight new 'strangers' were added to the group. Among them, two Orthodox Jews and two Muslims. Suddenly we noticed the absence of the most vibrant person in our group, Bartholomew. Dimas told us he was with his friend and would be along shortly.

We were so excited that we improvised the first of the project's many festivities to come. There, rich and poor, intellectuals and illiterates, Christians, Muslims, Jews and Buddhists ate, danced and spoke free of the world's prejudice. Our only goal was to share a bit of each other.

Not even Robespierre in his philosophical delirium could have imagined that the three pillars of the French Revolution — Liberty, Equality, Brotherhood — would be lived so richly by people who were so different from one another. The dreamseller, seeing our joy, told us:

'We are all different at our core: in the intrinsic fabric of our personalities, in the way we think, act, see and interpret existence. The dream of equality grows only when we respect each other's differences.'

But not all the pairs had been successful. My friend Edson returned with two black eyes. He appeared to have fallen down or been punched a couple of times. We were curious to hear the story.

He told us that, after succeeding in winning over people with his selflessness and kindness, someone had offended him. He said:

'A fifty-year-old man asked me if I was familiar with the Sermon on the Mount. I said I was.' Edson's voice caught in his throat. He was a little ashamed. Trying to encourage him, I asked, 'But isn't that a good thing?'

'Yes, but the problem is that he asked me to recite some of the words from the sermon, which I did enthusiastically because I knew the text by heart.' Edson paused again. He started to turn red. His silence provoked Dimas's question: 'But isn't that wonderful?'

'Yes, but when I got to the part where we're supposed to turn the other cheek, he asked me if I believed in that. Without batting an eye, I said I did.' He fell silent and blushed as the dreamseller listened closely.

'But that's wonderful, Edson,' Monica told him. Edson lowered his voice.

'Yes. I mean, no. At that moment, he slapped me on the left cheek. I've never felt so much pain, or so much anger. My lips trembled, and I wanted to strangle him. But I held back.

'Congratulations,' said Professor Jurema. 'That was truly a miracle.' But our friend's clothes were torn, his cheek was bruised and the dreamseller was suspicious.

'Why's your right eye black, too?' asked Solomon.

'After he hit me on the left, he asked me to turn and offer my right cheek. I didn't want to, but before I realized it he slapped me again. I wanted to grab the guy by the throat, but I remembered everything we've been through together. I remembered the gentle Jesus of Nazareth and the dreamseller's project. I held back. I don't know how, but I held back. He had heard of our project and he called me a 'nonsense seller.''

People started clapping, but he asked them to let him finish his story. Because he had failed. Finally, he finished explaining what had happened:

'Then he asked me for my right cheek

again. I was dripping with rage. I knew that Jesus had said to turn the other cheek, but not to turn the same cheek twice. I looked toward heaven, asked for forgiveness and started pounding the guy. But he was stronger, and he beat the hell out of me.'

It was no time to laugh, but we couldn't hold back. Even the dreamseller, who didn't approve of violence, was fighting back a smile. Then he gave us an unforgettable lesson.

'Being a human being without borders doesn't mean risking your life unnecessarily. Remember that I didn't call you to be heroes. Don't provoke, much less confront, those who offend you. Turning the other cheek isn't a sign of weakness, but of strength. It's not a sign of stupidity, but of great vision.'

He paused to allow us to assimilate his ideas, then continued:

'Turning the other cheek is a symbol of maturity and internal strength. It doesn't refer to the physical cheek but to the mental one. Turning the other cheek means trying to do good to someone who disappoints us, it means having the grace to praise someone who defames us, the altruism to be kind to someone who hates us. It means walking away from those looking for a fight. Turning the other cheek prevents murders, injuries and lifelong scars. The weak seek vengeance; the strong protect themselves.'

Edson soaked in these words like rain to dry earth. That episode helped him take a major emotional leap forward, polished his wisdom and expanded the frontiers of his mind. He contributed greatly to our movement.

The dreamseller's words penetrated all of us like a bolt of lightning. They had such an impact that the Orthodox Jews and Muslims who were present turned and hugged each other. I looked at my friend, Professor Marco Antonio. I remembered that I had come down hard on my enemies at the university. I never learned that those who turn the other cheek are much happier, much calmer and sleep soundly at night.

Jurema whispered in my ear, 'I taught for more than thirty years. But I have to admit that I produced many aggressive, vengeful, heartless students.'

And I thought to myself, 'So did I. Without realizing it, in the structured confines of universities, we produced dictators in the making.'

A commotion broke out as I was deep in thought. Bartholomew and Barnabas had finally appeared — completely drunk. Bartholomew had been so happy at finding his old friend that he let down his guard. He knocked back a few drinks to celebrate and got drunk on vodka again.

They had their arms around each other. Their legs got tangled up as they walked, and to keep from falling down, each clung to the other. They showed up singing a Nelson Gonçalves song:

> Bohemia, I'm back again, begging to
>   rejoin you.
> Crying for joy, I've come to see the
>   friends I left behind.

As if his bingeing weren't enough, Bartholomew looked at the group and yelled out his favorite phrase: 'Oh, how I love this life!'

'Shut up, Bartholomew!' we called out in chorus, laughing.

But he didn't shut up. Instead, almost falling over, he called out the dreamseller and questioned his project. His face flushed, and emboldened by everyone watching him, he said:

'Listen, chief, this whole deal about being 'humans without border,' that's old news. Real old, you know?' He tried, and failed, to snap his fingers to emphasize his point. He continued, 'Alcoholics have known about that for years and years and years ... No alcoholic is better than any other. They all kiss each other, they all hug, they all sing together. We don't have a country or a flag. You get what I'm saying?'

I watched the dreamseller. He had invested so much of his time in training us. He had had the patience of Job, and now, as his dream was becoming a reality, he had to deal with this mess. But the dreamseller just walked up to them and hugged them. And jokingly, he said, 'Some people can live outside the cocoon forever. Others need to come home now and then.'

And instead of being disappointed, he seconded Honeymouth's idea.

'It's true, alcoholics are human beings without borders, especially when they're not aggressive. Why? Because in certain cases the effect of alcohol blocks the memories that hold our prejudices and our cultural, national and social barriers. But it's better and safer to achieve that goal while sober, through the difficult art of thinking and choosing.'

And he began to dance among us, filled with energy. He understood that one person could not change another; it has to come from within. He knew, better than any of us, that the dangers of living outside the cocoon were many and unforeseeable.

Watching the dreamseller lovingly coach his 'students' who had strayed completely, I was convinced that the greatness of a teacher lies not in how he teaches his perfect students, but in how he teaches the most difficult ones. How many crimes against teaching had I committed? I had never encouraged a rebellious student or helped one who was struggling.

I took Jurema aside and told her, 'I've buried students in the basement of the educational system.'

Jurema, examining her own history, had the courage to confess:

'Unfortunately, so have I. Instead of encouraging creative rebellion, intuition and thoughtful reasoning, I demanded only the 'right' answers. We molded paranoid young predators, desperate to be number one, and not peacemakers, tolerant individuals who feel worthy of being number nine or ten.'

It felt like we were leaving behind our sociological infancy and entering into childhood. The celebration lasted till the early hours. We were drunk with joy. Barnabas was invited to join our team of dreamsellers, and he and Bartholomew became the most eccentric pair in the bunch. We didn't know whether they had been reformed or whether they would make us even crazier than we already were. But it doesn't matter. We, too, were learning to love this life.

The Living Dead

The dreamseller's fame was growing each day and was starting to seep into the world of finance. Businessmen and executives had heard about this unusual stranger, and because they were always eager to learn new inspiring leadership styles, they asked me to invite the dreamseller to give a lecture. They wanted to meet this man who was setting society on fire.

In my experience, the elite were only interested in three things: money, money, money. I almost told him immediately that the dreamseller wouldn't accept the invitation, but not wanting to be presumptuous, I passed along the news.

However, I was in for a surprise. After thinking about the invitation for a while, the dreamseller said he would talk to them, but in a setting of his choosing. And he gave me the address. It was a location I had never heard of. I didn't know the size of the amphitheater, whether it had air-conditioning and comfortable chairs. I only knew that his audience was used to luxurious accommodations and to getting their way.

I was told the audience would consist of close to a hundred businessmen and executives, of whom only five were women. There were entrepreneurs, bankers, owners of large construction companies, of supermarket networks, of retail chain stores and other sectors. They represented the richest and most powerful people in the state.

They were delighted that the dreamseller had accepted the invitation. But since I had always been suspicious of these people, I wanted to scare them, to tell them they had no idea what awaited them. I said that the dreamseller was so radical, he would make Lenin the communist seem ordinary. My jibe made them squirm, but I only doubled the threat. I told them that the dreamseller might call them capitalist vipers who lived to exploit the poor. They were not amused. They seemed to be rethinking the invitation, but even so, they wanted to hear this man's fascinating ideas.

The leaders received their invitations, and some found it strange that they didn't recognize the address, since they were used to attending events at the city finest venues. The night of the meeting, the dreamseller set off ahead of us. He seemed to want to meditate before the event. 'Could he be preparing for battle?' I thought. 'Was he asking God for the wisdom to be able to rattle these elite individuals? This is his golden opportunity to break the backs of the financial elite,' I thought. But I was wrong. I had no idea that what was about to happen would leave me at a loss for words.

We didn't know the address either, so we asked around as we walked. We were nearing the address, but couldn't find the location on the dimly lit street. Eventually, we came across another group of people who seemed lost, the businessmen and executives. They thought I'd given them the wrong address. But I assured them that it was the address the dreamseller had given me. Still, I thought they might be right. Maybe he had mistakenly given us the wrong address, since he didn't run in these high-society circles and didn't know exactly where the city's amphitheaters were.

The business leaders thought they'd been fooled. But we decided to go a bit further up the street together in search of the site. Suddenly, we found ourselves at the entrance to a huge, gloomy cemetery. It was the famous Recoleta Cemetery. We checked the street number the dreamseller had given us and the numbers matched. I thought to myself, 'If people thought the dreamseller was crazy before, they're sure of it now.'

'I don't mind confronting my mental demons, but this is too much,' Solomon said. 'I hate cemeteries, especially at night. Let's get out of here.'

I took his arm and asked him to stay calm. The elite participants were beginning to arrive in their luxury cars and to gather around the gates. Everyone was confused. For the first time, I humbled myself in the presence of that group, apologizing for the mistaken address.

Suddenly, just as we were about to leave, the gates of the cemetery swung open, their hinges creaking. Honeymouth clung to Angel Hand.

'I'd need a couple of bottles of vodka in me before I went in there,' he said trembling.

No sooner had Bartholomew said this than a strange, terrifying figure appeared. We couldn't see its face in the inky night. But it clearly was gesturing for us to step through the gates. Inside, under gas lamps throughout the cemetery, we saw the face of tonight's speaker, the dreamseller. The address was no mistake.

All of us, disciples and businessmen alike, moved slowly and apprehensively toward a wide open area where everyone could stand. We looked at one another for answers, all thinking the same thing: 'What am I doing here?' This would be the first time in history a leadership conference had been held in a cemetery. And it was appropriate. Because it would be the first time that the hurried world of the living would be discussed among the dead.

As we gathered around, the dreamseller used his deep, vibrant voice to greet the participants in an unusual manner:

'Welcome, all of you, the future rich residents of the cemetery. Please, make yourselves at home.'

The businessmen's legs weakened. They were used to great competitive battles, to taking phenomenal risks, but they had never faced a challenge like this. They had been knocked out in the first round by a stranger. I didn't know what to say or how to react, and those around me were frozen. Recoleta Cemetery is imposing. It's a cemetery for the wealthy. Its mausoleums are truly works of art.

Seeing us deep in thought, the dreamseller continued to let his ideas flow.

'The notable men and women of society lie here. Dreams, nightmares, secret feelings, visible emotions, anxiety attacks, moments of rare pleasure made up the lives of each human being who rests here. Their stories sleep here, forever. And other than their loved ones, no one ever thinks about them.'

We didn't know what the dreamseller was getting at, whether the conference had begun or even if there would be a conference. We only knew that his words were taking us on a journey through our own stories. That in the past of those buried here we might see our own future. His talk, which seemed intended to cause fear, began to take on an unexplainable tenderness. Then he made a request of all of us:

'Take ten minutes to read the gracious epitaphs on the front of the mausoleums.'

I had never taken the time to do anything like that. Despite the failing light, we began moving through the cemetery's passageways, reading the engraved messages that celebrated the existence of people now departed. So much longing! So many inscriptions! So many words laden with noble sentiments! Some messages said, 'To my kind and gentle husband, who will be greatly missed by his loving wife. May God grant him peace'; 'To our beloved father: Time stole you from us, but it can never steal the love we feel for you'; 'Dad, you are unforgettable. I will love you forever'; 'To my irreplaceable friend: Thank you for having lived and having been part of our lives.'

I don't know what happened to me when I

read those messages, but I became lost in emotion. I began to remember the ones I had lost. I never wrote a plaque for my father. Nor even thanked him for giving me life. His suicide blocked out my feelings. Not even for my brave mother had I written a message, other than the one I carry silently in my mind: 'I love you. Thank you for having put up with my rebelliousness.'

I looked to the side and saw that my friends and the businessmen were moved. They had traveled through time, opened the doors of their subconscious and encountered their excruciating frailty. They were men who ran companies with thousands of employees, but now they were simply mortals.

At that moment, I saw that the dreamseller had stripped them of their pridefulness, shut off their defense mechanisms, removed the security they took in their financial status. When he opened his mouth, he said something every businessman hates to hear, 'Where are the proletarians of today, and who are they?'

I thought to myself, 'These businesspeople won't stand for this.' No one answered. The question, though seemingly obvious, was not. Then he stood the theory of utopia on its head.

'You're today's proletarians,' he said.

I thought: 'What's he saying? Doesn't he know the audience he's talking to?' I thought the dreamseller had no idea what he was saying. But he quickly threw my thinking into a tailspin.

He said that Karl Marx (1818–1883) had left his native land and gone to Paris, where he met Friedrich Engels (1820–1895).

The two refined their ideas, joined socialist groups and initiated a lifelong collaboration. To them, the manner in which goods are produced and wealth distributed are the forces that shape all aspects of our lives: politics, law, morality and philosophy. Marx believed human history was governed by the laws of science and rejected all religious interpretations of nature and history. He thought these laws would help people, especially the working class, make their own history.

But this dream never materialized, he said. When a group of socialists seized power, they became ruthless, crushed their opponents, silenced dissenting voices, infringed on human rights and crushed the freedom they had preached. The working class did not construct its own history, rather, the ones in power wrote the history books. Religion was replaced by the cult of personality of those leaders.

'Their revolution was extreme,' he said. 'Unlike them, my dream isn't to destroy the ruling political system in order to rebuild it. I don't believe in change from the outside. I believe in change that begins from within, a peaceful change in our ability to reason, to see, to critique, to interpret social phenomena and, especially, to reclaim pleasure. My dream lies within people.'

After he showed that he knew what he was talking about, he said that when Marx launched his ideas, the project failed not because the ruling class didn't distribute income, but because they used political and financial power to oppress the working class. A small minority lived like princes while the majority lived like paupers.

Today, he said, this separation of the classes remained. Social inequalities hadn't been eradicated. In fact, with the advent of globalization, the system had created a new class of exploited people: 'You!' he emphasized again.

Again I thought, 'But aren't they the privileged ones? Don't they live in the lap of luxury? How can they be called an exploited class — the proletarians of this millennium?'

But to ground his ideas, the dreamseller crushed a popular saying of ours:

'In past centuries, before the system

developed, it took three generations for a family's fortune to disappear. So the old saying held true: rich grandfather, lordly son, poor grandson. But these days that saying doesn't hold up. A solid business can vanish in five years. A successful industry can be out of the market in a short time. Several fortunes over can be lost in a single generation.'

After that initial shock, the businessmen began to agree with this mysterious thinker.

'For your companies to survive, you can never stop competing. To stay ahead of the competition, you are forced to find ways to reinvent yourselves each year, each month each week.'

And he asked a basic question that everyone got wrong:

'Does the system crush companies that show weakness?'

Unanimously, they answered yes. But he said no.

'The system doesn't crush the *companies*. It crushes their *leaders*.'

He saw that doctors, lawyers, engineers, journalists — people of all professions — were being crushed in the same way. These masters of finance began to realize they weren't as rich as they thought. These proprietors of power began to understand they weren't as strong as they imagined.

288

Some in the audience were still skeptical. But the dreamseller loved skeptics. He could pin them down with the sharpness of his ideas. So he left no doubts:

'Ladies and gentlemen, the time of slavery has not been expunged from the pages of history but merely changed its form. I'm going to ask you some questions, and I want you to be completely honest. Anyone who isn't will have to answer to his own conscience. Tell me: Who has migraines?'

People were a bit embarrassed, but one after the other they raised their hands.

'Who has muscle aches?' Again, the vast majority raised their hands, this time more quickly.

Then he began asking countless other questions:

'Who wakes up fatigued? Whose hair is falling out? Who feels his mind is always racing? Who worries about problems that have yet to happen? Who feels like he's always hanging by a thread? Who loses his temper over the tiniest of problems? Who has wildly fluctuating emotions — calm one minute and explosive the next? Who's afraid of what the future will hold?'

Most never lowered their hands. They had all the symptoms. I couldn't believe what I was seeing. I rubbed my eyes and asked myself, 'Aren't these society's elite? How can their quality of life be this terrible? Aren't they the ones who drink the best wines and champagnes? Don't they dine at the best restaurants? Why are they so gravely stressed?' I was shaken.

My mind wouldn't reconcile the two images. The rich traveled in luxury cars, but they were paralyzed by their stress. They would go to their beach houses, but their emotions didn't surf the waves of pleasure. They slept on soft mattresses but lacked the mental comfort to sleep at night. They wore the finest suits but stood naked against the worries in their lives.

'What insanity!' I thought. 'Where is the happiness the system promised these people who've reached the top of their professions? Where is the peace for those who've accumulated riches? Where is the reward for competence? They take out insurance on their homes, their lives, their businesses, even against kidnapping. So how can they be so insecure?' The system, it turned out, crushed its leaders.

Midnight in the Garden of Broken Dreams

The dreamseller's questions in Recoleta Cemetery sent our heads spinning. I had attacked the business elite for years on end in my classroom, but I realized I needed to re-examine a few concepts. I began to understand that the system betrayed everyone, especially those who nurtured it most. It even affected celebrities, not just because they lost their private lives but because their success was fleeting. In this society, it was easy to become insignificant overnight.

In the name of competition, the system sucked out their last drop of mental energy. They expended more energy than many manual laborers, and were constantly fatigued from an overload of thinking. They were victors, but they didn't carry away the ultimate prize.

The stress was even greater for companies who specialized in production. There was an international price war, distorted by government subsidies that contaminated the value of products, and could crush companies on the other side of the globe. Now, add in the taxes on products coming in and out of the country, the disparity of wages paid to workers in different countries and the fact that some firms lowered their prices below the cost of production to corner the market. Survival was a hellish art.

It took its toll on everyone involved. Thirty-five percent of them had heart problems or were hypertensive. Fifteen percent had cancer, and some of those wouldn't live to see the New Year. Thirty percent suffered depression. Ten percent had panic attacks. Sixty percent had marital problems. Ninety-five percent exhibited three or more mental problems and most of those had as many as ten different mental issues.

Yes, the proletariat were still being exploited across the globe. But in developed and emerging societies, where labor laws were just and human rights were respected, the ones who were exploited were the those engaged in intense intellectual work, like managers, directors, business magnates, professionals, professors, journalists.

The oppression was so devastating that many executives took their problems home with them, even on vacation. Workers who had a decent salary but weren't in a position of leadership or management had time for friends, food, relaxation on weekends. They could go to bed and wake up without being suffocated by worry. But for the business leaders those simple pleasures were luxuries. In the best sense of the word, 'the serfs lived better than the feudal lord.'

It was then that I understood why the dreamseller said that success is harder to deal with than failure: The danger of success is that one can become a perpetual-motion machine. Marx and Engels would spin in their graves if they knew that the final stage of capitalism would attain the socialist dream: It would tax the elite more than the workers — physically, anyway.

Although there were exceptions. The problem for the working class was consumption: the compulsion to buy, to use credit cards, to live beyond their means. Capitalism, it turned out, made workers king and exploited the minds of those in power.

The interesting thing is that there were no statistics to tell us about this new group of exploited workers. They were apparently strong, self-sufficient demigods who needed no help, much less dreams. But they were not beings without borders; they were enslaved to this way of thinking. Aside from an annual medical checkup, nothing was done for them.

It was clear the dreamseller knew what he was talking about and to whom he was speaking, after all. But we didn't understand how he could know that. How could this ragged nomad possess that information? What kind of person is this who moves with equal ease among paupers and millionaires? Where does he come from?

Bartholomew couldn't keep quiet any longer after seeing these giants of industry admit their frailties. He raised his hand and told the dreamseller:

'Chief, these guys are in bad shape! But I think we can help them.'

It was the first time in modern history that someone so poor had called members of the financial elite paupers. It was the first time that a proletarian felt richer than society's millionaires. His utterance was so spontaneous that what had been tragic turned suddenly comical. The participants looked at one another and broke out in broad smiles. They needed to buy lots of dreams if they wanted to regain their mental health.

As if the night didn't hold enough surprises, another one arose in that darkened cemetery. Suddenly, from inside a tomb about fifty feet away, a terrifying figure with an old white coat over its head emerged with a horrifying cry: 'I am death! And I have come for you!'

Even the dreamseller was startled. And for

the first time in my life, I truly believed in ghosts. Our hearts jumped up in our throats, and reason completely leaped out of our bodies. Some started to run for the gates, but the ghost laughed and laughed.

'Take it easy, folks. Calm down! Why so nervous? Sooner or later we'll all be sleeping in a place like this,' it said.

The figure removed the coat from his head. It was that Bartholomew's worst half, Barnabas. Those two managed to make a joke wherever they were, even in a cemetery.

Every time we reached the heights of seriousness, they plunged us into wild laughter. They spoiled everything. If in the past, had they been students of mine, I'd surely have expelled them. But fortunately for them, they had found a patient teacher in the dreamseller. I didn't understand how he managed to love those two degenerates.

Seeing that the audience was still tense, Barnabas took a chocolate bar from his pocket, bit into it, and started in on a story of his own.

'I used to come to this cemetery drunk and depressed for a little self-therapy. Since the living seldom spoke to me because they thought I was drunk or crazy, and the ones who did speak to me insulted me or offered me fortune cookie advice, I'd come here to talk to the dead. Here, I could cry about my mistakes. Here, I could allow myself to be frustrated, a man who wanted to start all over, but I always failed. Here, I confessed that I felt like human refuse. Here, I asked God's forgiveness for everything: For my many drunken binges. For the 'one for the road' that left me sleeping in the park. For abandoning my family. I never had a dead person complain about my foolishness.'

The businessmen were moved by Barnabas's sincerity and his willingness to share his feelings, characteristics rarely seen in their circles. They desperately needed to open up but wouldn't dare show weakness. They couldn't be human.

Hearing Barnabas confess his woes, Bartholomew took the stage again. He embraced the other man and tried to console him as only Bartholomew could.

'Don't cry, Mayor. My problems are bigger than yours. I'm immoral.'

'No, mine are worse. I'm a pervert,' Barnabas stated in a louder voice.

'No, my mistakes are too many to count. I'm a scoundrel,' Bartholomew said in a still louder tone.

'No, no, you don't really know me. I'm completely depraved . . . '

Amazingly, they started arguing about

which one was worse. The businessmen had never seen anything like it. They only ever saw people bragging about who was better. We wanted to break it up, but we were afraid of making a bigger scene. And to show he really was the worst of them, Bartholomew lost his patience and said:

'I'm corrupt, dishonest, a liar, I don't keep my word, I don't pay my bills, I covet my neighbor's wife. I've even stolen your wallet when you were drunk . . . '

'OK, stop, stop, stop!' Barnabas said. 'You're right. You are the biggest good-for-nothing on the face of the earth.'

'OK, wait. Now, you're exaggerating, Barnabas!' Bartholomew said, now trying to defend himself.

Watching this madness, I looked up at the stars and said softly, 'God, take pity on these idiots. Please, shut them up.' But the businessmen loved watching them. If anything, they wished they could express themselves so honestly and openly as those two. They had worked beside their colleagues for years — or decades — but their spirits were sealed as tightly as the tombs that surrounded them in that cemetery. In the professional world they lived outside the cocoon; in their private lives, they hid inside. They didn't know how to be a shoulder to cry on. Instead, they disguised their feelings.

'Thank you, you two,' the dreamseller said to my surprise. 'You've made me recall my own imperfections.'

'You can count on me, chief,' said Honeymouth, shooting me a look. 'See that, Superego? You could learn a thing or two from me.'

Then the dreamseller began another story. Many species, he stated, had physical and instinctual advantages over humans. They saw farther, ran faster, leaped further, heard better, could smell aromas a mile away and bite down with incredible force. But we had something they didn't: a sophisticated brain with more than a hundred billion cells with which to think. Such a sophisticated brain should grant independence, he offered. Nevertheless, he asked his listeners:

'So why do our brains make us dependent on others, especially as infants? Rarely can a four-year-old child survive on his own, while other mammals and lizards the same age no longer have any contact with their parents. Some creatures are already in their full reproductive phase, and others are already elderly at the age of four. Why are we more dependent than the other species, despite loving independence?' he asked.

No one spoke up. They didn't know the

dreamseller was leading them into his marketplace of ideas, the warehouse where he kept his dreams.

An elderly businessman, at least seventy and apparently one of the richest in the audience, took me aside and said in a low voice, 'I know that man. Where does he live?'

'You wouldn't believe me if I told you,' I said, adding, 'I think you must be mistaken.'

'No, I know that extraordinary mind from somewhere,' he insisted.

Meanwhile, another businessman of about fifty, who had gone bankrupt three times but always made socially responsible investments, answered the dreamseller's question with a single word: 'Education.'

'Magnificent. Education is the key!' the dreamseller said. 'Our brain made us totally dependent on gathering the experience accumulated over generations of humans, from our parents to grandparents. The only way to get these experiences is through education. They're not genetically transmissible. Education is irreplaceable.'

Then he shook the participants by showing them how deeply their minds were being exploited — and how they could be passing on that mental exploitation to their children.

He explained that parents too often pressured their children to compete, to study incessantly, to take courses, to prepare themselves to survive in the future, without realizing that excessive pressure annihilates the creativity of childhood. It weakens existential values, closes them to new experiences, destroys their humanity.

'Do your children know about the failures in your lives?' he asked. 'Do they know how you overcame them? Do they know your fears and your worries? Do they know how courageous you've been? Have they explored your most important ideals? Do they know your philosophy on life, about your ability to reason, to analyze, to reflect? And have they seen your tears? Forgive me, but if they don't know any of this, then you're simply building machines to be used by the system. If they don't know these things, they're missing out on their humanity. And you're ignoring the very reason our brains made us dependent.'

Then he said something that really unsettled the crowd.

'For just thirty seconds,' he said, 'put yourself in your children's place and think about the epitaphs they would write for the entrance to your tomb.'

The suggestion alone sent many people into a nervous breakdown.

I would hate to know what my son would write about me. He doesn't know me. I always hid from him. 'How can someone living at the edge of society carry around this knowledge? What motivates him? What secrets is he hiding?' I thought.

Finally, the dreamseller took aim at his real target.

'The capitalist system brought about, and continues to bring about, unimaginable gains for society. But it runs a serious risk of imploding in less than a century. Maybe in just a few decades. But it won't happen the way socialists imagine, through class warfare. There is a problem that lies at its core: It produces freedom of expression and possession, but not freedom of simply being. Capitalism depends on our wants, not on our needs. It depends on chronic dissatisfaction as its engine for consumption. If at some point in time humanity were composed only of poets, philosophers, artists, educators and spiritual leaders, the world's gross domestic product would collapse, because, in general, these people are more satisfied with just what is necessary. The GDP might suddenly drop thirty or forty percent. Worldwide, hundreds of millions would be unemployed. It would be the greatest depression in history. There would be wars and endless conflicts.'

These arguments left some in the audience with jaws agape. The businessmen hadn't thought of that. But then, he started to sell the dream of relaxation.

'Getting back to the symptoms I asked you about, I'm going to ask one more question, and if you answer collectively I'll invite you to open a psychiatric hospital.'

The audience actually laughed.

'Who among you is forgetful? Who has memory lapses?'

Almost everyone raised his hand. They would forget commitments, everyday information, telephone numbers, where they had put items, people's names.

'Some people are so forgetful that they put their car keys in the refrigerator and look for them all over the house,' he said casually. People laughed. And he went on: 'Even funnier are the ones who look for their glasses without realizing they're wearing them. Others forget the names of colleagues they've worked with for years. The cleverest would ask, 'Say, what's your *full* given name?' when in reality they didn't even remember their first name.'

Some of the businessmen chuckled because they had used that tactic. I suspect that even the dreamseller had used it.

'Ladies and gentlemen, for those everyday memory lapses, don't go to a doctor. Why not, you ask?' he asked.

'Because he's forgetful himself!' yelled out an older man wearing a blue suit and striped gray tie.

They shook their heads at their own stressful lives. They were beginning to understand that the memory lapses, in most cases, were a desperate attempt by the brain to reduce the avalanche of worries.

Bartholomew had raised both hands, indicating that he was super forgetful.

'Chief, how come I always used to forget the names of my mothers-in-law?'

Sometimes we couldn't stand him. Barnabas, who had known him for years, jabbed back:

'Bartholomew's been married three times and lived with seven other women. He hasn't had enough time to learn their names to begin with.'

Honeymouth looked at the audience and opened his hands, as if to say, 'I never said I was a saint.' As hard as he tried, for better or worse, he just couldn't be normal

'I didn't choose you because of your failures or your successes,' the dreamseller told him, 'but because of who you are, because of your heart.'

'I'm forgetful myself, Bartholomew,' the dreamseller continued. 'Some people tell me, 'Teacher, my memory's lousy.' And I tell them, 'Don't worry, mine's even worse.''

I was forgetful, too, but I never would allow my students the same courtesy. I was a tyrant when it came to correcting exams. I recalled Jonathan, a brilliant debater, who nevertheless couldn't put the information down on paper. The other professors and I consistently gave him failing grades. Eventually, he failed out. We had called him irresponsible, but he might have been a misunderstood genius. We were the voice of the system. We tossed potential thinkers in the trash bin of education without a trace of remorse. Only now, after I learned to buy dreams of a free mind, did I realize I should have been evaluating my students' minds. And that might have meant giving the highest grades to someone who gets all the answers wrong.

I felt helpless and heartbroken at seeing all my shortcomings laid bare. I had been unforgiving even with my son. John Marcus suffered from mild dyslexia and couldn't keep up with his classmates. But I kept the pressure on, asking for more than he could give. If I'm being honest with myself, I wanted him to be an outstanding student in order to enhance my image as father and professor. Any message my son or my students would leave at my tomb wouldn't be one of praises and longing.

Jurema seemed to understand what I was thinking. She touched my shoulder and said quietly:

'Alexander Graham Bell said that if we tread the path that others have taken, at best we'll arrive at the places they've already been. If we don't sell new ideas so that students take new paths, they may end up right where these businessmen and -women are today, with ravaged health and broken dreams.'

One by one, the businessmen left, carefully observing the mausoleums they passed. Some of them remembered that from the sixteenth to the nineteenth century an inhuman system had bought and sold black-skinned human beings as if they were animals, locked them in the holds of boats and shipped them off to a terrifying future. Left behind were their friends, their children, their spouses, their freedom.

Today, the system had created a new, erudite slave. It paid them high salaries and gave them health benefits. Their future promised an endless crush of stress, anxiety, dog-eat-dog competition and forced mental labor. Left behind were their children, their spouses, their friends, their dreams. As the dreamseller said, history loves to repeat itself.

A House Divided

The dreamseller's latest conferences, especially the one at Recoleta Cemetery, were all over the media. People noted that even the giants of industry had been seduced by this enigmatic wanderer. The same questions that kept me up nights flooded their minds.

Some said he was the greatest imposter of our time. Others said he was a thinker far ahead of his time. Some argued that he was destroying peace in our society, while others said he was its most ardent defender. Some called him an atheist. Others, a vessel of unfathomable spirituality. Some believed he came from another planet, while others said he was the most human of us all. Maybe it was a mix of all of those things — or none of them at all. Discussing the dreamseller's identity was the topic du jour in bars, restaurants, coffee shops and even in schools. And the discussions were heated.

The more his fame grew, the more difficult his mission became. He neither gave interviews nor announced the following day's schedule. Even so he was in the news every time he spoke. When we got angry at the coverage that distorted his ideas, he would calm us down by saying, 'There is no free society without a free press. The press makes mistakes, but silence the press and society will plunge into an endless night without light. It will have a mind without voice.'

He couldn't go anywhere without being photographed. The dreamseller didn't appreciate being a celebrity and he was considering moving to another city or country. He thought of selling dreams in the Middle East, Asia, anyplace where people would see him as a mere mortal.

It was no longer possible to hold discussions in small venues. He was a magnet for crowds. Often hundreds would gather spontaneously to hear him speak. He would have to raise his voice, and even so, those farthest away in the crowd couldn't make out his words. His teaching was passed by word of mouth. He didn't like holding discussions in closed amphitheaters or using multimedia, preferring to speak outdoors. He liked that anyone who didn't agree with his ideas could freely and easily leave.

Companies wanted to sponsor him just to associate their image with his. They wanted their marketing to show they, too, were bold, innovative, unpredictable. The very idea of it sent shivers down the dreamseller's spine.

After his refusing countless gifts and offers of money for the use of his image, something unusual happened. Several well-dressed representatives of the powerful Megasoft Group approached us individually, without the dreamseller present, to make what they thought was a lucrative offer.

They first contacted Solomon and Dimas and me. They started out praising the dreamseller's social work effusively. Society had become more unified, kinder and more human since he had come onto the scene, they told us.

'We know that humility guides his life, that he hates fame, but we want to surprise him with an homage to all that he's done for society,' they said. 'This tribute won't be about giving him any kind of prize or money — we know he would never accept material goods. But we'd like to show our appreciation by offering to let him use the city's largest covered stadium, which our group owns, so he could address more than fifty thousand people all at once. His sermon would be televised, and later re-broadcast as a special prime-time event, to the entire country. Millions would get to hear his message.'

We were excited but suspicious about the offer. Still, the leaders of the business group seemed to have the purest of intentions. To seduce us further, they told us:

'Please don't deny us or society this privilege. Everyone wants and needs to hear the dreamseller's wisdom. His words could help save countless anguished people thinking of suicide, using drugs, wracked by their own demons. We insist on honoring him and giving the people of this country this gift. The only thing we ask is that it be a surprise.'

The entire group decided we should talk over this delicate matter. After reflecting on the proposal and analyzing the benefit to society, we felt it could be a good thing. After all, millions could be reached. Honeymouth and Barnabas were quite excited about that. Jurema was the only one who wasn't sold on the idea, she of all people, who still owned Megasoft shares. But she finally gave in.

We had to set up a secret plan to get the dreamseller to the stadium at the appointed date and time. That day, as we walked closer to the stadium, we could see traffic snarled in all directions and hundreds of people pouring through the main gates. When we came to a private entrance to the stadium, the dreamseller found it all strange and asked, 'Why do we have to come to this place?' And he seemed nervous.

Since we couldn't say anything about the tribute, we asked him to trust us and go along with our request. We told him we were going to a show, but when he continued asking questions, we backed him into a corner.

'Throughout all our time together, you've asked countless things of us and we've always obliged. Just this once, can't you go along with what we're asking?'

We knew it was a kind of blackmail, especially since the dreamseller had always listened to us and supported us. Still, he followed us without saying another word.

When we were about to enter the VIP room, he asked apprehensively, 'Who set up the event?'

'Some people who really care about you. Wait and see,' we said, without offering anything further.

The Megasoft executives were in a separate room, preparing the event. We found ourselves in a green room with a lavish buffet of fruits, cold cuts and juices. But the dreamseller didn't eat anything. He seemed to turn inward to reflect. The rest of us ate ravenously.

Barnabas stuffed a handful of seedless grapes in his mouth and muttered almost incomprehensibly, 'These guys are the best!'

Bartholomew, with three slices of salami and two of ham in his mouth, babbled, 'I'm starting to like those businessmen,' then immediately started humming to cover up what he'd said. We tried in vain to shush them.

The dreamseller sensed something in the air. He fidgeted and looked to the sides, uneasy, as if wishing he could go off alone and meditate. A long twenty minutes passed. When the time for the conference finally arrived, three glamorously dressed young women led us to the stage. The dreamseller trudged unusually slowly down the corridors. He seemed out of sorts.

Before directing us to our seats, the organizers of the event, wearing perfectly tailored suits, came to greet us. They greeted the dreamseller last.

They were five executives and the last one appeared to be the leader, maybe the CEO of one of the firms in the group. He shook the dreamseller's hand and, in a joking tone, said, 'Welcome to the stadium. And thank you for your delirious ideas. Great men have great dreams.'

The dreamseller, who was always in a good mood, usually never cared if someone called his dreams a delirium. But he just aimed a penetrating stare deep into the executive's eyes. The man was immediately flustered.

Until that moment, the dreamseller might have believed we would be attending a show.

The organizers took their seats to the right of the stage, and we sat on the left.

High on the stage was a huge screen, twenty-six feet tall and fifty-five feet wide. Other screens were scattered around the stadium. The master of ceremonies for the event appeared onstage, wearing a dark suit. He didn't mention the names of the executives or the sponsor. He did everything simply, as he should. In a resonant voice, he began to introduce the dreamseller. The immense crowd fell silent.

'Ladies and gentlemen, it is our great pleasure to present to you the most complex and innovative person to appear in our society in recent decades. A man with no marketing team, money or credit cards, and without revealing his origin or academic background, has spread his sensitivity and altruism throughout society. He has achieved a prestige that many have not. He has achieved a fame that is the envy of celebrities. He is truly a social phenomenon!'

At that moment, echoing his words, the crowd interrupted the presentation to applaud the dreamseller. We looked at the dreamseller and could see he wasn't happy. He, who always felt at ease wherever he was, who had a superb ability to adapt to the most diverse settings, seemed uncomfortable with the praise. But there was no denying that he was a social phenomenon. We followed him because he was an exceptional person. The master of ceremonies continued:

'Children and adults alike follow him. Icons of society and the common man listen to him. This man leaves political liberals speechless and conservatives amazed. For months we've been intrigued. The media, the authorities and even the man on the street asks: Where did he come from? What were the most important chapters in his story? Why does he seek to rock the pillars of society? What is his objective? We don't know. He calls himself only a seller of dreams, a merchant of ideas in a society that has ceased to dream.'

After defining the indefinable man that we followed, he called the dreamseller to the stage with a wink and a smile, and a joke that put the audience at ease. 'And now, I give you the seller of *nightmares*!'

It was then that the dreamseller realized this event had been staged in his honor. He rose awkwardly from his chair and headed for center stage. It was an emotional sight to see the crowd applauding him at length. We, his disciples, fell into step with them, and clapped wildly, emotionally. In turn, as he walked, I could see his lips moving, and he seemed to be telling himself, 'I don't deserve this ... I don't deserve this ... ' A microphone was quickly attached to his lapel while the applause continued.

It was a sight to behold. And a little unbelievable to know that a man in an old black coat with patched elbows and a wrinkled yellow shirt, an unshaven man with long unkempt hair who spoke in public yet craved anonymity, could be so loved. The applause died down and the audience awaited his words.

Onstage, he looked over at the event's organizers, but said nothing to them. Instead, he took a couple of unsteady steps and, staring out at the crowd, began with these words:

'Many kneel before kings because of their power. Or before millionaires because of their money. Or before celebrities because of their fame. But I humbly bow down to you, because I'm not worthy of your praise.'

The stadium crowd went crazy. People rose to their feet again and applauded. They had never seen an honoree solemnly honor the audience in attendance. He waited silently for the applause to die down before he continued. But as he was about to resume, the emcee interrupted.

'Ladies and gentlemen, before this mysterious and intelligent man graces us with his magnificent words, we would like to pay tribute to everything he has done for society,' he said.

We were confused. We thought the introduction had ended. The emcee looked at the dreamseller and asked him to kindly remain on center stage to watch an unusual film that had begun playing on the enormous stadium screen. At the same time, they cut off his microphone.

When the film began, we were expecting scenes of the countryside, flowers, valleys and mountains as tribute to the dreamseller. But the film didn't show springtime, rather the rigors of winter. And not a physical winter, but rather a harsh winter of the mind.

The film opened with the camera lens stepping through the main entrance of a large and rundown hospital. We could read that it was a mental institution, one of the few left in the region. The outer brown walls were peeling and cracks throughout the ancient structure formed odd horizontal fissures. The building was three stories high, a rectangular prison unlike the human mind, which revels in free forms and defies predictability. Instead, the building forebode claustrophobia and sadness.

The camera dove into the hospital and panned to different mental patients, some talking to themselves, others with trembling hands, some staring vacantly from the effects of drugs. The camera continued down hallways and revealed other patients sitting on uncomfortable benches with their gazes fixed on infinity or with their heads between their legs.

That the movie had no audio track and was deathly silent only added to the cold feel. We found it all extremely strange. The camera seemed to be handheld, and we figured whoever took this film must have been some kind of amateur. From time to time, the film cut to a live shot of the dreamseller's face. He looked worried, disconcerted. We couldn't imagine what was running through his mind, whether he was more confused than we were or whether he understood something about this tribute that we failed to grasp. Maybe he was feeling the pain of the patients in that hospital. And maybe the film would later show him showering that dreary place with his dreams.

Suddenly sound burst from the film as if someone had released the mute button. The entire stadium jumped, as if watching a horror movie, and they were startled to hear someone screaming from inside a room, 'No! No! Get away from me!'

A desperate mental patient was moaning

on the other side of a closed door. The camera moved in as the door opened slowly. A patient rocked back and forth on a bed, covering his face with his hands and tearfully calling out, 'Leave me alone! Get out of my life!'

The patient was wracked with uncontrollable anxiety, trying to flee from the monsters haunting his mind. He continued covering his face with his hands and rocking back and forth, like an autistic child. He was wearing a rumpled white shirt with its buttons in the wrong holes and his hair was disheveled.

The person filming him asked, 'What's making you depressed?'

The sound was muffled, but possible to make out:

'I'm scared! I'm scared! Help me! My children are going to die! Help me get them out of this place!' he moaned, panting, overwhelmed by unfathomable panic.

The one filming him repeated the question. 'I'm here to help you. Calm down. Why are you so worried?'

Shaken, he replied, 'I'm inside a house that's collapsing, a house that's fighting against itself.' Then the hallucinating patient spoke to the entities only he could see and hear. 'No, no don't destroy yourself! I'll be buried alive! You're suffocating me!'

The people in the stadium fell into a suffocating silence. We, too, felt our throats tighten. The patient said that the house itself was beginning to fight ferociously against itself. We were confused by the film. No one understood anything. We had never heard of a house battling itself. It was the height of insanity. We couldn't understand why the filmmaker would record this patient's mental breakdown. Maybe the dreamseller would come along and rescue him later in the film?

'Tell me what you see,' the cameraman asked.

Still covering his face, the patient's voice trembled:

'The roof is screaming, '*I'm* the most important part of this house! *I* protect it. I and *I alone* can withstand the sun and the storms . . . ''

The filmmaker wanted to know more about the hallucinations.

'Tell me more. The more you let out, the better you'll feel,' the cameraman said.

The patient began to shake and writhe in fear.

'The paintings! The paintings on the wall are shouting back!' he roared. 'They complain and complain and won't stop!'

'What do they say?'

'*We're* the most important things in this

318

house! *We're* the most expensive, the most precious thing you have! Everyone who comes through the door admires us!' the patient said. He broke out in a cold sweat and begged for the voices to stop yelling.

'Get out of my head! Leave me alone!'

At that moment, I remembered myself on top of the San Pablo Building. As much as I might have been suffering, I hadn't lost my mind; I hadn't been seized by hallucinations; I hadn't felt like a man trapped inside a dungeon his mind had created. I, who had been ready to kill myself, couldn't imagine the pain and suffering of this young man, who had fallen into the darkness of madness. His suffering sent shivers through the audience.

Monica, who had experienced the valleys of emotional misery in her own life, said, in a frightened, almost inaudible voice, 'What could make the human mind collapse like this, to make it reach the depths of despair?'

The suffering shown on the screen was so great and so captured our attention that some of us forgot why we were there. The dreamseller remained on center stage, his back to us, his gaze fixed on the screen. I couldn't imagine what he was feeling. He must have been sharing the same sadness we all were.

The patient turned his face into the corner and said, 'No one understands me! All they do is give me drugs!' He continued talking about his hallucinations. The furniture, he said, wanted to cannibalize other parts of the house. He shouted: 'The furniture wants to swallow the paintings. It's yelling at them! It's saying, 'We're the most important parts of this house! We give comfort and add beauty!''

I looked over at the executives of the Megasoft Group and saw them smiling. I thought to myself: 'How can they smile in the face of such pain? Maybe they know the movie has a happy ending. I mean, otherwise, they're psychopaths . . . '

The macabre film continued as the young patient wrestled with other parts of the house fighting all around him. Now, an imposing, domineering voice was shaking the patient's crumbling home. The cameraman, interested in capturing the smallest details of his mental break, asked again, 'Who is it that's upsetting you?'

The patient turned his back to the camera, removed his hands from his face, and placed them against the wall. His lungs fought desperately for air. The rise and fall of his shirt betrayed his panting. The cameraman persisted, without softening his tone: 'Talk to the monsters inside you! I'm offering you the chance to exorcize your demons.'

The patient fell back into his initial terror.

'I'm afraid! I'm afraid!' he screamed. 'Now it's the safe! The safe is threatening to destroy everything. It's threatening to devour the entire structure. It roars like thunder. '*I'm* the one who pays for everything. I'm the one that bought all of you. I brought you into existence. Bow down before me! *I* am the god of this house!''

The patient panted like an asthmatic. I thought at any moment he would have a heart attack. I had never seen anyone so weakened, someone so much in need.

At that moment, trying desperately to escape his prison, the patient turned his face to the camera and screamed hopelessly, 'We're going to be buried alive! I'm scared! So scared! Help, please! Everything's tumbling down!'

The camera zoomed in on the young patient's uncovered face for the first time. His panicked expression filled the gigantic stadium screen. And when we saw his face, it wasn't his house that we saw come tumbling down; it was our whole world. The floor seemed to shake beneath us, our bodies trembled. Our voices caught in our throats. We were paralyzed in our seats. The scene was unbelievable, surreal. The patient in the film was . . . the dreamseller.

Outside, I was frozen. But inside, my mind was a storm. My inner voice screamed, 'This isn't possible! We've been following a mental patient, a maniac? This can't be!' The sociological experiment shattered into a million little pieces. We'd been fooled. Our revolutionary leader showed his damaged, fragile form. I couldn't tell whether I felt rage for letting myself follow this man, or compassion for the misery he had suffered. I didn't know whether to feel sad or ashamed.

The audience was astounded. Like me, they couldn't bring themselves to believe that the person on stage was the same one in the movie. But the resemblance was unmistakable, despite our dreamseller's longer beard. My friends grabbed each other's arms, trying to shake themselves awake from a dream they wished they had never dreamed.

The event's emcee, so as to leave no lingering doubts, had them turn the dreamseller's microphone back on and asked him, as if he were facing an Inquisition, 'Sir, can you confirm that the man in the film is you?'

The audience of tens of thousands fell into a deafening silence. We were hoping against all hope that he would say no. That there was some mistake, that it was a lookalike or maybe a twin brother. But, true to his conscience, he turned to the crowd, fixed his gaze on his group of friends with tears in his eyes and said unequivocally, 'Yes, it's me. That man from that movie is me.'

Immediately, his microphone was cut off again. But the dreamseller didn't try to defend himself.

'A *mental* patient,' the announcer scoffed, shaking his head.

'Ladies and gentlemen,' he said, turning to the television cameras and now speaking in a high and mighty tone. 'We have finally discovered the true identity of the man who plunged this great city into disarray. This is the man who captured the imaginations of millions. Indeed, he is truly a great social phenomenon.'

Sweeping his hand toward the lonely dreamseller at the center of the stage, he said, sarcastically, 'Behold: The greatest imposter of all time. Society's greatest con man. The greatest swindler, the greatest illusionist and the greatest heretic of the century. And to show our gratitude, we confer on him the title of the greatest seller of lunacy, of nightmares, of trash and falsehood and stupidity that this society has ever produced.'

A lightning storm of flashes erupted. A stunningly beautiful model walked up to him and handed him a diploma. The organizers had planned everything down to the tiniest, insulting detail.

Incredible as it seems, the dreamseller didn't refuse it. Instead, he graciously accepted the scroll. We, his disciples, were perplexed. The audience was frozen. No one in the stadium dared say a word.

The muscles of my face as well as my ability to reason were paralyzed. My mind was roiling with questions: Had all the ideas we'd heard, ideas that had so swept us away, come from the mind of a psychotic? How is that possible? What had I done to my life? Had I dived into a sea of dreams or of nightmares? Had I been saved from a physical suicide only to suffer an intellectual one?

Psychotic or Sage?

After revealing that the dreamseller was, in fact, the young, tormented psychiatric patient from the film, the event organizers turned to us smugly, as if to say that we had been the biggest fools of all. They seemed to want revenge. 'But for what?' I wondered. What was behind this ambush? Why destroy a man's image so publicly? Why so much hate for a seemingly harmless human being?

Only later did we find out that one of the dreamseller's speeches was to 'blame' for the plummeting stock price of the La Femme fashion giant, part of the Megasoft conglomerate. Prices fell immediately after the dreamseller recommended emphatically, in the 'temple of fashion,' that designer labels should carry a warning that beauty cannot be standardized, that every woman has her own particular beauty, and that women should never identify with models who represented a genetic exception in the human race.

The real problem started when the CEO of the fashion giant — one of the organizers of the event — wrote an op-ed saying these were nothing more than the ramblings of a lunatic.

And if attacking a humble man weren't enough, he finished his thought with a quote that showed the depth of the Barbie syndrome: 'With apologies to all the ugly girls, beauty is important.' The statement had circled the globe, not only in newspapers but also on the Internet, generating heated debates in the media and producing a chain reaction of repudiation on the firm. Thousands had sent messages to the countless La Femme stores around the world opposing its philosophy. The company's stock fell by thirty percent in two months, a loss of more than a billion and a half dollars. It was catastrophic for the company.

Revenge, which exists only in the human species, reared its ugly head. Unmasking the man who had caused all the damage became a question of honor for the leaders of the company, a matter of survival. They wanted to publicly unmask the dreamseller to discredit his ideas and regain their credibility.

We didn't know where to hide in the stadium. We'd lost our courage, our adulation and our enthusiasm. I who had learned to love the dreamseller now couldn't find the energy to defend him. Now I understood the pain in John Lennon's famous phrase after the Beatles broke up: *The dream is over*.

'Our movement is dead,' I thought, and

figured the rest of the group felt the same way. But I was surprised by Monica and Jurema's defiant attitude.

'It doesn't matter if the dreamseller was or is psychotic,' they said. 'We were with him through the applauses and we'll be with him through the jeers.'

'Were women stronger than the men?' I wondered. I don't know, but I do know that they displayed an irrational idealism. Then, two of the men stood up in solidarity,

'If the chief's crazy, then I'm crazy, too!' Bartholomew yelled out.

Not to be outdone, Barnabas stood up emphatically.

'I don't know if he's crazy, but I do know he made me feel like a person again. And I won't abandon him now. You know what? *I'm* crazier than the dreamseller,' he said, then added, 'But not as crazy as you, Honeymouth.'

'Thank you, my friend,' Bartholomew replied, feeling flattered.

The dreamseller turned to leave and headed for the exit when the crowd started buzzing. We thought they might rush the stage to lynch him, and then, suddenly, they broke out in a chant that soon filled the stadium.

'Speak . . . Speak . . . Speak . . . '

The chant reverberated throughout the stadium until the entire building shook with nervous energy. The executives looked worried. The last thing they wanted was to start a riot that would give them more bad front-page press. So they turned his microphone back on and gestured for him to return to the stage and speak. Doubtless, they figured the dreamseller would crush what was left of his image by trying to worm his way out with superficial explanations and accusations. But clearly, they didn't know the depth of this man they were so eager to discredit.

He looked out at the audience, and then at us, his disciples. He gently raised his voice and, without fear of repercussions, he dissected his own history the way a microsurgeon does with the tiniest of blood vessels.

Softly, he told us his story, the most dramatic one I'd ever heard. Except that this time it was no parable; it was his true story, raw and uncensored. For the first time, the man I had followed exposed the very depths of his being. And I realized that I hadn't known him fully, either.

'Yes, I was mentally ill, or maybe I still am. I'll leave that for the psychiatrists and psychologists, and all of you, to judge. I was committed to an institution because I was suffering from a deep and severe depression accompanied by mental confusion and hallucinations. My depression was fed by a crippling feeling of guilt. Guilt over the indescribable mistakes I'd made with people I loved the most.'

He paused for breath. He seemed to be trying to rebuild his dismembered being, to organize his thoughts in order to tell his shattered story. 'What mistakes did the dreamseller make that unbalanced him?' I wondered. 'Wasn't he strong and generous? Didn't he demonstrate the height of camaraderie and tolerance?' To our surprise, he declared:

'I was a rich man, very rich, and powerful, too. I was more successful than anyone else of my generation. Young and old alike came to seek my advice. Every venture I touched turned to gold. They called me Midas. I was creative, bold, intuitive — a visionary, unafraid of uncharted territory. My ability to absorb a failure and come back stronger astounded everyone around me. But gradually the success I always thought I controlled came to control me, to poison me, to invade the intimate reaches of my mind. Without realizing it, I lost my humility and became a god — a false god.'

We were stunned by his words. I wondered,

'Could he really have been rich? What kind of power did he have? Or is he hallucinating again? Didn't he walk around in tattered clothes? Didn't we depend on the kindness of others just to survive?'

At hearing the dreamseller's admission, Bartholomew became emboldened.

'Aha, *that's* my chief! I knew it! I knew he was a millionaire,' Bartholomew said. Then, scratching his head, asked, 'Wait, then why were we always so broke?'

There was no good explanation. 'Maybe, like so many businessmen, he went bankrupt,' I thought. 'But could financial ruin trigger such a serious mental illness? Could it break someone's sanity and plunge him into the realm of madness?' My thoughts were interrupted when he continued his account.

'My only goal was to stand out, to compete, to be number one, as long as it meant playing by the rules,' the dreamseller confessed. 'I didn't want to be just another face in the crowd. I wanted to be unique. And so, I became a machine, tirelessly dedicated to success and making money. The problem doesn't start when we possess money, however much we have. It starts when the money possesses us. When I realized this had happened to me, I saw that money could, in fact, impoverish a man. And I became the poorest of men.'

I was flabbergasted at seeing this man, who had supposedly been so rich and powerful, remove his mask and become an unflinching critic of himself. I tried and failed to think of any leader in history who had ever spoken so courageously. I looked at myself and realized that I, too, lacked such bravery. His bold words began to invigorate me. My admiration for this man was being rekindled. Then, he told the story of how he, his wife and their two children were scheduled to go on an ecotourism vacation with friends to see one of the planet's few remaining great rain forests.

But, for him, time was a scarce commodity, he said. So he planned the trip months in advance. Everything was set, but at the last minute, he was asked to participate in a video conference with some of the company's investors. Vast sums of money were involved. His family and friends postponed the trip by a day to wait for him. The next day, he had to quickly resolve a business matter that had been dragging for months: He had to sign off on the purchase of another large company or lose it to his competitors. Hundreds of millions of dollars were at stake. The trip was postponed again. On the day they were finally set to travel, the board of directors of his petroleum firm presented him with a new problem. More make-or-break decisions had to be made.

'So as not to put off the trip again, I apologized to my wife, my children and our friends and told them to go on without me. I would charter a flight later and meet them there,' he said, his voice beginning to crack. 'My wife didn't like the idea. My seven-year-old daughter, Julieta, was sad, but she kissed me and said, 'You're the best daddy in the world.' Fernando, my loving nine-year-old son, also kissed me and said, 'You're the best father in the world — but the busiest, too.' I answered, 'Thank you, children, but someday Daddy will have more time for the greatest kids in the world.''

The dreamseller heaved a deep and heavy sigh. 'But that time would never come . . . ' He paused and started to cry. In a choked voice, overcome with emotion, he told the audience:

'While I was in the middle of a meeting, hours after they had taken off, my secretary rushed in to say there had been a plane crash. My heart started to pound. I turned on the news and heard that an airliner had crashed into a dense tropical rain forest . . . and there did not appear to be any survivors. It was the flight they were on. I collapsed to the ground and cried inconsolably. I had lost everything. There was no air to breathe, no ground to walk on, no reason to live. Between tears and pain, I put together a rescue mission, but we never found my wife and children's bodies; the plane had burned to a cinder. I couldn't even say good-bye to the most important people in my life, to look into their eyes or touch their skin. It was as if they'd never existed.'

Overnight, the man so many had envied became the object of pity, the indestructible man became the most fragile of beings. And to add to his indescribable pain, he was tortured by guilt.

'The psychologists who treated me wanted to ease my guilt. They tried to tell me I wasn't responsible for the loss. But I knew, indirectly, I was. They tried to protect me instead of making me face the monster of my guilt. But they couldn't ease my desire to punish myself. They were good doctors, good men, but I resisted and closed myself up in my own world.'

Still reading out from the chapters of his past life for the audience, he began asking himself aloud:

'What did I build? Why didn't I prioritize what I loved the most? Why did I never have the courage to cut back on my schedule?

When is it time to slow down? What is so important that it is more important than life itself? If you lose that, what does it matter if you have all the money in the world?'

What an unbearable burden. What colossal pain. As I listened to him, I began to understand that all of us, however successful, we all miss out on something. The warm sun sets on us all, no one sails forever on tranquil seas. Some lose more, others less; some suffer avoidable losses, others unavoidable. Some lose in the social arena, others in the theater of the mind. And if someone manages to get through life untouched, there is still something he loses: youth. I was a man of losses and I continued to be an expert in losses. But suddenly, recalling the last few months we had been together, I was startled. This man has lost everything in front of the entire world. How did he manage to dance? Why was he the happiest of wanderers? Why did he manage to always put us in a good mood? How did he manage to be so tolerant when life had been so unfair to him? How could he lead such a gentle life after having been the victim of such a brutal tragedy?

As I was pondering these questions, I glanced at the organizers of the event and saw they were visibly shaken; it seems they didn't know the true identity of the man they had mocked. I looked out at the crowd and saw people crying. They might have felt compassion for the dreamseller or, perhaps, some were recalling losses in their own lives. At that point Jurema squeezed my hands and told me something that surprised me even more.

'I know that story. It's *him*!' she said.

'Him, who? What are you saying, professor?' I asked, even more confused.

'It's him! The sergeants have laid an ambush for their own general. How is it possible?' Jurema was so worked up that she wasn't making any sense.

'I don't understand. Who is the dreamseller?' I asked again.

She stared at the leaders who had organized the event and said something that floored me.

'Incredible. He's standing on the very stage that belongs to him,' she said and could say nothing more.

My mind went into a tailspin, like a kite cut free of its string. Repeating her last sentence — 'He's standing on the very stage that belongs to him' — I began to understand what Jurema meant.

'I don't believe it! *He's* the owner of the powerful Megasoft Group? The sergeants laid a trap for their own general, thinking he was just a soldier. Could it be? But isn't he dead?

Or had he just gone into hiding? Then again, the dreamseller had severely criticized the leader of the Megasoft Group at dinner at Jurema's home. We must be dreaming!' I thought.

A film began to unreel in my mind. It struck me that the dreamseller had involved himself in many events linked to that corporation. He had rescued me at the San Pablo, a building belonging to the Megasoft Group. And mysteriously, they almost shot him at that same building. He had been beaten at the temple of computing, apparently at the behest of an executive of that same group, and had kept silent. A reporter from a newspaper owned by that group had slandered him, and he had said nothing. Now he was humiliated by leaders of the same corporation and hadn't rebelled. What was going on? What did it all mean?

I took a deep breath, trying to bring order to my whirlwind of ideas. I brought my hands to my face and told myself, 'This can't be true! Or is it? No, it can't be! We're experts at making up facts when we're under stress.' I took Jurema's arm and asked:

'How can one of the most powerful men on the planet sleep under bridges? How can a billionaire eat other people's leftovers? It makes no sense!' The professor shook her head; she was as upset and confused as I was.

Just then, the dreamseller seemed to be answering the questions on all our minds. He said his losses had been so great, his suffering so deep, that he began to lose all rational thought. He said he couldn't organize his ideas. He refused to eat and finally had to be committed to a psychiatric hospital. At the hospital, he began hallucinating just as we saw on the video. His brain seemed ready to implode.

In a firmer tone, he revisited the story that the organizers had used to destroy him publicly. He spoke of the second part, surely unknown to them.

'After the roof, the safe and other structures in that house fought against each other to claim supremacy, I heard another area of the house making itself known. But this time it was a soft, gentle, humble voice. It was a voice whispering beneath the ground, and it didn't terrify me.'

Looking out at the audience, the dreamseller stated:

'It was the voice of the foundation. Unlike all the other parts of that mansion, the foundation didn't want to be the greatest, the best, or the most important. It wanted merely to be recognized as part of the whole.'

337

I strained to understand what the mysterious man was trying to reveal, but it was difficult. But then it started to become clear.

'When I heard the voice of the foundation, all the other parts of the house condemned it vehemently. The safe was first. Bursting with pride, it said, 'You're an embarrassment to us. You're the dirtiest part of this house.' The conceited roof said, 'No one who has ever entered this house has even ever asked about you. You're completely unnoticed.' The beautiful paintings declared arrogantly, 'You're ridiculous to suggest you have any worth, at all. Just accept your lowly role.' The furniture was adamant: 'You're insignificant. Just look where you're located.' And so the foundation was rejected by all the other structures of the home. Humiliated, shunned and without any way to go on being part of that building, it decided to leave. And what do you think the result was?' he asked the crowd.

They all answered as one, even the children in the stadium: 'The house collapsed!'

'Yes, the house caved in. My house, which represents my personality, caved in because I dismissed my foundation. When it collapsed, I shouted at God: 'Who are you, and where were you when my world collapsed? Do you not intervene because you don't exist? Or do you exist and you simply just don't care about humanity?' I fought with the psychiatrists and psychologists. Fought with their theories and medications. I fought with life. I thought it so unjust to me, nothing more than a bottomless well of uncertainties. I fought with time. In short, I fought with everything and everyone. But when the foundation made itself heard, I was heartened, enlightened. And I understood that I had been profoundly wrong. More than anything else, I had fought with my own foundation. I had cast aside my values, my priorities.'

Hearing that explanation, we finally began to comprehend some of the secrets of this fascinating dreamseller.

He started to understand himself when he was able to interpret his hallucinations. The safe, he said, represented his financial power, which he had always valued. The roof was a metaphor for his intellectual capacity, which he had prized greatly for helping him overcome so many difficult tasks. The works of art represented his prestige and fame, and the furniture, all the luxuries and comforts in life.

'But I betrayed and neglected my foundation,' he said. 'I swept my love for my wife and children under the rug of my activities and mounting concerns. I gave them everything, but I forgot to give them the one fundamental thing that I had regarded only as trivial: myself. My friends were barely a consideration and my dreams were forgotten completely. How can one be a good father, a good husband and a good friend if the people we love are excluded from our agenda? Only a hypocrite could believe it, a noted hypocrite who so many held up as an example.'

He said bravely that he hid his mistakes, his shortcomings, his stupid attitudes, which represented the dirty part of his foundation, but which were also fundamental to the structure of his personality. Now I understand what he meant when he said that whoever fails to recognize his shortcomings has an outstanding debt to himself and to his humanity.

I began to further understand why this man had had such an effect on me. To get through to me, he had to be more than an ordinary man. He had to be more than a thinker, more than a brilliant mind, more than a teacher of uncommon sophistication. A man with those qualities might have attracted my admiration, but he wouldn't have captivated me as he did, wouldn't have broken down my prideful ego. The dream-seller had to be someone who had known the darkest valleys of fear, who had been mired in the morass of psychological and social conflict, who had been torn apart by predators of the mind and been lost in the mazes of madness. And, after surviving all of that, he remade himself with uncommon strength and written a new story based on his own experiences.

This, *this*, is the man I would follow.

His ideas were as incisive as a philosopher's, and his humor as vibrant as a clown's. His actions were a paradox, fluctuating between the extremes. He was sought out by icons of society, but he made no distinction between a prostitute and a puritan, an intellectual and a mental patient. His sensitivity overwhelmed us.

Whenever I saw someone on television being arrested by the police, he would hide his face in an effort to protect his image. The man standing on the stage in front of me wasn't hiding. I remember what he had said to the psychiatrist at the building where we met — that there were two kinds of insanity, and he had dared to say that his was the visible kind. Now, when his opponents had tried to ambush him inhumanely, he displayed his wounds in front of more than fifty thousand people, unashamed of his past. His honesty was crystal clear.

When I heard him confess that he had

betrayed his foundation, my mind was wracked by sociological concepts. Who isn't a traitor at some point? What puritan is not at some moment immoral to himself? What believer doesn't at some point betray God with his pride and his underlying desires? What idealist doesn't betray his beliefs in the name of hidden interests? What person doesn't betray his health in order to work a few extra hours? Who doesn't betray sleep by turning his bed into a place of tension? Who doesn't betray his children for his ambitions, arguing that he's working for them? Who doesn't betray his love for his spouse by failing to communicate in his marriage?

We betray science with our absolute truths, betray our students with our inability to listen to them, betray nature with development. As the dreamseller warned us, we betray humanity when we pick up a banner to call ourselves Jews, Palestinians, Americans, Europeans, Chinese, whites, blacks, Christians, Muslims. We are all traitors who desperately need to buy dreams. We all harbor a 'Judas' in our mind, a specialist in hiding our true feelings under the carpet of activism, ethics, morality, social justice.

It was as if he were reading my thoughts. He fixed his gaze on mine and then raised his eyes to the audience.

'My interpretation of that vision — regardless of whether some might call it a hallucination — made me realize that my mental illness started long before I'd lost my family.' He smiled and joked with the crowd. 'I warn you, ladies and gentlemen, you're dealing with someone who's been crazy for a while, now . . . '

The audience settled into smiles. The emotion of that scene is hard to describe.

'When I realized I'd betrayed my foundations, I had to find out who I really was. That's when I left the hospital and went off to find myself. It was a long road and I got lost many times on the way. But when I discovered myself, I left my nest and transformed into a delicate swallow, gliding down the streets and avenues, helping others who were also searching for themselves.' And he again demonstrated his sense of humor by saying, 'Careful, friends, this craziness is contagious.'

People smiled again and burst into applause, as if breathing in that contagion just as Bartholomew, Barnabas, Jurema and I — and so many others — had. I can still remember the day I was ready to give up on life and the dreamseller recited a poem that resonated with my own foundation. Even now, it echoes in my mind:

Let the day this man was born be
    struck from the record of time!
Let the dew from the grass of that
    morning evaporate!
Let the clear blue sky that brought joy
    to strollers that afternoon be with-
    held!
Let the night when this man was con-
    ceived be stolen by suffering!
Reclaim from that night the glowing
    stars that dotted the heavens!
Erase from his infancy all his smiles and
    his fears!
Strike from his childhood his frolicking
    and his adventures!
Steal from him his dreams and his
    nightmares, his sanity and his mad-
    ness!

This dreamseller's contagious ideas taught us
not to deny who we really are. His ideas were
an antidote; before meeting him, we had all
been 'normal,' and we had all been sick. We
wanted in some form or another to be gods,
not knowing that being a god means having
to be perfect, to worry about our image in
society, to give too much importance to the
opinions of others, to demand too much of
oneself, to punish oneself, to make constant
demands of ourselves. We had lost the joy, the

simplicity of being. We were brought up to work, to grow, to progress, and unfortunately also to betray our very essence in our short time in existence.

What kind of a madhouse are we living in?

If I Could Turn Back Time

Inspired after revealing and interpreting the story of the house, the dreamseller offered his final ideas. Once again he recited poetry in the desert, when his lips still thirsted. He looked out into emptiness, as if on another plane, and displayed an intimate relationship with a god I didn't know. Forgetting that he stood before the large stadium crowed, he called out:

'God, who are you? Why do you hide your face behind the curtain of time and why won't you help cure my foolishness? I lack wisdom, as you well know. With my feet I walk on the surface of the ground, but with my mind I walk on the surface of knowledge. I am too prideful if I think I know anything about this world. And even when I admit I know nothing, it's my pride that allows me to admit I know nothing.'

He lowered his eyes, glanced at the leaders who hated him, then at the audience, and delivered a philosophical speech that stealthily penetrated the depths of our being.

'Life is very, very long for making mistakes, but frighteningly short for living. And being

346

aware of that brevity erases my mind's vanity and makes me see that I'm simply a wanderer who is nothing more than a flicker in this existence, a flash that dissipates with the first rays of light. In that brief time between flickering and dissipating, I seek to find who I am. I've looked for myself in many places, but I found myself in a place without a name, in the place where jeers and applause are all the same, the place where no one can enter without our permission, not even ourselves.

'Oh, if I could only go back in time! I would achieve less power and have more power to achieve. I would drink a few doses of irresponsibility, position myself less as a problem-solving machine and give myself permission to relax, to think about the abstract, to reflect on the mysteries that surround me.

'If I could go back in time, I would find the friends of my youth. Where are they? Which of them are still alive? I would seek them and relive the uncomplicated experiences plucked from the garden of simplicity, where there were no weeds of status or the seduction of financial power.

'If I could go back, I would call the woman in my life, the love of my life, during breaks in meetings. I would try to be a more distracted professional and a more attentive lover. I would be more good-natured and less pragmatic, less logical and more romantic. I would write silly love poems. I would say 'I love you' more often. I would acknowledge freely, 'Forgive me for trading you for business meetings! Don't give up on me.'

'Oh, if only I could fly on the wings of time! I would kiss my children more, play with them more, enjoy their childhood the way dry soil absorbs water. I would go out into the rain with them, walk barefoot on the grass, climb trees. I would be less afraid that they would hurt themselves or catch cold and more afraid that they'd be contaminated by this society. I would try less to give them the world, and harder to give them *my* world.'

Beholding the magnificent stadium, its intricate columns, its expansive roof, its plush seating, he continued, intensely touched:

'If I could go back in time, I would give every penny I had for one more day with them, and I would make that day an eternal moment. But they went away, and the only voices I hear are those that remain hidden in the ruins of my memory: 'Daddy, you're the best father in the world — but the busiest, too.''

Tears streamed down his face, proving that great men cry, too. And he concluded with these words:

'The past is a tyrant and it won't allow my family to come back to me. But the present generously lifts my downcast face and makes me see that, although I can't change what I was, I can construct what I will be. They can call me crazy, psychotic, a lunatic, it doesn't matter. What matters is that, like all mortals, one day I will end the theater of existence on the tiny stage of a tomb, in front of an audience in tears.'

This last thought reached the roots of my mind. Breathing heavily, he ended his speech:

'On that day, I don't want people to say, 'In that tomb rests a rich, famous and powerful man whose deeds are recorded in the annals of history.' Or, 'There lies an ethical and just man.' Because those words will merely sound like an obligation. But I hope they say, 'In that tomb rests a simple wanderer who understood a little of what it means to be human, who learned to love humanity and who succeeded in selling dreams to other travelers . . . ''

At that moment, he turned his back to the audience and left the stage without a good-bye. The crowd in the stadium broke their silence, rising to their feet and applauding him uninterruptedly. His disciples couldn't hold back and burst into tears. We, too, were learning to lose the fear of showing our emotions. His supposed enemies also rose. Two of them applauded. The CEO sat still, not knowing where to look.

Suddenly, a boy broke through security, climbed onto the stage, ran after the dreamseller and gave him a long, heartfelt embrace. It was Antonio, the twelve-year-old boy who had been in such despair at his father's wake, the wake the dreamseller had transformed into a solemn act of homage.

'I lost my father, but you taught me not to lose faith in life,' the boy told him. 'I'll always be grateful . . . '

Touched, the dreamseller looked at the young boy and surprised him by saying, 'I lost my children, but you also taught me not to lose faith in life. And for that, *I* will always be grateful to *you*.'

'Let me follow you,' the boy said.

'How long has school been in you?' the dreamseller asked.

'I'm in the sixth grade.'

'You didn't understand my question. I didn't ask what grade you're in, but how long school has been *in you*.'

I had made teaching my life, my world, and even I had never heard anyone phrase a question that way, much less to a young boy. The boy looked confused.

'I don't understand the question,' the boy said.

The dreamseller looked at him and sighed. 'Well, the day you understand it, you'll become a seller of dreams like me, and in your free time you can follow me.'

The boy walked away confused, but then suddenly, something dawned on him. The stadium camera caught him just as his expression changed. He radiated pure joy. Instead of returning to his seat, he came over to us. We all wanted to understand what had happened, but none of us understood at the time.

The dreamseller headed toward the door, without a destination or an agenda or a map, living each day unhurriedly, blowing like a feather in wind. This time he left without inviting us to follow him. And we felt a deep sadness.

Would we ever see each other again? Had the dream of selling dreams ended? What would we do? Where would we go? Would I write other stories? We didn't know. We only knew we were children playing in the theater of time, children who understood very little about the mysteries of existence.

Who is the dreamseller really? Where does he come from? Is he one of the most powerful men in the world or a pauper with an uncommon imagination? To this day, we still don't know. But it doesn't matter. What matters is that we broke out of the prison of routine, and we left the cocoon to become wanderers.

Bartholomew and Barnabas touched me on the shoulder. I don't know whether they had understood everything that happened in the stadium or nothing at all.

'Don't follow us. We're lost, too,' they joked.

We hugged each other warmly. I had learned to love my fellow man in a way not found in textbooks. Despite our uncertain futures, we looked at one another and said, 'Oh, how I love this life!'

The other members of the group joined in the embrace. We might have been saying good-bye forever.

Before taking his last step off the stage, the dreamseller turned and saw us. Our eyes met, slowly and intensely. The image filled our hearts with joy. Immediately, our dream was reborn.

We ran across the stage and followed him, knowing that unpredictable adventures lay ahead of us — as well as unexpected storms. We left the stadium, joyfully singing our anthem.

I'm just a wanderer
Who lost the fear of getting lost
I'm certain of my own imperfection
You may say I'm crazy
You may mock my ideas
It doesn't matter!
What matters is I'm a wanderer
Who sells dreams to passersby
I've no compass or appointment book
I have nothing, yet I have everything
I'm just a wanderer
In search of myself.

THE END
(of the first volume)

Acknowledgments

I have met countless sellers of dreams along the way. Through their intelligence and their generous acts they inspired me, taught me and made me see my own smallness. They paused in their journey on the paths of existence to think about others and give of themselves while asking nothing in return. They made of their dreams lifetime projects, and not desires that shatter in the heat of the tempest.

I dedicate this book to my dear Geraldo Pereira, the son of the great editor José Olympio. It has not been long since Geraldo closed his eyes forever. He was a poet of existence, a fine seller of dreams in the universe of literature, as well as in the theater of society. He was my friend and counselor. I offer him the most grateful homage.

I dedicate this book to my esteemed friend and reader Maria de Lourdes Abadia, ex-governor of Brasilia. She sold many dreams in the Brazilian capital, of which I cite, especially her dreams for the underprivileged who live in and from the city's garbage. She gave back to them something fundamental to mental health: dignity.

To my esteemed friend Guilherme Hannud, an entrepreneur endowed with a noble sensitivity and a thirst for helping others. Through his social projects, he gave employment opportunities to hundreds of former offenders so they would have the strength to extricate themselves from the morass of rejection and achieve, despite the scars of the past, the inalienable status of human beings.

To my dear friend Henrique Prata and the excellent team of doctors of Pio XII Hospital, among whom I cite especially Dr. Silas and Dr. Paulo Prata (in memoriam) and my friend Dr. Edmundo Mauad. As compulsive sellers of dreams, this team transformed the small Barretos Cancer Hospital into one of the largest and best in the Americas by offering free treatment of the highest level to poor patients who would never have been able to pay for it. They proved that dreams prolong life and alleviate pain.

To my dear reader Marina Silva, who in childhood was punished by the vicissitudes of existence, but whose dreams of changing the world fed her courage and intellect and made her a senator and later an extraordinary minister of environment. Marina passionately yearns to preserve nature for future generations. Through her, I would like to dedicate this work to all the scientists of the Intergovernmental Panel on Climate Change who tirelessly battle to illuminate the mind of political leaders so they will take urgent measures to ameliorate the disaster of the greenhouse effect. Unfortunately, many of those leaders lie down in the bed of egocentrism and resist 'buying' dreams.

To the beloved Catholic friends and leaders, of whom I cite as representatives the priests Jonas Abibe, Oscar Clemente and Salvador Renna. In them, love of one's fellow man and tolerance ceased to be theory and entered the pages of reality. With surpassing love, they have sown dreams of a society suffused with brotherhood and altruism. To the beloved Protestant friends and leaders, of whom I cite as representatives Marcelo Gualberto, Aguiar Valvassora and Márcio Valadão. The pleasure of giving of oneself found in them a fertile ground. Wherever they go, they have spread the perfume of love and greatness of soul. To my countless Buddhist, Muslim and spiritualist friends. They have enchanted me with their dreams. To my atheist and agnostic friends, I was part of that group and know that many of them are outstanding human beings, dear dreamers.

I dedicate this novel especially to society's greatest sellers of dreams, the educators. Even with low salaries, they insist on selling dreams in the microcosm of the classroom so that students may stretch the frontiers of their intellect and become agents of change in the world, at least in their world. I have numerous professor friends in all fields. To represent them, I cite Silas Barbosa Dias; Dr. José Fernando Macedo, president of the Medical Association of the state of Paraná, not only an excellent professor of vascular surgery but a seller of humanism in medicine; and Dr. Paulo Francischini. Dr. Francischini has used one of my programs to notable effect to guide thoughts and protect emotion in masters and doctoral courses in his discipline, with the aim of molding thinkers.

To Jesus Badenes, Laura Falcó and Francisco Sole, brilliant executives in the Planeta firm, one of the largest publishers in the world. They do more than publish books; they sell dreams to nurture creativity and the art of thinking in their readers. To dear friends César, Denis, Débora and all the other members of the Planeta Brasil team. They were so excited about *The Dreamseller* that they stimulated me to write the continuation of this work. I especially thank my friend and editor Pascoal Soto for his intelligence and serenity. His opinions were of extreme value to the present work.

To my inspiring father, Salomão, who from childhood I watched selling dreams by taking needy sick people to hospitals for the simple pleasure of helping. He was always an excellent storyteller and an exceptional human being. To my cultured father-in-law, Georges Farhate. As incredible as it seems, among the dreams he sold, he taught us that it is worthwhile to believe in life when, at the age of ninety, he again ran for public office, while many young people of twenty or thirty feel old and alienated. To dear Dirce and Áurea Cabrera for their affection for my works.

To my beloved wife, Suleima, and my daughters Camila, Carolina and Claudia. They fascinate me with their astuteness, intelligence and generosity. I hope they will never come to love the worship of celebrity, that they will live the art of authenticity and understand that the most beautiful dreams are born in the terrain of humility and grow in the soil of nonconformity. I yearn for them not only to be in school, but for school to be in them, and for them to become dream-sellers until the last breath of life.

To my beloved patients. I not only taught them but also learned much from them. I learned much more from their deliriums, their crises of depression, their panic attacks and obsessive disturbances than from the restricted universe of scientific treatises. To all of them, my eternal gratitude. I found diamonds in the soil of suffering human beings. Whoever fails to recognize his conflicts will never be healthy, and whoever refuses to be taught by the conflicts of others will never be wise.

I have lived in a forest for close to twenty years, in a small and beautiful town that has no bookstore. In that unusual setting, I developed the psychological, sociological and philosophical ideas found in my books. I never expected that one day they would be read by millions of people, published in many countries and used in various universities. My dreams have taken me to unimaginable places.

instituto.academia@uol.com.br

We do hope that you have enjoyed reading this large print book.

Did you know that all of our titles are available for purchase?

We publish a wide range of high quality large print books including:
Romances, Mysteries, Classics
General Fiction
Non Fiction and Westerns

Special interest titles available in large print are:
The Little Oxford Dictionary
Music Book
Song Book
Hymn Book
Service Book

Also available from us courtesy of Oxford University Press:
Young Readers' Dictionary
(large print edition)
Young Readers' Thesaurus
(large print edition)

For further information or a free brochure, please contact us at:
Ulverscroft Large Print Books Ltd.,
The Green, Bradgate Road, Anstey,
Leicester, LE7 7FU, England.
Tel: (00 44) 0116 236 4325
Fax: (00 44) 0116 234 0205

THE CHRISTMAS SPIRITS

Whitley Streiber

George Moore is a modern day Scrooge, mean with his money, his time and his sympathies. A futures trader who drives his staff hard, George won't even let his assistant go home on Christmas Eve so she can look after her son. But on his way home that night, odd things start to happen . . . When he finally arrives back in his apartment, George is accosted by his old mentor in trading and greed, Bill Hill. Bill warns George that he will receive three visitors who will give him his only chance at salvation. But the thing is, Bill Hill is dead . . .

I MARRIED YOU FOR HAPPINESS

Lily Tuck

Nina sits at the bedside of her husband
Philip, whose sudden and unexpected
death is the reason for her lonely vigil. Too
shocked yet to grieve, she recalls the
defining moments of their marriage,
beginning with their first meeting in Paris.
Journeying through memories of events
that occurred in places as distant and
disparate as France, Massachusetts,
Mexico and California, Nina's recollec-
tions reveal the intimacies, secrets and joys
that shaped their lives together, and paint
a portrait of a forty-three-year-old marriage: an elegant elegy to a husband and a
meditation on how chance can affect both
a life and love.

IF THIS IS HOME

Stuart Evers

Mark Wilkinson has three names. He left his own behind in the rainy north of England. American immigration knows him as Josef Novak. And at the Valhalla, the mysterious complex where he sells lofty ambition and dark desires, he goes by Mr Jones. Since he was eighteen, Mark has been running away from his small town, his vanished mother, his broken father. But one night in Las Vegas, shocked by violence and ambushed by memories, he is propelled back to his real name and his real past. Back to Bethany Wilder: carnival queen, partner in dreams and tragic ghost.

HONEY BROWN IS MARRIED

Sara Judge

March 1950: ex-showgirl Honey Brown has married the farmer she adores — August Blake Esq. — and though she pines for the bright lights and glamour of the Windmill Theatre, her new mother-in-law, Doris, is determined to turn Honey into a respectable lady of the manor. To make matters worse, as well as the struggle to meet Doris's exacting standards, Honey feels increasing animosity towards dairy-man Nick. Why does she dislike him, when everyone else seems to find him so agreeable? When enmity between the two turns to disaster, Honey wonders if her life on the farm is really worth fighting for.

SCHRODER

Amity Gaige

As an adolescent, Erik Schroder — a
first-generation East German immigrant
— adopts a new name and a new persona
in the hope that it will help him fit in. This
fateful white lie will set him on an
improbably and ultimately tragic course.
Years later, amid a heated custody battle
with his estranged wife, Erik kidnaps his
six-year-old daughter, Meadow . . . From
the confines of a correctional facility, Erik
relates the story of their seven days on the
road as he tries to outrun the authorities,
and surveys the course of his life in an
attempt to understand and explain his
behaviour . . .

AN INVISIBLE SIGN OF MY OWN

Aimee Bender

When Mona Grey is ten, her father contracts a mysterious illness. His gradual withdrawal marks a similar change in Mona, who removes herself from anything — or anyone — that might bring her happiness. Numbers provide a kind of solace, and help her make sense of the world. As a maths teacher, Mona delights her pupils by encouraging them to find objects that take the form of numbers. But when seven-year-old Lisa appears with a zero that speaks of real turmoil, Mona realises she must find a way to reconnect with the world she has been afraid of for so long . . .